"Kate...wait. Don't go, not yet."

She was surprised when she realized that she had wanted him to say those words. "Why?" she asked, sitting back.

Nick's dark-as-dark eyes held hers. "Do you think," he said slowly, "that we could...start over?"

She couldn't pretend not to know what he meant—any more than she could ignore the fact that something was happening here. She could feel it, and she didn't like it.

"I don't know," she said. "I don't have time for...I mean, this isn't what I had planned...."

"This isn't what I had planned, either," he said. "But something is going on here, whether we want it to or not."

Try as she might, she couldn't look away from his face. "I don't know..."

For a moment she thought that he might bring her fingers up to his lips. Her heart began to pound. She'd always suspected there was much more to Nick Santos than he let people see, and she realized she was catching a glimpse of that private self now. That glimpse drew her to him, and she was suddenly shaken by how much she wanted to be with him. For a horrifying moment she almost asked him to come with her to her apartment. But though her body burned, and her skin tingled, she somehow managed to stop herself from blurting out the words that would change things between them forever.

Weddings by De Wilde™

Weddings by DeWilde™

PREVIOUSLY AT DeWILDES

Lawyers were champing at the bit to wrestle over the rights to the DeWilde name!

- A DeWilde wedding was interrupted by an outrageous stranger who proved to possess yet more family connections.
- The sophisticated image and spotless reputation of DeWildes' Sydney store was being tarnished by tacky T-shirts and unmentionable souvenirs!
- Maxine Sterling, the DeWildes' lawyer in Australia, found herself an unwilling guest at DeWildes Reptile and Wildlife Park, cozying up to crocs and their charismatic keeper, DeWilde Cutter.

Armed with new information, Nick Santos feels a sudden urge to head back to San Francisco, where his instincts tell him he may finally be able to put speculation about the missing DeWilde jewelry to rest.

Janis Flores is acknowledged as the author of this work.

ISBN 0-373-82547-1

ROMANCING THE STONES

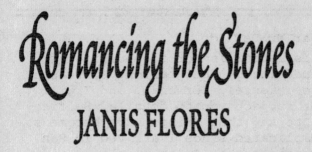

Romancing the Stones

JANIS FLORES

Harlequin Books

TORONTO • NEW YORK • LONDON
AMSTERDAM • PARIS • SYDNEY • HAMBURG
STOCKHOLM • ATHENS • TOKYO • MILAN
MADRID • WARSAW • BUDAPEST • AUCKLAND

Dear Mr. DeWilde,

This letter is for the purpose of tendering my resignation. My reasons are intensely personal, and I will not subject you to details. Suffice it to say that things have become so complicated since I arrived in San Francisco that I see no alternative but to resign from the case.

I know that you are very close to finding what you seek, and since the mystery of the DeWilde jewels has almost been revealed, you will no longer need my services.

Please believe me when I say that I wish I could have been part of the final coup. Unfortunately, as with so many things in life, it simply was not meant to be.

Sincerely,

Nick Santos

CHAPTER ONE

"GIVE ME THE STUFF or I'll cut you."

Dr. Kate DeWilde froze as the knife flashed silver under the fluorescent lights of the clinic. The blade came so close to her face that she flinched despite herself.

She knew the teenager standing in front of her meant what he said; desperation was evident in every taut line of his body. He gestured fiercely with the knife again. The sharp edge seemed to grow and expand until it was all she could see. She had to force her eyes away from it.

"You don't want to do this, Emilio," she said, willing her voice not to shake. "Taking drugs from me won't help you. You need—"

"Shut up!" Sweat beaded his forehead and matted his black hair. He used the hand that was holding the knife to wipe his face. "I need to think."

Kate couldn't just stand there. Her heart pounding, she said, "While you're thinking, why don't you let me take care of that injury?"

They both looked down at his left arm, which hung straight by his side. From what she had gleaned when he first burst into the clinic, he'd been involved in a gang fight. Blood from a wound he'd sustained flowed off his fingers and fell, drop by crimson drop, to the scuffed linoleum floor. Like a blossoming scarlet flower, the puddle of blood by his feet grew wider and potentially more lethal with every drop.

Emilio took a step toward her, his handsome young face twisted with anger and pain. He swayed, and Kate knew he was about to pass out. But he still had too tight a grip on the knife for her to make a grab for it, so she remained in place, her brain racing, trying to decide what to do.

She couldn't wait until he fell unconscious to the floor—though judging from the sickly pallor spreading under his smooth brown skin, that wouldn't take long. She knew she had to act quickly. She was backed into a corner behind the clinic's reception counter with Emilio—and the knife—less than three feet from her.

Forget about the weapon, Kate ordered herself. If she didn't, she'd be paralyzed by fear. She had to remember that she was a doctor. The boy before her—and he was a boy, for despite his tough-guy stance, Emilio Sanchez wasn't much more than sixteen—needed her help. It was her job to give it.

She tried again. "Please listen to me, Emilio—"

He leaped toward her so suddenly she couldn't defend herself. Before she could so much as raise her hands, he'd grabbed her by the throat and put the point of the knife right under her eye. His breath hot against her face, he snarled, "How do you know my name?"

She looked into his fierce black eyes. Her own senses were screaming with danger, but she could smell the fear on him. Or was that her own primal fright? With the knife pressing against her skin, she felt sweat begin to roll in great drops down her back. She had to will herself not to panic.

His grip tightened on her throat. "Answer me!"

She was about to choke. Somehow she managed to say, "Let go of me...and I will."

"Just tell me!"

"I know your name," she wheezed, "because you brought your grandmother into the clinic a few months ago. I remember Rosalinda Sanchez...and how proud she was of her grandson. She told me all about you, Emilio, about how you care for her and how you—"

"Enough! I don't want to hear any more!"

He spun away, releasing his hold on her throat. Thrown off balance, Kate almost fell. Grabbing onto the counter, she took a deep, gasping breath, feeling merciful air flood into her lungs. She thought she felt a thin trickle of blood oozing down her cheek, but maybe she imagined it. She shuddered. *It had been so close.*

She thrust the thought away. She couldn't dwell on what might have happened. She had to get that knife away from Emilio and treat his wound before it was too late.

"What would Rosalinda say about her grandson now, Emilio?" she asked. "What would she say if she knew you held a knife on her doctor?"

He whirled toward her again. "What do you know about my *abuela?* What do you know about anything?"

She was breathing easier now. "I know that if I don't take care of your injury, you're going to lose so much blood that you'll have to go to the hospital. I know that once you're there, the police will ask questions about how you were stabbed. I know that they will go to your grandmother and—"

"Ayiee!" he shouted. "Enough talk!"

She was afraid she had miscalculated, that he was going to jump her again. But then he looked at her, his young face twisting with uncertainty, and she allowed

herself a fleeting moment of triumph. In another second
or two, he was going to drop the knife or else surrender
it to her. She was just holding her hand out to him when
she saw a movement out of the corner of her eye.

Emilio saw it, too. They both turned as a man burst
into the clinic. The front door was still banging against
the wall when the stranger launched himself over the
counter and grabbed Emilio. Startled, the young Latino
shouted a curse in Spanish as the weight of the intruder
bore him back against the cabinets. He grabbed his as-
sailant as they crashed to the floor.

"I've got him!" the newcomer shouted at Kate.
"Run!"

Kate couldn't have run if she'd wanted to. Knocked
back by the flailing bodies, she was shoved up against
the counter.

Shouting and cursing, the two combatants rolled under
her feet, grappling with each other. Through the wild
tangle of arms and legs, she couldn't see who her supposed rescuer was, but she knew he was big.

She didn't care who he was. Furious that he had in-
terfered when she'd had the situation under control, she
waded into the melee and grabbed him by the arm.

"Let him go!" she shouted, pulling as hard as she
could. It was like trying to move a mountain. "Can't
you see that he's hurt?"

The stranger was on top of Emilio. With Kate pulling
at him and the teenager pummeling him, one-armed,
from underneath, he was clearly at a disadvantage. Finally, uttering an obvious threat in Spanish, he surged
to his feet. In the process, he grabbed Kate with one arm
and brought Emilio up with the other. They all stood
there, breathing hard.

Now that Kate had a chance to see who it was, she gasped, "You!"

"Yes, me," Nick Santos said grimly. He still had a grip on Emilio, who in turn was glaring murderously at him. Nick checked him out for additional weapons, then kicked away the knife, which had fallen to the floor. That done, he turned to Kate. "Where's the phone? I'll call this in and—"

"Call it in? You mean to the police?"

"No, to the local talent show—what do you think?" Nick said impatiently. "Of course I'm going to call the police. The last time I checked, threatening someone with a knife was a crime."

Kate reddened at his tone. "I can explain that."

"Maybe so. But I think that in this case, *he's* the one who's going to be doing the explaining."

"I'm not going to argue with you about that right now. He needs treatment. If you'd bothered to look, I'm sure even you could see that he's injured."

Nick glanced once more at Emilio, who was still losing blood. Then he caught sight of himself. Crimson stains smeared his white shirt, and there was blood on his suit jacket. He muttered an exasperated curse.

"I do now," he said. "Wouldn't you know, this is a new shirt."

Kate was outraged. "You care more about a shirt than you do about poor Emilio?"

Nick's dark eyes came back to her face. "Might I remind you that 'poor Emilio' was about to skewer you? Now, I don't know why, and I don't really care. There's probably all sorts of reasons, but I'd guess the one at the top of his list is drugs. Am I right?"

Kate didn't want to admit anything to this man, no matter how intense his dark gaze. When they had met so briefly last year, she had found his physical size almost overpowering, and now she was even more grimly certain that he used his height to intimidate people. Well, she wasn't about to be browbeaten by anyone. He could tower over her if he wished, and she'd spit right in his eye.

"It doesn't matter what the reason was," she said between her teeth. "The important thing is that he needs treatment, and he needs it now!"

"Well, fine. As far as I know, they have facilities down at the jail."

"I have facilities right here!" she retorted. "Now, please, let him go. He's my patient, and I'm going to treat him."

To show she meant business, she pointedly—and almost forcibly—removed Nick's hand from the teenager's arm. Completely ignoring the fact that Emilio had resisted her offer of help only moments before, she hauled him off toward an examination room. If the private investigator had had any intention of stopping her, she froze him with a look. To her satisfaction, he merely shrugged and leaned against the counter.

By the time she got Emilio into the examination room, he was too dizzy to fight anyone. Even before she suggested it, he lay down on the table and closed his eyes. Finally allowed to get down to business, Kate snapped on gloves and cut his bloodied shirtsleeve away. She was relieved to see that the wound wasn't as serious as she'd feared. It only required cleaning and a few stitches, which she accomplished as she always did, quickly and efficiently. When she was finished, she helped him sit up. He was still woozy enough to allow her assistance, but when he was upright, he remembered he was a macho guy and shrugged away from her grasp.

"I can do it," he muttered.

She didn't argue, and allowed him to get down from the table unassisted. But she watched him carefully and was concerned anew when he had to hold on to the edge of the examining table for a moment to steady himself. He still seemed dizzy.

"I think I'd better call someone to take you home," she said.

"No. One of my *vatos* will come for me."

He straightened, and even though she could see what an effort it was for him, she kept her expression neutral. She knew from experience how proud these Latinos were; in fact, from what she'd seen here at the clinic, sometimes pride was the only thing they had. She wasn't about to take it away from him.

She held out the antibiotics and painkillers she had dispensed. With a persuasive—she hoped—smile, she said, "All right, I won't insist, but only if you promise to take all of these. Until every one of them is gone," she added emphatically.

He shoved her hand away in contempt. "I don't need no pills."

"No, that's true. It's up to you, of course." She held them out again. "But if you don't take them, your arm could fall off."

He looked at her, and she shrugged. What she'd said wasn't technically true, of course, but she had learned a lot while working here that she would never have learned at the hospital. At first she'd been appalled at the way things were done at the clinic. But as one of the nurses had told her, in this environment, they did what worked. Many of the people in this extremely poor area harbored a basic mistrust of anyone in authority, and Kate had found out how difficult it was to gain even a modicum of acceptance—not to mention cooperation. She would never have taken this approach in another practice, but here she had learned to do what worked best.

Her words had definitely caught Emilio's attention. He looked down at his bandaged arm before glancing up at her again. Trying to be cool, he said, "You're puttin' me on, right?"

She shrugged a second time. "Do it your way and see."

He hesitated, then pocketed the medication. "I'll take it." He narrowed his eyes. "But only because I want to, you got that?"

Kate hid a smile. "I got it."

To her extreme displeasure, Nick Santos was still waiting in the reception area when they came out. She had forgotten all about him—no, that wasn't true. She hadn't forgotten him; she'd hoped that he would have tired of waiting and disappeared to do...whatever he had to do.

But there he was, all six-foot-four of him, still leaning indolently against the counter. The clinic, which normally would have held at least a half-dozen people even at this late hour, was totally empty. Unreasonably, she blamed the detective. By his mere presence, she was sure, he had scared everyone away. From what she had seen of him, he not only looked like a policeman but acted like one. And she knew that the people in this neighborhood could smell a cop from a mile away.

She challenged him with a determined look. "Emilio is going now," she said. "And I don't want you to stop him. He and I have reached an understanding, and I'm convinced that something like what...happened...isn't going to happen again."

Nick flicked a glance at Emilio, who stiffened, then he looked back at Kate. "Are you sure you know what you're doing?"

She lifted her chin. "Yes, I do."

He shrugged. "It's your clinic."

"Yes, it is."

Nick looked at her for a moment, then turned to the teenager. *"Y si sacas el cuchillo otra vez, tu culo es mio."*

Emilio hooked the thumb of his uninjured hand into his baggy, low-slung jeans. He had no intention of pulling his knife out again, but nobody was going to tell him what to do. Full of bravado, he snarled, *"No me asustas, puerco!"* You don't scare me, pig!

Nick's jaw tightened. *"Conozco muchos vividores como ustedes. Yo sè donde encontrarte, si lo necessito."*

Emilio's lip curled into a sneer. He didn't like being called a punk, but he wasn't sure if this guy meant what he said about coming after him if he had to. Jerking his head, he shot back, *"Si vienes a buscarme, te arrepentiras."*

Nick laughed sarcastically. "If I come looking," he said in English, *"you're* the one who's going to be sorry."

Emilio smirked, but he gave Nick a wide berth as he left the clinic. During her work here, Kate had picked up some Spanish, but the exchange had been so rapid-fire that she could only follow a few words. As soon as the door closed behind the teenager, she turned to Nick.

"What did you say to him?" she demanded.

Nick shrugged. "Just that he'd better be a good boy."

"Or?"

"Or Santa Claus won't come to visit this year."

Kate knew enough of the language to realize that Nick

hadn't said that at all. But she let it go because she wanted *him* to go. Annoyed that he made no move to leave, she was about to tell him that she had work to do, when their eyes suddenly met. Without warning, the hair at the nape of her neck rose, and she felt something move through her. It was as though she'd been touched by some kind of current. The sensation was enough to make her catch her breath. Just for an instant, it seemed...

Quickly, she broke eye contact. What was wrong with her? She was acting as though she were attracted to Nick Santos, when of course that couldn't be true. All that was happening was that she was still high on adrenaline after being threatened at knifepoint.

But still... She couldn't rid herself of the uncanny notion that he knew all about her, her thoughts, her desires...everything.

She turned away. She was being ridiculous. Nick didn't know anything about her, nothing at all—beyond what was in her file, which was something she was going to have to talk to her father about. Indignantly, she remembered that Jeffrey had given Nick dossiers on everyone in the family. That had been way out of line. If Nick was supposed to be looking for those damned jewels, why did he need to know anything about her? She hadn't stolen the stupid things. She knew nothing about them, and she intended to keep it that way.

She shoved her hands into the pockets of her lab coat and took the offensive. As disapprovingly as she could, she said, "Well! That was quite a scene here tonight. I hope you're happy."

He wasn't happy at all. Glowering at her, he said, "You should have let me call the police."

She knew he was right, but she felt obstinate enough

to say, "Why? So he could go to jail and have his life ruined?"

"You know, you bleeding heart liberals really get me," he said in disgust. "Ruining his life is something he chooses, not something that's done to him. He's not an innocent bystander here. He's responsible for his own choices."

He was right again, damn him, but she wasn't ready to surrender. "He *is* an innocent bystander," she insisted. She made a sweeping gesture with her hands. "Look around you, Mr. Santos—not the clinic, but the neighborhood. What do you see but poverty and despair? Emilio didn't choose to be born into an environment like this. It's not his fault!"

"That's true. But he can still choose whether to stay or get out of it. And pulling a knife on someone isn't a move up in my book."

"He was scared and hurt—"

"Those aren't excuses."

"No, but they're mitigating factors."

"Not to me."

She gave him a furious look. "And what do you know about it?"

"I know more than you do, *Doctor,*" he said, using the Spanish pronunciation of the word. Then he sneered just as Emilio had a few minutes earlier. In doing so, he looked so much like Emilio's older brother might have that Kate was quiet. Nick took advantage of her silence by continuing harshly, "I grew up in an environment just like this, *Doctor.* So don't ask me what I know about it."

Kate had known nothing about his background. Nor would she have guessed if he hadn't mentioned it. Embarrassed, she stammered, "I...I'm sorry. I...didn't know."

"You mean because I don't have an accent like our little friend?" he said contemptuously. "Well, I did once—yes, just like 'poor Emilio.' But you know what? I worked my way out of it, just like I worked my way out of the barrio. And if I did it, others can, too. All you have to do is want it bad enough."

Kate knew that wasn't all that was necessary. At another time, she would have said so, too. But there was no way she wanted to get into that line of argument.

"I'm sure you—" she started to say, then she noticed that Nick was bleeding, too. "You're hurt!"

He glanced at the gash on his hand and shrugged. "It's nothing. Just a cut."

She was horrified. "Emilio cut you?"

He hesitated. "I have to admit, I'm tempted to say he did it on purpose—just to see if it would help change your mind about that kid." He looked down at his bleeding hand and added, almost regretfully, "Actually, it happened during the struggle. If he could have, I'm sure he would have stuck me but good. This one was an accident."

"Well, I treated him, I guess I can treat you. Come on, let's—"

Almost smirking at her grudging tone, he said, "Please don't bother. I wouldn't want to be any trouble."

"It's no trouble," she said. Still irritated that he'd called her a bleeding heart, she grabbed his arm and pulled him over to the counter. As she swabbed the cut with antiseptic, she felt compelled to mutter, "You're wrong about Emilio. I know he wouldn't have hurt me."

Nick grunted as the medication stung. "He was faking

it pretty good, then. Because when I looked in the window—''

Kate was taking longer than she needed to bandage
Nick's gash. She always noticed hands, and despite herself, she had to admit that Nick Santos had wonderful
hands, strong and square and capable-looking. His fingers were well-shaped, the nails blunt—just like his personality, she thought. But when he mentioned looking
in on her, she dropped him as though she'd been scalded.

''You were *spying* on me?''

''Don't get your dander up again,'' he said, examining
the bandage she had put on him. ''Good job.''

She waved the compliment away. ''You haven't answered my question. Why were you watching us?''

''I wasn't *watching* you, Doctor. I was coming to see
you.''

''Why?''

''To ask you some questions.''

''You should have called and left a message on my
answering machine.''

''I did—about five times. But apparently you only use
the service to record messages, not to listen to them.''

She flushed. He had her there. She'd been so tired this
week, working double shifts here at the San Francisco
City Free Clinic and putting in time at the hospital, that
when she finally stumbled home to her apartment, it was
all she could do to take a shower and fall into bed.
Checking her messages had been the last thing on her
mind. She knew that if there was a real emergency,
someone would page her.

Annoyed that he seemed to have caught her at yet
another disadvantage, she snapped, ''If you wanted to
ask me anything about the great search for the missing

jewels, you've wasted your time. I don't know anything about it, and I don't care.''

"Having traveled practically around the world and back again tracking down those damn things, I'm beginning to feel the same way. But I still need to know a couple of things.''

"Well, ask someone else, then,'' she said. "I'm not involved, and I don't want to be. And now that I've told you everything I could possibly tell you about my father's little project, I think you should go. You're scaring people away—people who *need* me, I might add. I want to get back to work.''

"You sound like you don't approve of the fact that your father hired me.''

"I'm not sure that I approve of my father right now, period.''

"You're angry with him because of the divorce?''

She was angry about a lot of things, none of which she intended to confide in him. "I don't think that's any of your business,'' she said haughtily.

"You're right. It isn't.''

"You mean we actually agree on something?''

"We do. But I won't bet it will happen again.''

With that, he smiled a slow, easy smile that inexplicably reminded her of New Orleans and the French Quarter on a hot, steamy night. She'd been there once, and she remembered a street musician playing a horn on a sweltering evening. The sensuous melody had wafted through the Quarter past midnight, calling to lovers, quickening the blood.

At the memory, Kate felt something stir inside her. Hastily, she looked away. This was absurd, she told herself. Midnight and a steamy New Orleans? She must be more tired than she thought.

"I really have to get back to work," she said. She looked at him, daring him to contradict her. "Unless you have any more questions?"

He shook his head. "Not right now." Shoving himself away from the counter where he'd been leaning, he headed for the door. "But I'll be back."

"Next time, make an appointment."

He had the last word after all. Before he went out, he turned. His dark gaze met hers. "I will. But next time, maybe you'd better pick up your messages. You never know when one might be important."

CHAPTER TWO

THE BAR OFF MARKET STREET was so crowded, noisy and dim that Nick had to stop in the doorway to let his eyes and his ears adjust. He was standing there, searching for the person he had arranged to meet, when a woman came up to him. She was wearing six-inch heels, a micro-mini that barely covered her crotch, and a see-through blouse that left nothing to the imagination—especially since she wasn't wearing a bra.

"Hey," she said throatily. "What's up, handsome? Can I help you with something?"

Nick smiled sardonically. In his work, he'd had a lot of experience with situations like this, so he said, "Another night, maybe."

"You sure? I could show you a real good time."

She moved even closer to him, her unbound breasts in the very low-cut blouse rubbing against his chest. He wouldn't have been a living, breathing male if he hadn't briefly entertained a tempting image of what might happen if he accepted her invitation, but when she began to fiddle with the buttons of his shirt, he grabbed her hand.

"Sorry," he said. "I'm here to meet someone."

She smiled slyly, her full lips glistening with lipstick that looked magenta in the smoky light. "I can make you forget her."

Another image flashed into Nick's mind—this one of Kate DeWilde. As tired as she had looked tonight at the clinic, her face pale, her green eyes shadowed, she had been so much more appealing than this woman, younger, fresher....

Why was he wasting his thoughts on Kate DeWilde? She had almost attacked him for trying to save her life. What was the matter with her anyway? He felt outraged all over again just thinking about it.

But that had nothing to do with the woman moving with what she obviously hoped was sensuous promise against him. She wasn't his type, but he didn't see any point in hurting her feelings. "I'm sure you could," he said to her, "but not tonight, thanks."

She pouted again, but it was a formality this time. Her eyes were focused on the entrance and he knew she was already assessing new prey. With a meaningless smile, she moved away just as Nick spied his friend sitting at the bar. He began threading his way through the crowded room.

"Hi, Max," he said, sitting down on the bar stool that his friend, by some miracle, had managed to save for him.

Maxine Roybal turned to him with a grin. Slightly built, with incredible blue eyes, short, frizzy blond hair and a year-round tan, Max had once been a beat cop like Nick but was now a detective second grade with the San Francisco Police Department. In a deliberate parody of the woman who had just made a pass at him, she purred, "Hi there, handsome. What can I do for you?"

Nick grinned back at her. "I see you've been keeping an eye on our friend over by the door."

"Hard to miss her, wouldn't you say?" Max put out a hand. "It's good to see you, Nick."

He pushed her hand aside and gave her an affectionate hug as the bartender set a beer in front of him. He and

Max had been friends longer than they'd been partners on the force, and when they'd been partners, they'd made a good team. He didn't see her much now; he was always off on jobs, and she was married to her career. She'd almost quit the force when he'd gotten shot in that drug bust; she'd blamed herself until he'd gotten out of the hospital and come around to her apartment to kick her ass into counseling. She hadn't spoken to him for a while after that, but it had been worth it. Even though he'd been disabled out of police work because of the damned limp that bullet had left behind, he enjoyed his work now as a private investigator, and Max had gone back to the department and risen fast. Things had worked out.

"It's good to see you, too," he said. He lifted the beer. "I guess I can thank you for this."

She clinked her own glass with his. As always, she was drinking bourbon straight. "My pleasure, B.D.," she said, using the nickname she'd given him when they'd been partners. It stood for Bulldog, since he'd been known for never giving up until a case was solved. She smiled wryly. "I owe you one, anyway. More than one, if I remember correctly. You covered my back a lot in the old days. I just wish—"

He dismissed the painful part of his past with a wave of his hand. "Enough of that. You deserve what you got. And I'm better off. So, how are you, Max?"

She took the cue. Her eyes twinkling, she said, "I could complain, but it wouldn't do any good." She poked him in the shoulder. "But how about you? When you called, you said you'd been busy."

He winced. "I've logged so much time in the air this past year that my frequent flier miles could take me to the moon and back."

"I'm envious. It sounds pretty exciting."

"Let's just say it's been interesting. This family I'm working for—" He shook his head. "They've got more branches than the Bank of America."

"I know you can't tell me what it's about, but are you close to wrapping things up?"

"You're right—I can't tell you much. But I can say that after traveling back and forth across the globe, all trails seem to lead to San Francisco—except for one niggling detail back in Australia. If I don't finish up now, I'm out of ideas."

"You've never been out of ideas. You'll know what to do—you always have. Remember when we were growing up in the old neighborhood? You could have joined the local gang like all the other kids, but you were too smart for that."

Nick curled his lip. "Join the Mariachis? That blowhard gang of losers? They went out of business, I hope."

"It's pretty hard to have a gang when most of the members are in jail or dead from street violence."

He shook his head in disgust. "What a waste. And to think that could have happened to us."

"It wouldn't have happened to us, especially to you. You never bought into all that macho crap, and I was always too busy working or studying to be a gang *chica*."

He laughed at the memory. "Not to mention that your parents and my grandmother would have strung us up by our thumbs if we'd even given that gang a second look."

"How is your grandmother?" Max asked.

He sobered. "She died a few years ago, not long after I finally convinced her to move up to Sonoma County. At least I got her out of the neighborhood."

"I'm sorry to hear she died, Nick. She was a wonderful lady." She pressed his arm and said with a nostalgic smile, "You know, I can still taste her homemade tortillas."

He put his hand over hers. "I can, too. In fact, even now I get cravings for the *huevos y papas* she used to make." He grinned once more. "We had a lot of those when I was growing up."

"So did we. Eggs and potatoes were cheap. I'll never forget the time you were teasing her in the kitchen while she was cooking, and she lifted that frying pan, pretending to go after you with it—"

"And just then one of those damned Mariachis drove by and shot off a gun. The bullet hit the frying pan and knocked her flat." Nick's jaw tightened. "I was ready to do murder that night."

"I remember. Thank God she was able to talk you out of it. If you'd gone after them, you could have been killed."

Nick stared down into his almost-empty glass. "I owe my life to my grandmother. She saved me from making a lot of mistakes. That's why tonight when I saw that kid—"

"What kid?"

"Oh, some young *pachuco* over at the free clinic. I was going by and happened to look in just after this punk pulled a knife on the doctor there. I went in and took it away from him."

Max was more resigned than surprised. "Just another Saturday night in the barrio, right? Then what happened? No, never mind—" She eyed the bandage on Nick's hand. Since his injury obviously wasn't serious, she teased him a little. "You used to be quicker than that, B.D. Looks like you got the worst of it."

"You can say that again," he agreed. "And no thanks for my trouble. The doctor jumped all over my case and made me let the kid go."

"Great. You help the guy—"

"Not a guy—a woman." He thought about it. "A rather nice-looking woman, I have to say."

"Same old Nick. Ever the ladies' man. You had girls hanging all over you even back in school."

"Only because I acted like a tough guy," he said ruefully. He shook his head again. "The swaggering hero who quickly abandoned his swagger when his grandmother came in sight."

Max laughed. "Yeah, but you were *so* romantic with those dark, brooding stares and the way you used to slouch in the school hallways. I have to confess, I was half in love with you back then myself. But what about this woman doctor? Did I detect a note of interest?"

He looked at her in exasperation. "I can't believe it. Even after all this time, you're still trying to fix me up!"

"Only because you're *so* good-looking, and such a catch," she teased him.

He ignored that comment. "The answer to your nosy question about this woman is a simple no. I'm not interested in anyone right now, especially a bleeding heart doctor from a rich family who's trying to work out guilt feelings about her background by dabbling in things she knows nothing about and will never experience."

Max sat back in surprise. "Whew! She really got under your skin."

"No, she did not. I was just making a simple statement of fact."

"A little too vehemently, if you ask me."

"I didn't ask you. And you know exactly what I mean, Max. We've both seen it before, too many times to count. These do-gooders come down here from their very comfortable lives to tell us how to live ours. They're filled with the milk of human kindness, until something inevitably happens to make it curdle. Then they run back home crying about how they tried, but what can you do with people who just won't cooperate?'' He snorted contemptuously. ''They think that all the bad stuff will go away if everyone would just learn some manners.''

''You're sure you're not being too hard on her? Maybe she's sincere.''

''They're *all* sincere. Until a little good old home-cooked violence shatters the fantasy.''

''Now, now, no reason to be bitter, B.D.''

''I'm not bitter, just realistic.''

Max finished her drink. ''Boy, she really *did* get to you.''

''Now, Max, I told you—''

The beeper on Max's belt suddenly went off. With a grin, she stood. ''Saved by the bell,'' she said. ''Gotta go. It was nice talking to you, B.D. And if you stick around for a while, give me a call. We can talk about old times when—'' she grinned wickedly ''—when we were young, and everything was possible.''

He scowled. ''I never believed that, and neither did you.''

She dropped a sisterly kiss on the top of his head. ''Of course we did,'' she said. ''That's why we became cops.''

WHEN KATE LEFT THE CLINIC that night, her friend and mentor, Dr. Sheila McIntyre, chief surgeon at the exclusive San Francisco Golden Gate Hospital, was waiting for her. When Sheila saw Kate, she opened her door and got out of the car, a low-slung black Porsche. She stood there, one foot on the frame, watching as Kate approached.

"You look tired," Sheila said. "Bad night?"

Kate thought of Emilio's desperate face, the pain he had tried to hide behind his tough-guy stance. "No more than usual," she lied. She knew that Sheila would try, but she'd never understand what had happened tonight.

Sheila didn't press her. She got back inside the car as Kate opened the passenger door and slipped into the soft leather seat herself. To her annoyance, Kate found herself thinking of Nick Santos as Sheila started the car with a roar. Why was she thinking of him? He'd made no secret of the fact that he disliked her intensely *and* disapproved of who she was and what she believed in. In fact, she thought indignantly, what right did he have to judge her? And what right did he have to come barreling into the clinic tonight and attack that poor, innocent boy…?

Grimacing, she had to admit that Emilio Sanchez wasn't exactly innocent. But he *was* poor, and he *had* needed help.

Besides, she could have handled the situation without Nick's interference. If she had needed help, she could have called for assistance—911 was only three numbers away.

Sighing, she had to admit that wasn't true, either. For a few minutes tonight, the only thing that had existed in her world was that knife, held right under her eye by a scared and angry boy. She could still see—

Quickly, she turned to Sheila. "Thanks for picking me up tonight. The mechanic said I should have my car back tomorrow."

"No problem," Sheila said. But as they started away

from the curb, she added, "We've talked about this before, Kate. As long as you insist on working at that place, you should make sure that you get home safely. I wasn't going to leave you to the mercy of a cab that probably wouldn't have shown up."

"Now, Sheila—"

"I know, I know." Sheila looked at her as they stopped for a red light, then reached pointedly across her and locked the car door. "Obviously you haven't changed your mind or come to your senses and quit."

Kate put her head against the backrest and wearily closed her eyes. "Don't start, Sheila, please. I'm not in the mood to argue."

"Nor am I. But I am your friend, and I'm worried about you."

The light changed to green and she shifted into first gear. "I never have liked the idea of you working in this area. It's too dangerous. You know it, even if you continue to refuse to admit it."

"It's not—" She started to argue, but she knew she wouldn't sound convincing, especially after what had happened tonight. So she said instead, "Someone has to help the people here."

"I agree. But does it have to be you?"

"If not me, then who?" she asked, sitting up again. She gave Sheila a challenging look. "You?"

Sheila shifted on the seat. "Now, Kate, you know I'd help if I could. But with all the demands of my practice—"

"You could set some time aside if you really wanted to."

"The same thing could be said about you," Sheila argued. "I've asked you for months to join my staff."

It was Kate's turn to look away. "I'm not sure I want to concentrate on surgery."

"You were *meant* to be a surgeon, Kate. You know it. I've never seen finer hands on anyone—" She smiled at her. "Except for me, of course."

Kate smiled faintly in return. "You told me you'd give me some time to think about it."

"I *have* given you time."

"Not enough. Please, Sheila, you know I have to do this."

"So you say. I just don't understand why."

"I've told you why. I've lived such a life of privilege. I feel obligated to give something back."

"You give something back every day just by being the person you are. And you give even more by being the doctor that you are. But you could do so much *more* good by concentrating on surgery, with a specialty in neurosurgery. Think how many people you could help—people who desperately need you."

"The people at the free clinic need me, too," Kate said, feeling herself becoming defensive. "And something that happened tonight proves it. A boy came in—a teenage gang member who'd been involved in a fight. He was injured and scared. He said he wanted drugs, but he was really asking for my help."

"*What?*" Sheila was so shocked she almost braked the car to a stop in the middle of the road. "And you... Never mind, don't tell me. You helped him, right?"

"Of course. Naturally, I didn't give him drugs, but just when he was about to surrender his knife to me—"

"This fellow had a *knife?*"

"He was just a kid," Kate insisted.

"A kid with a knife, you mean."

"Sheila, let's not get distracted by the damned knife, all right? The point is—"

"The point is exactly the one I tried to make earlier! After what you just said, it should be obvious even to you that these people are dangerous!"

"Oh, for heaven's sake!" Kate exclaimed. "You sound just like Nick Santos!"

Sheila stopped the car in front of Kate's apartment house. "Who's Nick Santos?"

Kate sighed. "He's the investigator my father hired to look into some family business."

"And this Santos fellow was there tonight, too? Why?"

"I don't know why, and furthermore, I don't really care! If you'll listen for just a minute—"

"Kate! Can you hear yourself? Just a moment ago, you calmly announced that some gang member came into the clinic and held a knife on you. Don't you see that you've completely lost perspective here?"

Angrily, Kate opened her car door. "I think you're the one who's lost perspective! You're acting as if you have the right to make decisions for me, but you don't. For your information, *I* decide where I practice medicine and which clients I treat. Not you, and certainly not Nick Santos!"

And with that, she got out onto the sidewalk and slammed the car door.

Sheila called out to her when she was halfway up the steps to her apartment house. "Wait, Kate—wait!"

At the pleading note in her friend's voice, Kate had to stop. Jerkily, she turned back to the car. "What is it?"

"Kate, please, I'm sorry," Sheila said. "I didn't mean

to make you angry. I'm just worried about you. All your friends are."

Kate bit back a retort. She knew Sheila meant well; concern was evident on her friend's face. "I'm sorry, too," she said. "I didn't mean to snap at you. It's just been…a long night." Then, because she wanted to re-assure herself as much as Sheila, she added, "And I appreciate your concern—really, I do. But I can take care of myself."

Sheila didn't look convinced. "I want to think that, Kate. Believe me, I do. But when you tell me a story like the one you told me tonight, about a kid coming at you with a knife, I can't help it…" She shook her head helplessly. "I don't know how you do it."

"Someone has to," Kate said gently. "Maybe one day, it will be you, too."

HOURS LATER, LONG AFTER Sheila had gone, Kate stood by her bedroom window in her nightgown, staring blindly down at the deserted street. As exhausted as she was, she couldn't sleep. Jumbled images kept flashing through her mind—Emilio's taut face, the blood drip-ping onto the floor, the knife whipping through the air, the blade touching her cheek. She saw Nick Santos mak-ing his flying tackle; she saw Sheila's worried face.

Oh, how brave she'd acted, Kate thought derisively. She'd told them all what a big girl she was; she'd as-sured everyone that she could handle whatever came at her, even a knife.

But the incident with Emilio had happened hours ago, and she couldn't get it out of her mind. She'd tried a cup of tea to calm her nerves; she had even swallowed some brandy, something she rarely drank. Neither had helped.

As she stood there, she looked down at her hands. What would Sheila think of her surgeon's hands now, Kate thought. Even after all this time, she was still shaking like a leaf.

CHAPTER THREE

SINCE HER NEW STORE HAD opened in December, Grace DeWilde had made it her practice to arrive at Grace every morning before eight o'clock—when she was in town, that was. It seemed that she'd become a will-o'-the-wisp these past few months, traveling the world and back, when what she should have been doing was staying right here in San Francisco, attending to her precious business. *Thank God for Rita,* she thought, as she had a thousand times since she'd hired her assistant. If it hadn't been for Rita these past few months, she would have been out of her mind with worry—especially when that terrifying fire broke out. There had been endless details to take care of, but finally—finally!—the store was back in business.

And so was she. The roller-coaster ride that had been her life for the past year had finally come to a screeching halt in Las Vegas in April, and now she had become something she had never dreamed she would be: a divorced woman.

For most of the past thirty-odd years, her life had been mapped out for her. She had married Jeffrey DeWilde and worked by his side to make the DeWilde bridal stores an international success. They had been happy years. Though the store had four branches worldwide—in Paris, Monaco, New York and Sydney—Grace and Jeffrey had stayed at the flagship store in London, raising their three children, the twins, Megan and Gabriel, and their youngest, Kate. A native of San Francisco, Grace had immediately made England her own. She had loved the energy and excitement of London, yet reveled in the pastoral life at Kemberly, the family's country home.

Then, little more than a year ago, that well-ordered life had entered uncharted territory. A misunderstanding…a husband's infidelity…a broken trust. But she had survived—she *would* survive. And opening Grace had been her salvation.

Banishing all thoughts of the past, Grace let herself in through the back door. The store wasn't officially open until ten, but she had eagerly accustomed herself to making use of these early hours to attend to the myriad details involved in the running of what had turned out to be one of the most successful new retailing ventures in San Francisco.

At the thought, she allowed herself a brief glow of pride. From the moment of the grand opening, the store had been overrun by a veritable flood of potential brides. Every one of them—from girls in their late teens to mature women of a certain age—had come in with the sparkling eyes, the flushed cheeks and the telltale blush that every woman in the world possesses when talking about, thinking about or dreaming about the most magical day of her life.

And the brides didn't come in alone. They were accompanied by their friends, their bridesmaids, their maids and matrons of honor, their parents, the grooms' parents, and even, on occasion, the bashful grooms themselves. After all, this was the nineties, and men were expected to participate in the planning of such a special day.

On numerous occasions, Grace, Rita and the other employees had had to hide their amusement over the confusion of men who were asked by their enthusiastic fiancées whether they preferred Chantilly lace or alençon—or perhaps guipure would be a better choice? And what about galloon? When the doors were closed, they'd all collapse with good-natured laughter at how bewildered the males of the species had been over the shapes or designs of bridal headdresses, or the merits of crystal buttons over pearl to complement a certain gown. Such were the mysteries of females, for whom no detail was too small to be given careful consideration.

Not that Grace minded, but the crush of people all this activity entailed was so great that at times she might better have been occupied with the business of giving parties instead of overseeing the grand, glorious and giddy enterprise of assisting a bride in the planning of her most singular day.

On this particular June morning, Grace arrived even earlier than her usual time at the store. Among other things, she wanted to go over the invoice records before Rita sent them out to the accountant. Locking the door behind her, Grace began walking through the display areas, amazed at the fresh rush of pride that rose within her every time she surveyed the store—*her* store. It was hard to believe she had come so close to losing it only two short months ago. She had been in Las Vegas, waiting out the residency requirement for her divorce from Jeffrey, when Rita called to say a fire had broken out in the accessories storeroom on the second floor. Fortunately the fire had been quickly contained, but not before considerable water and smoke damage had occurred. The feat of cleaning up the store and replacing damaged stock had been nothing short of miraculous. Anyone looking around now would never have guessed there had even been a fire.

Squaring her shoulders, Grace resumed her morning inspection with a tour of the dressing rooms. As she had with every other detail in the store, Grace had planned the dressing rooms carefully. Each was the size of a small bedroom, with cream-colored walls and pale rose carpeting. Each had a dais in front of floor-to-ceiling three-way mirrors, and every mirror had been specially selected to be free of distortion. The glazier had assured her when she ordered the mirrors that there was no such thing as a "fat" or "thin" mirror, but Grace knew better—as did every woman who had ever tried on a bathing suit in a store. Smiling in agreement, she had nevertheless insisted on inspecting all the mirrors personally, and chose only those that offered the most flattering reflections.

In addition, all the dressing rooms were luxuriously appointed, with rose-colored velvet settees, soft lighting and an end table or two for the coffee or tea that was served in china cups and saucers. Grace wanted the prospective bride and her attendants to be as comfortable as possible when selecting the gowns that were to be the crowning glory of the day.

Satisfied that the fitting rooms were ready, she headed toward the front of the store. As she emerged into the vast display area, she stopped and looked around with pleasure.

At this hour, the sun was just coming through the new leaded windows that flanked the front doors. The effect was enchanting. A rainbow of color cascaded through the windows, shimmering on the carpeting, softening the angles of the display cases, and caressing the curves of the mannequins who were dressed to present special gowns.

One mannequin in particular caught Grace's eye. Since the store's opening, she and Rita had made a habit of posing a single model in the center of the floor—a subtle reminder that on her day, the bride would be the center of attention. They changed the mannequin's attire every week, and everyone who worked in the store was delighted when they realized that Grace now had customers—past, present and future—stopping by regularly just to see what the model was wearing that week.

Today, the dress was one of their newest discoveries, a magnificent off-the-shoulder froth of the finest silk moiré and beaded reembroidered alençon lace. The detachable train was folded gracefully over the model's arm, and the several dozen pearl-and-crystal buttons down the back added to the beautiful lines of the design. As Grace slowly walked toward it, the dress shimmered in the morning light as if with a life of its own. It was so beautiful it almost took her breath away.

Sighing with satisfaction, Grace slowly turned and inspected the rest of the store. Details had always been important to her, and to that end, every glass surface sparkled, the plush carpet was unmarked, and not a speck of dust was in sight. After straightening an imaginary wrinkle in the featured bridal gown, she turned and went upstairs to her office.

She'd been tired last night when she went home, and the work she hadn't been able to clear away was still on her desk. She sat down, surveyed the mess and decided to start with the pile of orders that had been checked and initialed by Rita, then placed on Grace's desk for her to sign. She was just reaching for the stack when Jeffrey's face suddenly flashed into her mind.

Since she'd awakened this morning, she'd been doing her best not to think about Jeffrey, but as she realized with a sigh, that was an impossible task. She couldn't help it, she thought mournfully. Divorced they might be in the eyes of the law, but in her heart, she still thought of him as her husband.

Tears filled her eyes. Blinking rapidly, angry at herself and impatient with her tears, she sat back. Squeezing her lids shut, she willed herself not to cry, but in spite of her efforts, a tear made its way between her lashes and trickled down her cheek.

"Damn it," she muttered, reaching for a tissue from inside a desk drawer. "You don't have time to cry."

Trying to distract herself, she looked at her calendar. She had a very busy day scheduled: six brides-to-be coming in for fittings, and who knew what else? She didn't have room for tears; the way the day was shaping up, she'd be lucky to find time to draw a breath.

Still, the tears kept flowing, and she reached for another tissue. Angrily, she blew her nose and tried, as Rita would have said, to buck herself up. Instead of feeling sorry for herself, she should concentrate on the good things this past year had brought. So much had happened since that awful day she'd decided to leave Jeffrey— more than she could ever have imagined. She had a beautiful apartment in a city she had grown to love again, and she had the store, which was succeeding beyond her wildest dreams. She had a wonderful assistant and friend in Rita Shannon Mulholland, and long ago she'd come to regard Rita's husband, Erik, as another son. And even if she and her husband were...no longer married...at least all her children were speaking to her once more.

Blowing her nose again, she told herself how much

she had to be grateful for. It was ridiculous to feel so depressed. She had to snap out of it.

With determination, she forced herself to sit up and reach for the pile of orders. Summoning the fierce concentration that had aided her in the past, she made herself go through the work, page by page, until at last that particular stack was done. By this time, her employees were starting to arrive, and relieved that she wasn't alone anymore, she went downstairs.

Her two seamstresses, twin sisters Magdalena and Estrellita Rodriguez—or Lena and Lita, as they preferred to be called—were already in the sewing room when Grace stopped in the doorway. With their magic fingers and even nimbler tongues, they were favorites, not only with the staff but with the customers, as well. The only problem was, they never stopped talking.

"Ah, good morning, *señora*," Lena said cheerfully, interrupting her dialogue with her sister when she saw Grace at the door.

Lita, who had the same round face and snapping black eyes as her sister, turned to Grace with an identical smile. An ornate barrette in her mouth, she was twisting her long black hair, now threaded with silver, into a little knot atop her head.

"Good morning, *señora*," she said, speaking around the hairpin. "I was just telling Lena what we needed to do today."

Lena sniffed. "Not that I needed telling. I know what we have to do."

Grace tried not to smile. This was one of many now-familiar rituals with the two women. "I just wanted to say good-morning," she said. "We've got a busy day ahead—"

"Oh, don't we know it!" said Lena.

"We're looking forward to it!" added Lita.

Grace laughed. "It's always wonderful to see suc
enthusiasm. You inspire me, so I think I'd better finis
up in my office before the store opens."

She was just heading toward the stairs when Rit
breezed in the back door. As always, Grace's energeti
assistant seemed to bring in a gust of fresh air with he
and Grace smiled at Rita with genuine pleasure.

"Well, good morning," Grace said. "You seem to b
in a good mood today."

"I'm always in a good mood," Rita teased her. Sh
poked her head into the sewing room as she went by
exchanged some quick banter with the Rodriguez sisters
then beamed at Grace. Her eyes sparkling, she said
"Erik came home last night."

"Ah," Grace said. "Now I understand why you loo
so chipper."

"I have reason to be. Erik's been gone a long time."

"Yes," Grace said solemnly. "Let me see. I think it'
been three whole days this time?"

Rita laughed. "Well, it *seemed* a long while."

"To newlyweds, I imagine it does," Grace agreed
"So, how are things going with the Sutcliff project?"

"About as frantic as usual. Ever since Erik got in
volved with Bob Sutcliff, it's been one thing after an
other. You can't believe the work involved—not to men
tion what a giant headache it is—putting together all th
financing for a worldwide chain of hotels."

"And Erik's enjoying every minute, right?"

"Too true," Rita said wryly. "I've decided that it'
my job to make sure he doesn't love it so much that h
forgets to come home."

"No chance of that, my dear. The man is head ove
heels in love with you."

"As I am with him," Rita said dreamily. "That's why it's not *such* a chore to make sure he gets quite a welcome when he comes home."

Grace laughed again. Before she could stop it, a memory of how she and Jeffrey used to—

Quickly, she shut off that train of thought. Rita was wearing a stylish chapeau this morning, and she gestured at it with a wave of her hand. "That hat looks wonderful on you."

"Thanks." With a flourish, Rita took it off and struck a model's pose. "What do you think?"

Grace was stunned. "You changed your hair!"

Ever since they'd known each other, Rita had worn an almost severe asymmetrical wedge cut. Grace had always thought it suited her assistant, who was sophisticated, no-nonsense, sharp and efficient, just like the style. But this morning, Rita looked so changed that Grace could only stare. Gone was the wedge; in its place was a mop of soft curls. Lita and Lena had obviously heard her exclamation and rushed out to inspect the new do.

Rita blushed as they all surrounded her. Finally she said, "All right, someone has to say *something*. Do you like it or not?"

"*Ai, querida mía!*" Lena exclaimed. "You look divine!"

"It's true!" Lita agreed. She turned Rita around, then gently touched the new curls. "You look...so soft."

Rita laughed. "I'm not sure that's the way an executive assistant is supposed to look."

Lena crossed her arms over her ample bosom. She exchanged a quick look with her sister, and they both nodded and smiled again, as if they shared a secret. Then

Lena said, "Yes, but it is the way a new mother might look, is it not so?"

Grace caught her breath. When she saw that her assistant was blushing furiously, she exclaimed, "Oh, my Rita, is it true?"

Rita couldn't keep the wonderful news to herself any longer. With a giddy laugh, she said, "Yes, I found out for sure last week, but I couldn't tell anyone because I was waiting for Erik to come home so he'd get the news first. Isn't it wonderful? We're going to have a baby!"

"Congratulations!" the seamstresses chorused joyfully, smothering Rita with hugs and kisses before remembering to give Grace a chance. Laughing and waving, they returned to the sewing room, chatting gaily in Spanish.

For her part, Grace was so flabbergasted she hardly knew what to say. She gave Rita a delighted hug, then teased, "I guess your views about waiting to have children went the way of the wedge haircut."

Rita's expressive eyes twinkled. "I always said I would have children...someday. I guess that day came a little sooner than I planned."

"I'll bet Erik is over the moon."

Rita flushed charmingly. "He was...pleased."

"And your family?"

"I told them this morning. Already they're suggesting names."

"Goodness. Are you going to find out ahead of time whether it's a boy or girl?"

"No, I want it to be a surprise—when *she* arrives."

They were laughing when suddenly they were interrupted by a furious banging at the front door. They looked at each other, then glanced in unison at the clock. It was barely nine. The store wasn't open yet, but after a renewed onslaught of pounding, it was obvious they couldn't ignore whoever was out there.

"I think I'd better find out what's going on," Grace said.

"I'll come with you."

As they hurried to the front of the store, they could see a hysterical-looking young woman with one of the store's signature silver-and-pale-rose dress bags over her arm. Written in graceful deep rose script up the entire side of the bag was the name of the store. The young woman was clutching the bag to her as though it were a lifeline.

"Why, that's Amy Harrington," Rita said in surprise as she and Grace headed toward the door. "Didn't she pick up her gown just last week?"

"Yes, she did," Grace said. "Oh, dear. I wonder what she's doing here."

Rita had barely unlocked the front door with her key before Amy rushed in, tears streaming down her cheeks. "Oh, Rita…Mrs. DeWilde!" she wailed. "The most terrible thing has happened. This is the worst day of my life!"

Over the years, Grace had heard this cry too many times to count from brides-to-be who had been equally as distraught as the young woman in front of her. In her experience, the disaster could range from a simple problem of a few seed pearls coming unfastened from the gown to a major crisis like the groom running off with another woman—or man. Grace didn't know what Amy's particular dilemma was, but she said soothingly, "Now, now, my dear. There's no need to be so upset. Whatever it is, we can fix it."

Amy looked from her to Rita and back again. Tragically, she cried, "No one can fix this! Oh, I just don't know what I'm going to do!"

"Why don't you sit down and tell us what the problem is," Rita suggested. "Would you like a cup of herbal tea to help calm your nerves?"

"A cup of hemlock would be more like it!" Amy cried. But she allowed Rita to lead her to a nearby chair. Once there, she plopped ungracefully down, only to spring up again. "I can't believe this has happened! My dress—my beautiful dress! It's ruined!"

Grace and Rita carefully avoided looking at each other. Cautiously, Grace asked, "What do you mean... ruined?"

Amy burst into renewed tears. Clutching the dress bag to her chest so tightly that Grace winced at the thought of what it was doing to the gown inside, Amy sobbed, "I can't wear it! I tried it on this morning and it's...too tight!"

Grace was so relieved she barely suppressed a laugh. "Is that all?" she said gently. "We can—"

"Nobody can fix this! I've gained ten pounds. *Ten pounds!* I look like a stuffed sausage! I couldn't even do up the zipper because I thought I'd rip the whole thing!"

Amy collapsed onto the chair again, sobbing miserably. "Dean and I should have just gotten married down at City Hall. Now if I try to wear this dress, I'll be a laughingstock at my own wedding!"

"No, you won't," Rita said calmly. She tried to pry the dress bag from Amy's grip. "Here, let me just...have this—" She finally succeeded in wrenching the bag away. "We'll take this to our seamstresses, they'll work their usual magic, and *voilà!* Your gown will fit perfectly again."

Amy looked up, naked hope on her face. "You're not just telling me that, are you? Do you really think they can fix it?"

"I'm sure of it," Rita said. She held out her hand. "So, come along. We'll put you in one of the dressing rooms, and before you know it, you'll be on your way."

"But the wedding is Saturday!"

"Plenty of time," Rita said. But as she gave Amy a reassuring smile, she also crossed her fingers behind her back so that only Grace could see the gesture. They both knew the Rodriguez sisters' schedule this week. The seamstresses were so busy they'd hardly have time to go home and come back again, much less alter an already-finished gown.

Grace stepped in. "Rita's right, Amy. There's nothing to worry about. Lena and Lita are absolute wonders. They'll have you on your way in no time."

Amy stood, still looking uncertain. "I hope you're right."

"We are. You'll see."

The bride-to-be dared a tiny smile. "I don't know how to thank you."

"No thanks are necessary," Grace said. "We're here to make sure that your day is just as beautiful and lovely as you want it to be. And the last thing you need to worry about is how your dress fits. That's *our* job."

Amy drew a shuddering breath. "I'm still so upset, I hardly know what to do. Oh, Rita, how did you ever manage to get through your wedding?"

Rita laughed. "If it's any comfort, on that day I was a nervous wreck."

"But I remember the photos you showed me. You looked so calm! And you were so beautiful. I'd never seen a red bridal gown before. It was so unique."

"It was that," Rita agreed.

Her glance met Grace's, as they both recalled the day of Rita's wedding to Erik Mulholland the previous December. Over Grace's protests, the bride and groom had scheduled the ceremony to coincide with the store's grand opening. Once Rita had convinced Grace that this was what they really wanted to do, Grace had surrendered, and together with her cousin Michael Forrest, a PR wizard, they had planned a marketing campaign that had enticed the public and attracted the attention of none other than the society editor of the *San Francisco Chronicle*.

For weeks before the actual day, people who passed by the store had been treated to window displays of fabrics from which Rita's wedding gown might be made. One week, the material had been a glorious black velvet, with a pair of long white gloves casually placed nearby. The next week the display was of emerald-green antique silk, with an antique family Bible accompanied by calla lilies as the bridal bouquet. Yet another time it was traditional white organza and satin, with a veil of gauze so fine it was almost impossible to see.

Each week, public interest grew, until on the day of the wedding, three television crews, plus reporters from newspapers as far away as Ukiah and Crescent City, crowded outside the store for a glimpse of the bride, the groom and their attendants as they arrived by carriage for the reception, which was held at the store.

Grace could still remember the oohs and aahs as Rita alighted from the carriage, proudly assisted by her handsome new husband in a white tuxedo. The bridal gown had been simplicity itself, made of a rich deep crimson velvet that had never been displayed in the window, so luxurious in texture that it almost begged to be caressed.

Every movement of Rita's slim body in the crimson sheath caused mysterious and beckoning shadows to appear and disappear in the soft folds of the gown, so that she had truly resembled a living flame as she'd walked down the aisle, her beaming father in his white tux holding her arm.

In her free hand, she had carried a stunning bouquet of red poinsettias, sprays of green mistletoe and white orchids surrounded by clouds of baby's breath. Her only jewelry, apart from her engagement ring, had been a matching pair of diamond earrings Erik had given her the night before.

She had needed no other ornamentation. As a special present, Grace had asked her daughter-in-law, Lianne Beecham DeWilde, to design a bridal headpiece to accompany the crimson gown. The result was magnificent—a smart little hat fashioned from the same crimson velvet as the gown and covered with shimmering pearls and sparkling green tourmalines.

To carry out the Christmas theme, Rita's attendants—her four sisters, plus two friends—wore forest-green velvet and carried white orchids. Her niece Betsy was the flower girl, and her nephew Todd was ring bearer. As far as Grace was concerned, it was one of the loveliest weddings she had ever attended.

The *Chronicle*'s society editor agreed, and not long after, while Rita and Erik were still on their honeymoon in Tahiti, the editor returned to do a story and pictures about the store. By then, San Franciscans already knew about Grace, but when the article appeared in print, the world found out about the store.

And not even a note of congratulation from Jeffrey.

There I go again, Grace mused with a sigh. She had promised herself not to think about Jeffrey today, but he kept intruding on her thoughts no matter how she tried to put him out of her mind.

Fortunately, it was time for the store to open. Two of her saleswomen, Anna and Linda-Marie, came in shortly before Grace unlocked the front door for the second time that morning. It was as though the floodgates opened. Two women walked in, then two more, followed by an entire bridal party. In fact, they were so busy that Grace stayed down on the floor to help. She didn't have time to think about Jeffrey again; in fact, she didn't have a second to think about lunch until early afternoon. She was about to go up to the office to fetch her purse when yet another customer came into the store.

"Anna," she said, gesturing to the saleswoman.

But the older woman who had entered the store walked over to Grace. "Are you Grace DeWilde?" she asked.

"Yes," Grace said, suppressing a sigh. She had been so looking forward to a quiet lunch. "May I help you?"

"My name is Marguerite Kauffman," the woman said. She held out a delicate hand. "Your daughter Kate and my granddaughter Erin are friends."

"Is that so? Then what a pleasure it is to meet you, Mrs. Kauffman."

"Please, call me Marguerite."

"And you must call me Grace. Did you come in today because your granddaughter is getting married?"

Marguerite Kauffman laughed. "I suppose she will eventually. Though I'm not at all sure. You know how young women are these days. They're so much more independent than we were."

"That's certainly true," Grace agreed, thinking of Kate.

"But we also have another connection."

"We do?"

"A long time ago, I knew Dirk DeWilde."

Dirk DeWilde—Jeffrey's uncle, Grace reflected. Dirk had managed the New York branch of DeWilde's in the forties, until he had mysteriously disappeared—along with half a dozen of the most precious pieces from the family's renowned jewelry collection. When a missing tiara turned up in New York, Jeffrey had sent his private investigator, Nick Santos, on a quest to try to locate the rest of the pieces and perhaps find clues to Dirk's disappearance. So far, a bracelet had been recovered in Australia, where Dirk had immigrated, and a new roster of relatives had been added to the DeWilde family tree.

Grace's mind flashed back to the Bible she'd seen on her recent trip to Australia. Maggie Cutter had shown it to her, and inscribed therein had been Maggie's parents' names: Dirk DeWilde and…Marguerite DuBois. Grace looked quickly at the little woman smiling before her. Could it be…? For a moment, she thought she saw a resemblance between Maggie and this woman. Could Marguerite Kauffman be Maggie's mother?

She shook her head, feeling foolish. Even though Marguerite was not exactly a common name, it was too much of a coincidence to think that this woman and the Marguerite mentioned in Maggie's Bible were one and the same. What was she thinking?

"My goodness," she said. "How in the world did you know Dirk?"

Marguerite smiled. "I met him in New York. He was somewhat of a black sheep in your family, wasn't he?"

"Not my family—my…er…my husband's family." It was too difficult to go into the fact that Jeffrey was no longer her husband and that his family wasn't hers anymore. So she just said, "But yes, he was. I guess

we'd call him an independent spirit now, but then..."
She laughed. "As I recall from family lore, it was one
scandal after the other with Dirk."

"Yes, I can imagine. I remember him well."

On impulse, Grace said, "I was just about to go
around the corner and have a bite to eat. Would you like
to join me?"

"I'd be delighted."

Astonishingly, Grace had located a tiny café near the
store whose English proprietor knew how to make a
proper cup of tea. The owner, Eloise Grayson, also made
some of the best tea biscuits Grace had ever tasted on
this side of the Atlantic. Grace often popped in for a
taste of the country she had lived in for all thirty-two
years of her married life. Once she and Marguerite were
seated, with the tea steeping in the pot in front of them
and a freshly made plate of scones at her elbow, she
invited her table companion to elaborate about her acquaintance with Dirk.

Marguerite's dark eyes turned nostalgic. "We met
when I lived in New York. I was...married at the time,
and he came to visit friends who happened to live next
door. He knew how unhappy I was, and he used to cheer
me up." She smiled shyly. "He was so handsome...so
charming."

Grace said dryly, "Yes, so I heard." She glanced co-
vertly at Marguerite, then decided to take a chance. "I
never knew Dirk, of course, but I seem to remember
that somewhere along the line he...disappeared. You
wouldn't happen to know about that, would you?"

Marguerite reached for her cup of tea. Grace wondered if she had imagined that the other woman's hand
shook slightly, when Marguerite said, "You know, I do
remember something about that." She smiled as she

carefully set the cup down. "I have to say, it didn't surprise me. From what I know about Derrick, he always was looking for adventure. I can easily imagine him going off to seek his fortune."

Or to avoid having to explain a major jewel theft, Grace thought cynically, though she said nothing to Marguerite. Apart from not wanting to reveal private business to a total stranger, she was beginning to think that she had made more of Marguerite's acquaintance with Dirk than was actually there. Instead, she murmured, "Perhaps you're right."

For a moment, Marguerite looked as though she wanted to say something more, but Eloise returned to their table just then to ask if they wanted more tea. After she left, there was a moment of awkward silence, until Grace launched into some of her funniest stories about the hazards of being in the bridal business. At last she glanced at her watch.

"Oh, good heavens," she exclaimed. "I'm so sorry, Marguerite, but I must get back to the store."

"I understand. I didn't mean to take up so much of your time."

"Oh, I enjoyed it." Waving away Marguerite's offer to pay, she took the check. "I hope we can talk again."

"I'd like that," Marguerite said. "In fact, I was wondering if one day you would have time to come over to Napa and have lunch with me."

"An invitation to the wine country? Who could resist? I'd love to come, Marguerite."

"Good," the woman said, pleased. "My husband is gone now, so we don't make the wine we once did, but in its day, Vignoble Winery produced some of the finest reds in the valley."

Grace couldn't hide her surprise—or her embarrass-

ment. "I'm so sorry, Marguerite. I never connected you
to the Kauffman who owns Vignoble Winery."

"Perhaps that's because I leased some of the vineyards to another winery after Edward died," Marguerite
said. "But I couldn't sell Vignoble, especially the house,
which has its own history."

"I've read about your home," Grace said delightedly.
"I'd love to see it."

"Then I'll call you sometime next week and we can
set a date." The older woman hesitated. "I'm so glad
we've met, Grace. I've looked forward to it for a long
time."

"Well, thank you," Grace said uncertainly. She
wasn't quite sure what Marguerite meant; it seemed a
curious thing to say. But she quickly decided she was
reading more into the remark than was warranted. She
wasn't usually like this, and, unreasonably, she blamed
Jeffrey. She was off kilter today, and it was all because
he kept popping up in her mind.

Damn you, Jeffrey, she thought after she'd said goodbye to Marguerite and was hurrying back to the store.
She still missed him as much...no, more, she thought,
than she had on the day she'd walked out on their thirty-
two-year marriage.

WHENEVER SHE HAD TO GO to the city, Marguerite
Kauffman took a limousine. It wasn't that she mistrusted
her own driving, but the hour and a half drive there and
back was exhausting at her age—especially on an occasion like today.

Not that her meeting with Grace had been stressful,
she thought. As she had always suspected, Grace
DeWilde was a lovely, vibrant woman, and it had been
a pleasure to meet her at last.

It was just that the circumstances of the meeting had caused her much anxiety. She still wasn't sure she'd done the right thing, but after so many years, she had to do *something*. And everything she'd heard or read about Grace DeWilde had been so encouraging. If she couldn't tell this woman her secret, whom could she tell?

As the big limousine purred smoothly back to Napa, Marguerite looked down at her hands, clenched tightly in her lap to prevent them from shaking. She'd taken the first step of many today. Who knew what tomorrow would bring....

CHAPTER FOUR

A FEW DAYS AFTER the incident at the clinic, Kate met her mother for lunch. Before she arrived, she had decided that she wasn't going to mention what had happened with Emilio. Both her parents were already upset enough at the idea that she was working in such a bad part of town; if they found out that she'd been threatened with a weapon, she'd never hear the end of it. So when Grace asked her about her work, she responded with a smile.

"It's very satisfying," she said. "Every time I put in a shift at the clinic, I feel so… I don't know, rewarded. I know that sounds corny, but it's true. The people there are so appreciative about any medical care at all. It's been such an eye-opener for me."

"I'll bet," Grace said, digging into her salad. "I have to confess, Katie, that while I admire you greatly, I still don't like to think about you working in that area."

"Now, Mother—"

"I know, I know, I've said it before. But I'm your mother. I'm entitled to worry, no matter how old you are."

"But it's not necessary," Kate said, mentally crossing her fingers at the white lie. Aware of Grace's raised eyebrows, she went on quickly, "And it's not so bad. I mean, the neighborhood is very run-down, but what can you expect? Unemployment is rampant, the poverty rate is high.... I'm amazed the people there function as well as they do. They're the ones to be admired."

Grace reached across the table and pressed her daughter's arm. "You've always been so kindhearted, Kate. Remember all those wounded creatures you used to bring home and nurse back to health? I think it's absolutely wonderful that you've become a doctor and I'm so proud of you." She sighed. "But I have to admit, I never expected you'd choose to work at a free clinic in a depressed area."

Kate grinned, ignoring her mother's concern. "Neither did I. But when the opportunity came up, I jumped at it. As I told Sheila the other night, I've had so much all my life, and now I feel obligated to give something back."

"That's all well and good, Kate, and I realize it's unworthy of me, but I still wish you could find some other way to do it."

"Oh, Mother, you sound just like Sheila."

"That's because Sheila is also concerned about your welfare," Grace said pointedly. "But no more of this! Tell me what you've been up to lately. Dare I ask if there's any room in your busy life for romance?" Grace's eyes twinkled mischievously.

Kate laughed until a sudden image of Nick's dark, sardonic face flashed into her mind. "There aren't any men in my life," she said, "if that's what you mean. I simply don't have time."

"But—"

"Now, don't start your antennae waving, Mother," Kate warned. "The men I know from the hospital are just friends—and as busy as I am. We hardly have time to read the newspaper, much less think of relationships. There will be time for that after I finish my residency."

Grace raised her hands in defeat. "All right, then, tell me about Sheila McIntyre. She must be a real dynamo to be head of surgery at such a young age."

Relieved to be on a safer subject, and resolutely shoving all thought of Nick Santos from her mind, Kate said enthusiastically, "Sheila is a wonder. She's smart, compassionate, talented—"

"And she wants you to join her surgical team."

Kate looked down at her own salad. "Yes, well, that's in the future—*if* I decide I want to go into surgery. I don't know yet."

"And how *will* you know," Grace said gently, "putting in so much time at that clinic?"

"It's only three nights a week," Kate said defensively. "And besides, I enjoy it. Sometimes, I think that's what I was meant to do."

Grace studied her daughter's face with concern. "Sometimes I worry about you, Katie. You always have taken too much on your plate. I do hate to say it, darling, but you look tired. Are you sure you're getting enough rest?"

Kate laughed. "No intern or resident ever gets enough rest, Mother. That's the nature of the profession." Wanting to distract Grace from issues that would never be resolved between them, she said, "Enough about me. Tell me about you and the store. I saw another mention of Grace the other day in the society section of the *Chronicle*. From what it said, you must be outfitting every bride in the Bay Area—and beyond."

Pleased that her daughter had noticed, Grace teased, "Why, Kate, don't tell me you actually have time to read the society pages!"

Kate made a face. "I hardly have time to read my mail. In this case, I have to confess that one of the charge nurses at the hospital showed me the item. But still, it seems that congratulations are in order."

"The store is going well, much better than even I anticipated, especially for such a new business."

"Well, I'm not surprised! You've always had a knack for retail. Everyone agreed that you were the driving force behind..." Kate stopped, biting her lip. "I'm sorry. I shouldn't have mentioned—"

Grace reached across the table and gave her daughter's hand a reassuring squeeze. "Don't be silly, dear. It's ridiculous trying to have a conversation where we have to watch every word in case either of us mentions your father or DeWilde's."

"I know, but—"

"No, it's all right. The situation isn't quite so... painful now."

"Isn't it?" Kate waited for her mother to answer, but when Grace was silent, she said tentatively, "You know, we hardly ever talk about Dad."

Grace gestured helplessly. "That's because I don't quite know what to say."

Kate sighed. "I guess there isn't anything *to* say. It's over now." She glanced up at her mother. "Isn't it?"

Grace hesitated. "As far as the marriage, yes. But I still..." As Kate watched, all the sparkle seemed to fade from her mother's features. "Every time I think that your father and I are starting to communicate, things fall apart again."

Her appetite gone, Kate put down her fork. "Mother, did you actually *want* a divorce?"

"I don't think that anyone ever *wants* a divorce, Katie."

"You're not answering my question."

Still avoiding Kate's eyes, Grace stirred her coffee.

"That's because you ask too many questions," she said gently. "I don't want to hurt your feelings, darling, but...would you mind if we talked about something else? The truth of the matter is that I don't know what I feel now. When I think that a marriage that lasted over thirty years just...disintegrated, I..." She stopped and shook her head. "I'm sorry, but I just can't talk about it."

Moved, Kate put her hand over her mother's. "I understand—or at least, I'm trying to. Obviously, I've never experienced what you're going through, but I want you to know that, no matter what, I'll always love you."

Grace smiled at her gratefully. "Thank you."

Kate felt she had to add, "And I love Dad, too."

"I'd be disappointed if you said anything else," Grace assured her.

"I'm glad," Kate said, relieved. "Because I don't want to take sides. I love you both—just as Gabe and Megan do. And I know from my own experiences, meager as they are, that no one on the outside can ever fully comprehend what's happened in a relationship." She smiled painfully. "Sometimes I think that the people involved can't explain their actions, either."

"That's certainly true," her mother agreed. "And while we're talking about your father, I wanted to tell you that the detective Jeffrey hired is back in San Francisco."

Before Kate could stop herself, she said, "I know."

"You do?"

Silently, Kate cursed her slip of the tongue. But she couldn't backtrack now. "Yes, I do. Mr. Santos... stopped by the clinic the other night."

Grace studied her daughter and smiled. "You'd never

make a good poker player, Kate. I gather you're not very pleased about Nick's reappearance.''

"I'm not," Kate said with a scowl. "He interrupted me in the middle of…treating a patient. And he was rude.''

"My, that is news," Grace said mildly. "He was very nice to me when he called.''

"He called you? What did he want? You've already told him that you didn't know anything about those stupid jewels. Did he think you were hiding something, or was it just that he didn't believe you?''

"Goodness, Kate, don't put the man on trial simply for doing his job.''

"I'm not putting him on trial. I just don't think he should be bothering you.''

Obviously trying not to laugh, Grace said, "To put your mind at ease, my conversation with Mr. Santos was very brief. He wanted me to know that he was back in San Francisco for a while—in case I'd thought of anything, since we last met that might be useful to his investigation.''

"And what did you tell him?''

"I couldn't tell him anything. As everyone knows, I'm definitely out of the loop as far as DeWilde business is concerned.'' Grace paused a moment, then asked, "Why did he come to see you?''

"Oh, who knows?" Kate said impatiently. "Who cares? I don't have time for some guy who thinks that just because Dad hired him, he can poke around in things that aren't any of his business.''

"What exactly did he do?''

"Well, he—'' Kate began indignantly, only to stop. She didn't want to talk about Nick Santos—especially with her mother, who always seemed to have the ability to see right inside her. And what she didn't want her mother to find out was that she couldn't seem to get Nick Santos out of her mind. To her intense annoyance, she'd been thinking about Nick ever since that night at the clinic. His handsome face would pop into her thoughts during rounds at the hospital; she'd remember something else about him when she was treating a patient at the infirmary. In her mind's eye, she'd see his strong, square hands when she was writing a prescription; she'd recall how intense his glance had been the night Emilio had threatened her with that knife.

Even worse, the memory of those dark eyes of his seemed to bring warmth to her cheeks...and heat to other regions of her body. It galled her to admit it, but she was affected by him in a way she'd never been by any other man.

And she didn't like it one bit.

"He what?" Grace prodded.

Kate avoided her mother's glance. "Never mind. Let's just say that he caught me at a bad moment at the clinic. I wish he'd do what he's supposed to do and be on his way."

"Why, Kate," Grace said, "you sound as if you don't like Mr. Santos."

"I don't."

"You hardly know the man. It's not like you to be so judgmental."

"Yes, it is," Kate insisted. "You always told me when I was growing up that that was one of my failings. And obviously," she added with a frown, "it's something I still need to work on."

"But you never said what Nick wanted when he came by the clinic," Grace commented.

Avoiding her mother's eyes, Kate replied, "The truth

is, we never did get around to why he just *happened* to stop by. I had an...emergency, and after that I was so miffed with him I sent him on his way.''

"Oh, Kate!" Grace sighed.

"Well, I couldn't help it! I wasn't going to drop everything just because he showed up.'' Kate realized she sounded shrill and lowered her voice. "If he wanted to talk to me, he should have made an appointment.''

"Yes, I suppose you're right.''

"I am right! You wouldn't like it if he barged in on you when you were busy, would you?''

"No, I wouldn't," Grace soothed.

Kate shot her mother a suspicious glance as she reached for her water glass. "We seem to keep hitting on touchy subjects today.''

Grace laughed. "So it seems. Well, I have something to ask you that is guaranteed not to be controversial. Do you know a young woman named Erin Kauffman?''

"Erin?" Kate was surprised enough to forget her displeasure about Nick. "Of course I know her. She's a nurse at the hospital and we immediately struck up a friendship when we met. But how did you know about her? Have I mentioned her before?''

"I believe you have. But my memory was jogged when her grandmother came into the store a few days ago—a lovely woman named Marguerite.''

"I've met Mrs. Kauffman before. She's actually Erin's step-grandmother. Erin took me to her home. It's an estate in the Napa Valley and the family winery was called...let me see—''

"Vignoble.''

"Yes, that's right. It's a beautiful place. In fact, I'm going out there again very soon for Erin's birthday party.''

"I might be going there soon myself. Marguerite and I had tea, and she invited me for lunch one day. We're supposed to get together sometime soon."

"You'll love the place, Mother. In some ways, it reminds me of Kemberly. In fact, I remember a portrait over the fireplace in the living room there that is similar to the one of Grandmother at—"

Kate stopped, a look of astonishment coming over her face.

"What is it?" Grace asked.

"You know," Kate said, "I hadn't thought of this before, but…" She looked at her mother. "Remember that pin you used to wear occasionally—you know, the one from the DeWilde collection that's in the shape of a cat sitting on a crescent moon?"

"Of course I remember. It was one of my favorite pieces. Jeffrey used to laugh—" Grace's voice caught momentarily, but she collected herself and continued, "He used to tease me about my lack of good taste, since it was by far one of the lesser items in the collection. But still, I loved the whimsy of it. Why do you ask?"

"Because I'm suddenly remembering the picture I saw of Marguerite Kauffman at Vignoble," Kate said. "It didn't strike me at the time, and it probably wouldn't have now, except for all this business of the missing DeWilde jewels. But I believe that in the picture, Marguerite is wearing a pin very similar to the one of the cat on the moon. Isn't that odd?"

"Very odd," Grace agreed.

They looked at each other. Then Kate said, "You don't think—"

For a moment, Grace's expression had turned distant, as if she was suddenly remembering something. But at

Kate's question, she gave her head a slight shake and started to laugh.

"I'm sorry, darling," she said, "but for a few seconds there, my imagination was working overtime. When you mentioned the pin, I thought how interesting it would be if Marguerite was connected to the theft of the jewels. After all, as I remember it, there were three of those pins, one for each of the brothers—Charles, Henry and Dirk. So Dirk would have had one.... But that's quite ridiculous, isn't it. It has to be a coincidence."

Kate thought it was absurd, too. "You're right. I mean, what are the odds of the grandmother of a nurse who works at the same hospital as I do being involved in the mystery of the stolen DeWilde jewels? It's too much."

Grace looked pensive a moment, as if considering what she was about to say. "You know, though, there is something I haven't told you. Marguerite Kauffman did know your great-uncle Dirk for a time when he lived in New York."

Kate's eyes widened in astonishment. "Wow! Now, that is a coincidence! You don't suppose she does know something—"

Grace waved her hand dismissively. "Not unless she were the mystery woman who went to Australia with Dirk. But I think that would be most unlikely. And I'm sure if Dirk had mentioned anything to Mrs. Kauffman about the jewels, she would have told me. As for the similarity of the brooches, I imagine we could find dozens of replicas based on the original DeWilde design. I think we'd best leave the detective work to Nick Santos."

Kate knew her expression must reflect the distaste she felt at the mention of Nick's name. Unwilling to meet her mother's assessing gaze, she glanced down at her watch.

"Oh, dear. I really have to be going. If I don't hurry, I'll be late for Sheila's consultation. She has a patient scheduled for surgery who's presenting symptoms of—''

Hastily, Grace held up her hand. "You don't have to regale me with all the gory details."

"All right," Kate said with a mischievous gleam in her eye. "But you'll be sorry. It's an interesting case."

Grace shuddered. "I'll take your word for it."

"If you insist." Kate took the check from her mother. "I'll get that. It's my turn to pay."

"But—"

"No buts," Kate said firmly. "I'm a real doctor now. I can afford to take you to lunch."

After Kate paid the bill they walked out to the sidewalk. Before they headed in opposite directions to their respective cars, Grace gave Kate a hug.

"I'm so glad you made time for me in your busy schedule," Grace said. "I did enjoy lunch."

"So did I," Kate said, returning the embrace. She added with mock severity, "And it wasn't a matter of 'making time' for you, Mother. I enjoy seeing you, too."

"I know." Tenderly, Grace put her hand under Kate's chin and stared into her eyes. "It's just that I worry about you."

"I know you do. But there's no need, I promise you. You should stop worrying about me and look after yourself."

"But I'm fine, darling. Things are going so well at the store—"

"It's not the store I'm talking about."

"Oh, yes, I see. Well, I'll be fine about that, too."

Kate took her mother's hand. "Are you sure there's

nothing I can do—I mean, to help where Dad is concerned?''

"I wish there were, Katie. But as we said, the thing is done. It's time to…to move on.''

"Yes,'' Kate said sadly. "I suppose you're right.''

GRACE WAS PREOCCUPIED as she drove away from her luncheon date with Kate. She was thinking about Marguerite Kauffman, and for the life of her she couldn't get that cat pin out of her mind. She tried to laugh at herself—after all, it was an incredible leap to believe the woman had had something to do with the theft of the DeWilde jewels simply because she had once worn a pin similar to one in the collection.

"You're being absurd,'' Grace chided herself. It wasn't like her to allow her imagination to run wild, but for a moment the idea had been so tantalizing. She had pictured herself solving the mystery of the missing jewels before Nick Santos could, and sending them to Jeffrey as a…

A what?

She frowned, wondering what she'd do if by some miracle she *did* manage to get her hands on the jewels.

Would she throw them in Jeffrey's face as a sort of "so there!'' gesture?

When she thought about it, she had to admit that the gesture would probably give her great—if fleeting—satisfaction. But she knew that, in the end, it would only make things more tense between them.

Still…

She caught herself. Why was she thinking about those silly jewels? It was one thing for Jeffrey to make a personal mission out of finding the damned things, but it had nothing to do with her. Or did it?

She answered her own question. Of course not.

Grace drove into the garage near the store and parked the car. She was opening the door when something else struck her, and she halted, half in, half out of the car. Her mind racing, she examined the conversation she'd had with Marguerite... Marguerite, who had at one point called Dirk DeWilde by the name *Derrick.*

She hadn't stopped to think about it at the time, but it jumped out at her now. According to what Nick had learned, Jeffrey's uncle Dirk DeWilde had changed his name after he'd immigrated to Australia. That meant that when Marguerite had met him in New York, he was still known as Dirk. Yet during their conversation, Marguerite had called him Derrick at least once. Grace was sure of it.

Preoccupied, she locked her car, trying to view this new development calmly. Even so, she felt a thrill race through her. She couldn't wait for Marguerite to call and invite her to Vignoble for lunch. If she was right about this, Marguerite Kauffman knew more about Dirk/Derrick than she'd revealed so far.

Maybe, Grace thought with rising excitement, Marguerite did know something about the missing jewels.

NICK SANTOS STOPPED the rental car outside the tall, decorated iron gates of Vignoble Winery. Far down the long, tree-lined drive, he could just catch a glimpse of the house.

House? he thought with a touch of irony. The place was a mansion. It was so big it could have been a hotel—and he could only see part of it.

What he could see was impressive, he had to admit. In his travels, he'd had his share of incredible sights: the twin buildings of New York's World Trade Center, the

Eiffel Tower in Paris. He'd been to Buckingham Palace in London and visited the gambling casinos of Monte Carlo. He'd marveled at the Opera House in Sydney and strolled through a colorful market in the Provençal village of Gordes.

But something about this vast fieldstone house in the Napa Valley held him. He wasn't sure what it was—the softness of the light as the late afternoon approached twilight, or the scented air, already laden with the promise of grapes. Maybe it was the vines themselves. It all seemed to point to a different age, a time when life was slower...more elegant.

Vineyards stretched in every direction as far as he could see. On this afternoon in June, the leaves were deep green, alive, rustling slightly from the caress of a gentle breeze. The afternoon sun cast a sepia glow over the landscape, and the valley looked like an antique photograph of some long-lost Eden.

The estate was so far off the main road that traffic sounds were nonexistent; it was so quiet Nick could hear the call of one bird to another as a little family of quails, all in a line, scurried across the road right in front of him before disappearing into the bushes.

He watched the birds until the last tiny tail vanished under the leaves. Then he sat back, the car's vinyl seat creaking beneath his weight. Through narrowed eyes, he studied what he could see of the Kauffman house. He drummed his fingers on the steering wheel, then stopped. The noise, as muted as it was, sounded much too loud in the silence. Abruptly, he opened the car door and got out.

Mindful of the quiet, he carefully shut the car door and leaned against it. But instead of thinking how best to approach Marguerite Kauffman, whom he had tracked halfway around the world and back, he was thinking of someone else—someone with auburn hair the color of dark flames, someone with eyes that reminded him of a glade in a deep green forest.

He snickered at himself. How poetic, he thought. Scowling, he shoved his hands into his trouser pockets. He had a job to do, and he'd better get to it.

The problem was, he hadn't been able to get Kate DeWilde out of his mind since that incident at the clinic. He wasn't sure why; he hardly knew her. But every time he remembered looking through the clinic window and seeing that kid standing there with the knife to her cheek, he had the same sinking feeling in the pit of his stomach. If she'd been hurt...

But she hadn't been hurt, he reminded himself; she'd just been scared—for about two seconds. After that, she'd gotten mad at *him*. Some gratitude that was for possibly saving her life.

"Forget it," he muttered. "Forget her. You've got a job to do, and you'd better get to it."

When they'd been on patrol together, his partner Max had told him time and again that no man would ever really understand a woman, so why even try? Besides, he didn't want to get involved with someone like Kate DeWilde. If he attempted it, he'd be out of his league. He'd known women like Kate before. They were what he'd cynically learned to think of as "high maintenance." The DeWilde family were the royalty of retailers, and Kate had grown up in a world of wealth and privilege. Nick had seen enough of that privileged life in his dealings with the family to realize that he would never fit in—nor did he want to. He and Kate were at opposite ends of the pole. All they had in common was that he was doing a job for her father.

A job, he reminded himself, that he'd better get back to. He'd traveled thousands of miles; he'd talked to dozens of people in this quest to find out what had happened to the missing DeWilde jewels. This was his last lead and he couldn't afford to get distracted—especially not by a woman.

Frowning, he turned and scrutinized the house once more. He had to find a way to get in there; he had to figure out how to talk to the old woman without raising her suspicions.

He stood there for a long time, just staring at the house. Finally, he got back into the car and started the engine. Another little quail family scattered as he headed slowly down the road back to the highway, but this time he hardly noticed. As he turned toward San Francisco, he formulated a plan—of sorts. If it didn't work, he thought, he could always throw caution to the wind and break into the house.

Of course, breaking in was a last resort, he decided hastily. It was not only the mark of an amateur, but an idea he was sure Jeffrey DeWilde wouldn't sanction.

Maybe he could charm his way in, he thought with a deprecating grin. He'd done it before on other cases; he could do it again.

He grew serious as he crossed the Golden Gate Bridge. There was one thing he had to take care of before he did anything else. It had been niggling at the back of his mind, and he knew he wouldn't have any peace until he looked after it. Sighing, he passed the sign for Nineteenth Street, took Highway 101 and turned onto Van Ness. Before he knew it, he was heading downtown, about as far down as he could get.

It was time, he'd decided, to apologize to a certain doctor named Kate.

CHAPTER FIVE

KATE WAS HELPING Rosalinda Sanchez out of the examination room and back into the reception area where Emilio was waiting, when she glanced toward the door and saw Nick Santos. His long legs crossed at the ankles, his hands in his pockets, he was leaning against the doorjamb in the front entrance, staring at her. She felt her spine automatically stiffen at his indolent pose and the unreadable look in his eyes, but she finished assisting Rosalinda, and guided the elderly woman to her grandson with a smile.

"Your *abuela* is going to be fine, Emilio," she said. "It's just a bad cough, and I have something to help her with that."

Emilio's dark eyes held hers. "No hospital?" he said, trying to hide his anxiety behind a tough-guy stance.

Kate shook her head. "No hospital. If she takes her medicine, she will be fine." She dropped her glance pointedly to the teenager's arm; the knife wound he'd sustained in that gang fight was healing nicely. She couldn't resist. "Just like your arm. You took the medicine, didn't you?"

His eyes gleamed. "I didn't want my arm to fall off."

Kate realized that he was actually teasing her, and she laughed. "That's good," she said. "It would have been a much bigger problem to handle that way."

He smiled, too—a tentative, reluctant smile, as if he

was still loath to trust her. But it was a start, Kate thought, and she was pleased. She'd seen him around since that terrifying night, walking past the clinic, looking in—almost as though he wanted to enter but couldn't make himself do it. Tonight he had come with his grandmother. She turned her attention back to Rosalinda Sanchez. "Now, Mrs. Sanchez," she said slowly and carefully, "I want you to take the medicine I gave you every day. And you must call me if the cough gets worse. Will you do that, please?"

The elderly woman smiled, placing a gnarled hand over Kate's. "I will call," she said. "And I will take the medicine. I know you will help me. You helped my grandson. Didn't she, Emilio?"

Emilio had no choice but to nod. "*Sí, abuela,*" he said. His glance flickered to Kate before he looked back at his grandmother. "She helped me." Then he turned to Kate. "Do we do anything else?"

"Yes, she must come back next week, so I can check her again. And, Emilio, if you have any questions, any at all, you must call. Promise?"

He nodded. Then, as if it were shaken from him, he said, "Thank you, Doctor. We are grateful for all you have done."

"I'm glad we're here to help," Kate said. She looked at Rosalinda and smiled. "I will see you next week."

As the two left the clinic, Emilio eyed Nick before giving him a wide berth. Nick stared back at him for a moment with an unreadable expression, then he nodded to the elderly woman and bowed slightly to her before moving politely out of the way.

Kate watched the little interplay and wondered why the place seemed to be empty—or nearly so—whenever

Nick Santos showed up. With no other patients to treat at the moment, she couldn't ignore him.

Ousted from his idle position by the door, Nick began to walk toward her. She noticed that his slight limp seemed more pronounced tonight, but maybe she only thought that because she was trying so hard to concentrate on anything other than those dark eyes of his, which never seemed to leave her face.

What was he doing here, anyway? she wondered. She wished he hadn't come. She wished someone would come in so she would have an excuse to go about her business. She wished she were anyplace but here.

It was so *unnerving,* she thought angrily. She hadn't been able to get this man out of her mind for nearly a week, and now that he was actually here, she didn't want to talk to him. She didn't like these convoluted feelings he aroused in her, and because she was uncomfortable, she took the offensive.

"What are you doing here, Mr. Santos?" she asked.

He smiled that insolent smile that irked her so. As though it were obvious, he said, "I came to ask you a few questions."

"What kind of questions? I told you a long time ago that I don't know anything about the DeWilde jewels. And if you want the truth, I couldn't care less about the whole mess."

"If it's any consolation, I feel so frustrated I'm almost beginning to reach that point myself. I've been tracking down clues for over a year and don't feel any closer to resolving this mystery than I did a year ago."

She looked at him suspiciously. "That sounds strange, coming from you. Even if it were true, I can't believe you'd make such an admission."

"That goes to show how little you know about me."

He took a step closer. His physical presence was so intimidating that she had to will herself not to step back. Stiffly, she said, "I know as much as I want to know."

"Since we've already had one close encounter, why don't you just call me Nick?"

"That close encounter, as you call it, nearly cost me a patient. Emilio is coming around—with no thanks to you."

"No great loss as far as I'm concerned. You don't need a patient who threatens you with a knife."

"I told you, he was confused and frightened that night."

"He was confused, all right, and he was definitely scared. But I guarantee, it wasn't for any of the reasons you'd probably like to think."

"And just how do you know what I think?"

He studied her closely for a few seconds, and she stared right back. Then he said, "You know, you're right. I don't know what you think. Maybe we should go and have a cup of coffee so you can enlighten me."

The invitation caught her completely off guard. "I...I can't do that," she stammered.

"Why not?"

"Well, because...because..." She looked around the reception area of the clinic, as if she hoped to find a reason written on the walls. "Because, in case you hadn't noticed, I'm on duty here. I can't just...leave."

"The clinic closes at eleven. It's almost that now. I'll be glad to wait."

She didn't want him to wait. "How do you know I don't have a date?"

"Do you?"

Of course she didn't. In fact, she hadn't had a date in longer than she could remember. She couldn't even count on Sheila to bail her out. She was in Seattle for a few days, attending a medical conference.

"I'm sorry, but I can't," she said, scrambling for a convincing excuse. "I have…a lot of reading to do when I get home."

It sounded as ridiculous to her as it obviously did to him. When she saw his amused expression, she stiffened. He was laughing at her, and she lifted her chin defiantly.

"What's so funny?" she demanded.

He immediately tried to look solemn. "If you want the truth, I think it's interesting that you're not afraid of a punk with a knife, but you're afraid to have coffee with me."

"Me, afraid?" she said, her voice rising. She lowered it with an effort. "That's ridiculous!"

"Then you'll come after all? I promise, I'll be mindful of all the…reading you have to do, and won't keep you out too late."

He was totally infuriating! But he had also neatly boxed her in, and if she tried to refuse a second time, it would look as if she *was* reluctant to go out with him. She tapped her foot, considering. She didn't see any way out, but she decided that even if he had bested her in this particular battle, she didn't have to be gracious about it.

"All right," she said. "But we'll have to take two cars. I'm not coming all the way back down here again."

"Can't blame you for that," he said easily.

Before she could answer, he went over to the cracked Naugahyde couch shoved against one wall and sat down. The battered end table by his elbow had a few ancient magazines scattered on it, and he reached for one.

"Tell me when you're ready," he said. He looked

innocently at her. "Unless you want me to help with something?"

"Oh, no, I think you've done enough by scaring all my patients away, thank you very much."

He exasperated her further by burying an obvious smile behind the curling, stained pages of an outdated *Sports Illustrated.* She glared at him for a few seconds, then she turned and went into the nearest examination room. She closed the door and leaned against it, wondering why he had this adverse effect on her. Her heart was pounding; she felt light-headed and almost short of breath. If she didn't know better, she'd think she was having some kind of anxiety attack.

Well, she was, she decided grimly, as she shoved herself away from the door and began busying herself with the jar holding the tongue depressors. And she was furious with herself for letting him do this to her. Nick Santos meant nothing to her. She didn't know him, and she didn't *want* to know him. The only reason they'd ever met was because he'd been hired to do a job for her father—a job in which she hadn't the slightest interest. She had too many other things to care about, things that really mattered, like people and their illnesses. She didn't have time to worry about who stole what jewels, and when.

So, if that were the case, she told herself sternly, she ought to be able to handle Nick Santos better than this. If she couldn't, she shouldn't have agreed to go anywhere with him, not even for something as innocuous as a cup of coffee. Annoyed at her confused feelings, she turned to check the supply cart. In any other clinic, the cart would have held commonly used instruments like thermometers and oto-scopes. Here at the free clinic, it was covered only by a paper towel. Anything of value was kept in a locked cupboard, because in this neighborhood, things that weren't tied down had a way of walking off by themselves. So she couldn't even use the excuse of putting away her instruments as a delaying tactic.

After she straightened the towel, she looked around again for something else to do. But the room was as clean as it could be. She couldn't do anything more—unless she wanted to wash the floor. It was eleven o'clock, and she had sent her nurse-receptionist, Mary, home early, so she didn't even have an ally out there. She had no choice but to go out and face Nick Santos again. She took a deep breath and returned to the reception area. Once there, she made a show of checking the front desk, arranging the telephone and the desk set, then leafing through the big appointment book that was ignored more than it was filled in. Finally, she had to turn to Nick.

"I guess we can go now," she said. "Where would you like to meet?"

"You choose," he said.

"We'll have to take two cars," she reminded him, hoping he'd change his mind.

"So you said. Lead the way."

She took Nick to a coffee shop near her apartment, where the waitresses on the graveyard shift knew her. The place was open all night, and she often stopped in on her way home from the hospital or the clinic when she was too tired to sleep or when she just needed some understanding, uncomplicated company after a particularly grueling day.

But she had forgotten that this was a night that Roz Makinney worked. As soon as she walked in with Nick, Roz straightened from talking to a man at the counter, did an exaggerated double take, grinned and gave Kate a thumbs-up sign. Grabbing a coffeepot, Roz stuck a pencil behind her ear and sashayed over as Kate and Nick were sliding into a booth.

"What can I get you?" Roz drawled.

"Just coffee for me," Kate said.

"The same," Nick added.

Roz grabbed two mugs from a cart and poured their coffee with a flourish. "You know what?" she said to Nick. "You look like an apple-pie-à-la-mode kind of guy to me. How 'bout it?"

Nick grinned. "Sounds good to me. Kate?"

"No, thank you," Kate said. For some stupid reason, her stomach was in knots. She couldn't understand it. What *was* this man doing to her?

"Be right back," Roz said cheerily, and sauntered away.

Kate watched her go until she realized that Nick was staring at her again. Almost accusingly, she demanded, "Why are you looking at me like that?"

He seemed surprised. "I was just thinking about you and that old woman at the clinic tonight. You know, I believe that's the first time I've seen you smile. You should do it more often. It looks good on you."

Kate wasn't sure what to say. Caught off guard by the compliment, she looked down at her coffee cup. "Sometimes, at the clinic, there's not much to smile about."

"Then why do you go there?"

She was exasperated again. "You know, I'm getting tired of everybody I know asking me that."

"Hey, no offense. It was just a simple question."

"It didn't sound simple at all. I know you think I don't know what I'm doing, and that I shouldn't be there."

"I never said you didn't know what you were doing. That's your interpretation. But since you mention it, maybe it's not a good idea for you to be there."

"Why not?"

"Well, the obvious reason is that you don't *have* to be there. It's dangerous."

"So?" Her green eyes challenged his. "*Life* is dangerous. People can get hurt—"

"Walking across the street. I know. But that's not what we're talking about. I doubt even you would say that doctors should have to demonstrate their self-defense skills at the same time they take the Hippocratic oath."

"You're talking about what happened with Emilio. I told you—"

"I remember what you told me. But you don't know these people like I do."

"*These* people?"

He sighed. "You're getting liberal on me again."

"Why do you persist on *labeling* people?" she snapped.

"It's easier that way."

"Easier! I can't believe—" Kate began hotly, only to be interrupted by Roz, who reappeared bearing a huge piece of pie with two scoops of ice cream melting down the sides.

Ignoring the waitress's curious look, Kate reached for her coffee cup and forced a sip past tight lips. Roz set the plate in front of Nick, asked if they wanted anything else and finally went away. She'd barely gotten out of earshot before Kate slammed the coffee down and leaned forward.

"What did you mean when you said it was easier to label people?" she demanded.

Nick picked up his fork. Shrugging as he cut a piece of the pie, he said, "I don't think now is the time to talk about that. Why don't you just let me get to know you a little better, to provide me with some more background for my case, and leave it at that?"

Kate didn't want to answer any questions. All she wanted to do was to get out of here. It had been a mistake to bring him here; it had been a mistake to go anywhere with this man. He made her feel tongue-tied and uncomfortable, like a girl out on her first date.

"Go ahead and ask then," she said abruptly. "But I don't have much time. I've got a full day at the hospital tomorrow, and then tomorrow night I—"

"You have to be back at the clinic."

"Yes, I do." She narrowed her eyes. "I can't imagine you'd have a problem with that. After all, it's none of your business, is it?"

He held up his hands in mock surrender. "You're right, it's not. Did I say it was? I don't like things to be complicated. In fact, the only reason I came to the clinic tonight was to apologize."

That took her aback. Suspiciously, she asked, "For what?"

"Not for saving you from that young thug, that's for sure."

She bristled again. "I tried to tell you—you didn't have to save me. Before you came barging in that night, Emilio was about to give up the knife."

"That's one interpretation. To me, it looked like he was about to stick it to you."

"Emilio wouldn't do that."

"Why, because he's young and innocent? Don't kid yourself, doc. I've seen kids his age kill without a second thought."

"I feel sorry for you, Nick. You're so cynical."

"I'm not cynical, just realistic. I told you, you don't know these punks."

"I have more faith in those 'punks' than you obviously do. And one day you'll see that I'm right. All that kids like Emilio need is a chance."

Nick shook his head. "I can see that I'm not going to change your mind."

"No, you're not. But if it's any comfort, that's one thing you *are* right about."

He wasn't amused. "I just hope you won't get hurt by your sweet little innocents."

"And I hope that one day you'll realize you're being too hard on them."

"Maybe this wasn't such a good idea after all," he said, starting to slide out of the booth. "It's been nice, doc—"

"Just a minute."

"What?"

He halted in surprise. As he stared at her, Kate wondered why she had stopped him. Only a moment ago, she'd wanted him to go; now she was trying to think how to get him to stay. What was going on with her?

Nick was obviously also wondering why she had delayed him, so she said quickly, "I wanted to ask you a question."

He sat back down. "What is it?"

Now that she had his attention again, she said the first thing that came into her head. "Why did you become a private investigator?"

He studied her a long moment, clearly debating whether she was serious. But he finally said, "Because I could no longer be a cop."

"You were a cop?"

"Yep. Carried a gun and a badge and everything."

She sat back. Well, she had suspected it, hadn't she? Behind the cool demeanor, she'd detected a certain tension, as if he were in a constant state of alert.

Not that she knew much about policemen, she told herself hastily. But one of her college roommates had briefly dated a police officer, and Kate remembered that he'd had the same watchfulness about him that Nick had.

She knew she had no right to ask, but for some reason, the words just came out. "So you quit to become a private investigator?"

"I didn't say I quit. I said I could no longer be a cop."

"I'm sorry. I misunderstood. What happened?"

Once again, she'd blurted the question before she thought. As she felt herself flush, she wondered what was wrong with her. She wasn't the kind to pry. And none of this was any of her business.

The problem was, she always seemed to lose her usual self-control around Nick. She could deny it all she liked, but something had happened to her tonight. She still disliked the man for generating these strong, inexplicable feelings in her, but at the same time she was curious about *why* he had such an effect on her. It couldn't be that she was...interested in him, could it?

Maybe, she decided hastily, she was just trying to understand why he was so critical of the clinic and her work there.

She was still sitting there in confusion when he said, "I was ousted from the force because the powers that be believed I couldn't do the job properly after I'd been shot."

"You were shot?" Instantly, Kate's mind flashed to the gunshot injuries she'd seen while working at the clinic. She'd quickly discovered that the reality was so much more grisly than photographs in medical textbooks. She started to feel genuine sympathy for him until he grinned wickedly at her.

"It was a real bullet, too," he said. "You know, the kind your little punks use to prove how grown-up they are."

She wasn't going to get drawn into another argument about the people who came to the clinic. Instead, she asked, "Where were you shot?"

He grinned again. "Right here in San Francisco."

When she realized he was making fun of her, she stiffened. "I didn't mean that," she said with dignity. "But you're right. I had no reason to ask. This time, it's none of *my* business."

He saw that he had offended her. "I'm sorry," he said. "I didn't mean to make you angry."

She didn't want him to apologize; that would only make it more difficult to dislike him. Starchily, she said, "I'm not angry."

"Good, because we were getting along so well."

"Were we?"

"I thought we were. Now I'm not so sure. I apologize again. I guess I just don't like to talk about that time in my life."

She knew he was being honest, and once again she was caught off guard. Her tone softening, she said, "I understand. I shouldn't have asked."

"No, no, it's all right. I can understand your interest. After all, you are a doctor." He paused. "A nosy one, but a doctor."

His smile was too disarming; she found herself smiling in return. "Thank you—I think," she said. "But I respect your privacy. Let's just pretend that I didn't ask.''

"No, I want to tell you," he said, looking surprised himself. He took a deep breath. ''I was shot in the back during a drug bust when I was a beat cop. My partner always blamed herself, but it wasn't her fault.''

"Your partner was a woman?''

He laughed at her look of astonishment. ''You don't think I could work well with a woman?''

Embarrassed, Kate lied, ''Of course I do.'' Then she had to add, ''I was just thinking that she'd have to be some kind of woman, to put up with you.''

"She was. Max is quite a gal.''

"A *gal?*''

He laughed again. ''Uh-oh, I'm being politically incorrect again, aren't I. Well, for your information, Maxine Roybal wouldn't mind at all. In fact, she often describes herself as a tough broad. And she is. In my opinion, she was better than half the guys on the force. Still is. She's now a detective second grade with the SFPD.''

"I'm impressed.''

"You should be. She's a special person.''

"I'm sure she is,'' Kate said. She didn't want to talk anymore about this Maxine Roybal, detective second grade. She felt… She wasn't sure what she felt. Could it be a twinge of jealousy?

Appalled, she told herself that was absolutely ridiculous. She wasn't envious in the slightest; it was just that she didn't want to talk about Nick's partner when, as a physician, she was much more interested in his injury.

Quickly, she said, ''You were telling me about being shot.''

"There's nothing much to tell.'' He shrugged. ''The

creep who shot me walked on a technicality, but he left me with a permanent reminder of our little encounter."

"You still have the bullet in your back?"

He shot a glance at her from under eyebrows black as midnight. "No, they took that out. I was talking about the limp."

She couldn't say she hadn't seen it, so she nodded matter-of-factly. "Oh, yes, I see. Well, it's hardly noticeable. You must have done a lot of physical therapy."

When he stared at her for a long moment, she thought she'd made a mistake in referring to it so lightly. Then he laughed. "I did. But even so, you should see me on cold days. It hurts like a son of a...well, it bothers me some, and it shows."

Touched by the fact that he was being so candid with her, she said, "I'm sorry, Nick."

"It's just the breaks of the job."

She knew it was much more than that; she could hear the regret he tried to hide in his voice. Thoughtfully, she said, "You know, I've often felt that everyone who thinks guns are cool—especially kids—should be compelled to stand around an inner city emergency room one night and see exactly what happens to someone who has been shot. I'm sure that the experience would convince them never to touch a gun again in their lives."

"It'll never happen. Too hard on their little psyches."

She sighed. "I see we're back to the cynicism again."

He apparently thought better of continuing the subject, which was obviously going to lead to another disagreement. "You're right. Would you like some pie?"

She had forgotten all about the pie Roz had brought. She looked down now at the huge piece still sitting in front of him. The ice cream had melted enticingly all over the crust. She hesitated, then shook her head. "No thanks."

He glanced over at Roz, who was deep in conversation with another customer at the counter. He leaned forward and whispered conspiratorially, "Come on, you have to help. I can't possibly finish this, and we don't want to hurt her feelings, do we?"

"No, but I don't—" She stopped, reconsidering. "Well, maybe a few bites," she said. "It does look good, and I just remembered, I only had time to grab a bagel for dinner."

"A bagel? Then let me order you something substantial."

She grabbed his arm as he started to signal the waitress. "No, no, it's okay. This'll be fine. Just don't give me any lectures about skipping my veggies. Ice cream and apple pie have got three of the main food groups covered, right?"

"Right," he said, pushing the plate to the center of the table. "I knew that you were basically a woman after my own heart."

"Oh, you did, did you?" she said, picking up her spoon and scooping up some ice cream. "And how do you figure that?"

Solemnly, Nick reached across the table and used his napkin to wipe away a dribble of ice cream at the corner of her mouth. Embarrassed, she began to take the napkin from him, and for an instant, their fingers met. It was the first time all night that they had touched, and Kate felt something flash right through her. Quickly, she looked at Nick to see if she'd just imagined the jolt, and for a few scintillating seconds, they gazed at each other over the napkin.

Then she realized that she was still holding his hand,

and she released her grip. Nick dropped his arm, and they both looked down at the table.

"I...I think I'd better get going, after all," she managed to say. "It must be getting late."

"Yes...it must be," he agreed.

"You don't have to come," she said. "Stay and finish your pie."

As she reached for her purse and started to slide out of the booth, he said, "Kate...wait. Don't go, not yet."

She was surprised when she realized that she had wanted him to say those words. "Why?" she asked, sitting back.

His dark-as-dark eyes held hers. "Do you think," he said slowly, "that we could...start over?"

She couldn't pretend not to know what he meant— any more than she could ignore the fact that something was happening here. She wasn't sure what it was yet, but even before he'd made the simple gesture of wiping the ice cream from her lips, things had changed. She could feel it, and she didn't like it.

"I don't know," she said. "I don't have time for... I mean, I don't want... This isn't what I had planned...."

She wasn't making any sense and she knew it. He sensed her confusion and reached for her hand. His palm felt warm, and hard, and strong. She found herself entwining her fingers with his.

"This isn't what I had planned, either," he said. "But something is going on here whether we want it to or not."

Try as she might, she couldn't look away from his face. "I don't know—"

For a moment, she thought that he might bring her fingers up to his lips. Her heart began to pound.

"I don't know, either," he said. "But...I'd like to be friends."

Friends? Was that what she wanted? She drew in a shaky breath and said cautiously, "I...I think I can handle friends."

He sounded uncertain himself. "Good. That's a step, isn't it?"

Kate had always seen him as the strong, silent type, self-possessed, confident. But for the first time since she'd met him, he looked unsure of himself, and she was intrigued.

She'd suspected there was much more to Nick Santos than he let people see, and she realized she was catching a glimpse of that private self now. That glimpse drew her to him, and she was suddenly shaken by how much she wanted to be with him. For a horrifying moment, she almost asked him to come with her to her apartment. But at the last second, she held back. Her emotions were running high, but she was still aware that with some bridges, once crossed, there was no going back.

Though her body burned and her skin tingled, she somehow managed to stop herself from blurting out the words that would change things between them forever. Instead, she said simply, "I think I'd better go home."

He hadn't released her hand. "When can I see you again?" he asked.

She tried to look away from his intense stare. "I...I don't know. My schedule is so complicated, and I—"

"You must have *some* time off."

"Well, I have to go to a birthday party for a friend of mine on Saturday. I promised months ago. But I can't imagine that you would like—"

"It sounds perfect," he said.

She was so tense that she laughed. "I don't know

about that, though the party's being held at an estate in the Napa Valley. It's owned by my friend's grandmother, a delightful lady named Marguerite Kauffman.''

Something changed in his eyes. She wasn't sure how to read his expression, but suddenly she wanted him to come with her....

"It's very beautiful there. I'm sure that if nothing else, you'll enjoy the countryside, especially at this time of year."

He was still looking at her intently, then he gave her fingers a squeeze and let go of her hand. "I'd like to come," he said at last. "What time shall I pick you up?"

She was sure that she sensed a reserve in his tone, but she was too pleased he'd accepted her invitation to wonder about it. "Around noon, I think. That will give us plenty of time to get up there."

She was giving him her address when Roz came over to the booth. "Well, well," the waitress said. "I see that you liked the pie."

Kate looked down at the nearly empty plate. She knew she must have helped polish it off, but right now she couldn't remember tasting a bite.

CHAPTER SIX

KATE SPOKE TO HER MOTHER by phone just two days before she was to go with Nick to Erin's birthday party in the Napa Valley. She hadn't intended to tell Grace that she had invited Nick to come with her; it just came out.

Not that it was supposed to be a secret, she thought hastily. It was just that she didn't want to get into a big discussion about why or how she'd changed her mind about him. After all, she'd been so critical when they'd had lunch, and she knew her mother would pick up on her change of heart. Sure enough, Grace did.

"You invited Nick Santos to Erin's party?" Grace repeated in surprise, after Kate had opened her big mouth. "But, darling, I thought you didn't like him."

"Well, I didn't," Kate said. "But...things have changed. We had coffee the other night, and I realized that I might have... misjudged him."

"Really," Grace said casually. "How so?"

"Oh, Mother, I don't know. He isn't the way I thought he would be. He comes off tough and cynical— which he is," she amended quickly, then added, "but underneath... I don't know how to explain it. Anyway, before I realized what I was doing, I was telling him about this party, and asking if he wanted to come with me."

"I see," Grace said.

"You sound as if you don't approve."

"Now, Kate, don't go putting words into my mouth. Why should I possibly object if you and Nick are seeing each other?"

"We're not *seeing* each other! I just asked him to a simple little party."

"All right, dear, you don't have to bite my head off."

"I'm sorry. I don't know why I'm so sensitive about this."

"I don't know, either, Kate. After all, it's not for me to approve or disapprove. You're an adult, capable of making your own decisions. I'm not going to interfere."

"There, you see! You *do* disapprove. Is it because Nick is working for Dad?"

For a moment, there was silence at Grace's end. Then she said, "That's ridiculous, Kate. The fact that Nick Santos is working for your father has nothing to do with anything. I hope you and Nick have a wonderful time at the party."

Kate let the matter drop, but after they'd hung up, she was still uncertain about her mother's reaction. For a moment there, she was sure she'd heard some reservation in Grace's voice. But she quickly dismissed that notion. Maybe, since *she* was so unsure about this, she was projecting her feelings onto her mother.

"It's only a party," she finally muttered. "It's not as if you're getting engaged to the man. Get a grip."

She had plenty to do to keep her mind occupied until the party. In addition to early rounds at the hospital, she was scheduled for two double shifts at the clinic. She was glad she was going to be so busy; it gave her less time to think about Nick Santos.

"You seem a little preoccupied, Kate," one of the

charge nurses observed later that day. "Is something wrong?"

Kate looked blankly at her. "No, why?"

The nurse gestured. "You've been staring at that chart for the past five minutes."

Kate glanced down. The page was blank. Embarrassed, she scribbled her orders on it and handed it to the nurse.

"Thanks," she muttered. But she could feel the woman staring after her as she hurried off, and all she could think of was how much she wished Saturday would come and go, so she could get her mind back where it belonged.

GRACE SAT IN HER OFFICE, staring at the telephone. She'd been trying to think of a way to approach Marguerite Kauffman again without sounding pushy. But after the conversation with Kate that morning, getting together with Mrs. Kauffman seemed even more imperative. She wanted to talk to Marguerite before Nick Santos did.

She was just reaching for the phone when it rang. When she answered, she was surprised to hear that it was Marguerite. "Well, this is a coincidence," Grace said, when the pleasantries were out of the way. "I was just about to phone you."

"Really?" Marguerite sounded pleased. "I hope it was to ask when we might get together. I did so enjoy talking to you the other day."

"The pleasure was mine."

"I know it's terribly short notice, but Erin tells me that your Kate will be here for her party this coming Saturday, and I wondered if you could possibly join us, too."

Grace, who had been desperately trying to figure out a way to wangle an invitation to Vignoble without sounding too eager, looked in dismay at her calendar. When she saw that Saturday was totally blocked in, she almost groaned. What with everything else, she'd forgotten all about the Hancock wedding descending on the store. But there it was, in big block letters, filling the entire day.

"I'd love to, Marguerite," she said, "but I just can't. An important wedding is in two weeks, and the bride and all her attendants are coming in—again—for yet another 'final' fitting on Saturday. I have to be here. I promised the mother, who is beside herself at this point. Her daughter has changed her mind six times now."

"Oh, dear," Marguerite said, disappointed. "I wanted to—but it doesn't matter. I understand about your commitment. And as I said, it was short notice. Perhaps another time."

"I hope so."

Marguerite hesitated. "I do have to come into the city late this afternoon for an appointment. I seem to be issuing impromptu invitations by the score today, but if you have time, we could meet for an early dinner. I usually have a driver, but it's his day off, so I'll be driving in myself. My night vision isn't what it used to be, and I've promised my granddaughter I won't drive late at night."

Thanking whatever benevolent deities had dropped this opportunity into her lap, Grace accepted at once. "As it happens, I'm free tonight. I'll be delighted to meet you, wherever and at whatever time you wish."

"That's wonderful!"

They agreed on six o'clock at a restaurant not far from the store. Grace was so anxious that she arrived a full fifteen minutes before the hour and spent the time trying to figure out what to say. She had to be careful how she approached Marguerite. After all, could hardly come right out and ask Marguerite if she was Dirk's mystery lady. Just because they'd known each other in New York didn't mean they'd run off together to Australia.

Still…

Then she thought of something else. Even if Marguerite *was* the one who had gone with Dirk, she might not know anything about the jewels. Grace didn't know much about Jeffrey's uncle, but if he'd been brazen enough to steal the gems in the first place, he might be secretive enough to keep it even from the woman he supposedly loved.

And that was another thing, Grace thought, increasingly anxious. How was she going to go about mentioning the jewels? It was a sensitive subject, and she most definitely didn't want Marguerite to think she was implicating her in the theft.

Deciding that she would have made a terrible spy, Grace ordered a glass of wine. By the time Marguerite walked in at precisely six o'clock, Grace had decided that she ought to abandon this entire quixotic quest. It had been silly to think that she could get her hands on the remaining jewels, when Nick, whose business it was to take care of problems like this, hadn't been able to locate them. And why was she worrying about the DeWilde collection, anyway? It was no longer any of her business.

That decided, she was breathing a sigh of relief when Marguerite sat down, smiled at her and dropped her bombshell.

"I wasn't quite candid with you the other day when we first met, Grace," Marguerite said, unfolding her napkin and placing it across her lap. "Do you remember when I mentioned that I had known Dirk in New York?"

Did she remember? Grace almost laughed aloud. She'd been doing practically nothing but thinking about the implications of the remark ever since. But she just nodded and said, "Yes, I remember."

Marguerite hesitated. "Well, the truth of the matter is—"

Just then, the waiter came bustling up to the table, and Marguerite looked at him with impatience. He was oblivious to her disapproval, intent on delivering a well-rehearsed spiel about that day's specials. He'd barely finished when Marguerite made a dismissive gesture and said, "I need a few moments to think about this. Would you mind coming back later?"

"Certainly, madam." He beamed, anyway. "In the meantime, may I get you some more wine...or an appetizer?"

Grace looked at her half-empty glass. "No, I'm fine," she replied. "Marguerite?"

"Yes, I'll have a glass—the same as my friend," Marguerite said impatiently. Her expression almost willed the man to go away.

Once he had left, Marguerite turned back to Grace. "I was talking about Dirk—or Derrick, as he called himself later."

With an effort, Grace kept her expression neutral. But inside, she was fairly quivering with anticipation. What was Marguerite going to tell her? As casually as she could, she said, "Yes?"

Marguerite flushed. As Grace waited for her to continue, she found herself studying the older woman's features, imagining how attractive she must have been when she was younger and had first met Dirk. A thrill of recognition coursed through her and she could barely contain her excitement. *Why,* she thought suddenly, *Marguerite does look just like Maggie Cutter in Australia!* Could it be...?

Grace tried to get hold of herself. Her mind was galloping ahead, with so little concrete evidence to go on.

"I've never spoken about this to another living soul," Marguerite went on at last, "but as I told you, I've been following you and your career for years now—especially since you came to San Francisco and started your own store here. I...I know it's presumptuous of me, Grace, but I feel that I can trust you."

Grace was touched. "Of course you can trust me, Marguerite."

"I'm so glad, Grace. I...I need a friend right now."

Despite Marguerite's brave front, Grace could see that the woman was struggling to keep her composure, and her heart went out to the older woman. Her emotional pain was evident in the shadow that seemed to cloud her eyes and the tension that tightened the soft lines of her face. Instinctively, she reached for Marguerite's hand.

"What is it?" she asked. "You can tell me anything."

Tears filled Marguerite's eyes. Obviously embarrassed, she took out a lace-trimmed handkerchief. As she dabbed at her face, she said, "This is ridiculous. I can't remember the last time I cried."

Grace smiled, a little sadly. "I know what you mean. Until this past year, I hadn't shed a tear in longer than I could remember. Then it seemed that every time I turned around, I was blubbering."

"It's so annoying."

"It is, indeed."

They smiled at each other, then Marguerite crumpled

the handkerchief and put it back in her purse. "I have to admit, I do feel better. But before that overzealous waiter returns with our wine and wants to know in detail what we'll have to eat tonight, I have to say what I came to say. And the truth of it is that, long ago, I left my husband and ran off with Dirk DeWilde to Australia."

This time, Grace couldn't keep her feelings in check. So, she *had* been right! Marguerite saw her expression and smiled.

"I see that my big confession isn't exactly the surprise I thought it would be," she said wryly.

"It's not that," Grace said. "I have to admit, I *had* guessed. But to hear you say it—"

"How did you guess?"

"It was something Kate said when I mentioned that you had come into the store. Apparently, when she went out to Vignoble, she saw a portrait of you there in which you're wearing a certain pin."

Marguerite's expression turned faraway, as if she were reaching into the past. "Oh, yes, that whimsical little cat on the crescent moon. Dirk gave that to me when we were in Australia—to celebrate our...time together. I always loved that pin."

"So did I," Grace said, with her own nostalgic smile. "There were three of those pins in the DeWilde collection, one for each of the brothers—Dirk, Henry and Charles. I was given Charles's pin by his wife—my mother-in-law. I often wore it when Jeffrey and I..."

Her voice caught as she remembered the many happy times she had worn that pin with Jeffrey. Setting aside the memories, she steadied herself and went on. "He used to tease me about my choice, because it was one of the most minor pieces among a dazzling array of real gems."

"We women can be quite silly and sentimental at times, I agree," Marguerite said. "I knew I was taking a chance that someone would recognize the pin when I wore it for that portrait, but I couldn't help myself. Of all the things that Dirk gave me, that pin was the most precious to me."

All the things Dirk had given her? Grace thought, feeling another thrill. Was Marguerite referring to other jewels—perhaps even some of the pieces that Dirk was rumored to have stolen? She wanted desperately to ask, but then she noted Marguerite's expression and knew that now wasn't the time. Marguerite looked so wistful that she couldn't possibly grill her about the missing jewels.

Instead, she said, "It isn't silly to be sentimental— especially where the men we love are concerned." She paused before she added painfully, "Sometimes, in the end, sentiment is the only thing we have left of them."

Marguerite nodded her head silently. After the waiter came and took their order, the two women spoke of other things—Grace's store, Marguerite's years spent running Vignoble Winery. But as they parted that night, Grace knew that their conversation about Dirk wasn't finished. Marguerite had more to tell, but until she was ready, Grace had no choice but to bide her time.

TWO DAYS AFTER GRACE and Marguerite had dinner in downtown San Francisco, Kate was preparing for her outing with Nick Santos. It was Saturday, and she couldn't believe she actually had a whole day off.

In fact, she thought, she couldn't recall when she'd had so much time away from the hospital and the clinic. She'd slept in this morning until seven o'clock—an unheard-of indulgence she hadn't allowed herself since she'd entered medical school. To celebrate, she'd taken a cup of coffee back to bed and lingered luxuriously there.

But by seven-thirty, she was up and cleaning her apartment. Then she washed her hair and did a couple of loads of laundry. By eleven, she was still racing around, and all because in one hour she was going to see Nick Santos again. Why was she so nervous? It wasn't as though she'd never gone out with a man before.

"For heaven's sake!" she muttered to herself. Too agitated to sit, she started to fold and put away the clean laundry. As she worked, she suddenly wondered how Roz Makinney would handle this situation.

The thought made her laugh. If she were Roz, things would be so simple. All she'd have to do was don skin-tight pants, a revealing blouse, pile her hair as high as possible on her head and put on false eyelashes. When she greeted Nick at the door, she'd assume a seductive pose, grab him by the shirt, pull him inside and ravish him the rest of the day—and probably far into the night—until they were both exhausted.

She considered the possibility. Now that she thought about it, maybe it wasn't such a bad idea.

What was she thinking?

Appalled, she quickly shoved the rest of her clothes into a dresser drawer and walked over to her closet to choose what to wear. But once she was standing in front of her wardrobe, nothing seemed right. She pulled out a silk dress. Too fancy. She looked at jeans. Much too casual. What next?

Aware of time passing while she dithered about something so inconsequential as what to wear, she yanked out a pair of cream-colored linen slacks and a matching silk blouse. The outfit seemed acceptable until she got it on. When she looked at herself in the mirror, the neutral color made her feel as though she'd faded into the woodwork.

She had to do something—fast. Wishing too late that she had made time for some much-needed clothes shopping, she rummaged through her usually neglected jewelry box and unearthed a wonderful wood and bead necklace that her parents had brought back for her from a trip to Africa. She remembered matching earrings and she dug around until she found those, too. Newly bedecked, she reexamined her reflection. It wasn't spectacular, but it would have to do.

The doorbell rang just then. She was so nervous she actually jumped.

This is ridiculous, she told herself as she stood in the center of the bedroom, hands clenched. If she didn't pull herself together, Nick was going to think she was an absolute idiot. She took a few deep, calming breaths and went to answer the bell.

"Hi," she said brightly when she opened the door. But as soon as she saw him, her heart began to pound again—and this time it had nothing to do with nerves. On the other occasions she'd seen him, he'd been in a suit. Today, he was wearing light slacks and a green shirt. Hanging casually over one arm was a gingercolored sports jacket. In his other hand he was holding a bouquet of pink carnations surrounded by ferns and baby's breath. He held the flowers out to her.

"For you," he said in that deep voice that caused a shiver to run down her back.

"Why...thank you." She took the bouquet from him, surprised and pleased. It had been a long time since a man had brought her flowers, and for a moment, she just stood there. Then she said, "Let me just put these in water, and we can go."

She stepped aside so that he could come in, then she escaped to the kitchen. She was just reaching for a vase when she realized that Nick had followed her. When she turned, he was standing in the doorway watching her.

"What is it?" she asked.

He smiled that sensuous half smile of his. "I was just thinking how different you look today."

"What do you mean...different?"

Shoving himself away from the doorjamb, he came toward her. "Why do you sound suspicious at everything I say?"

Hastily, she retreated to the sink. "I don't. It's just that you have...a way of putting things."

"In this case, I meant it as a compliment."

"Oh. Well...thanks."

"Do you want help with those?"

Blankly, she looked down. She had forgotten she was holding the flowers and the vase. She was so rattled at the moment that she couldn't remember getting the container out of the cupboard. Whirling around, she stuck the vase under the faucet and turned on the water. It was incredible that Nick's mere presence in her kitchen was having such an effect on her. She couldn't understand it. She was less nervous assisting at the most complicated surgeries. All this man had to do was to walk into view, and she fell apart. What was going on here?

Whatever it was, she decided grimly, it was going to stop. There was no doubt that Nick Santos was a good-looking, sexy man—but he *was* only a man. There was absolutely no reason for her to be acting like a silly schoolgirl around him; she was too old for that.

With renewed resolve, she turned off the water, stuck

the flowers in the vase, fluffed them up a little in an attempt at an arrangement, put the whole thing on the counter, and turned calmly to Nick.

"They're beautiful," she said, trying to tell herself that she was imagining the heat from his dark eyes. "It's been a long time since anyone brought me flowers."

"That's hard to believe."

"It's true," she replied, feeling herself becoming unnerved beneath his gaze. Suddenly exasperated by the unfair advantage he always seemed to hold over her, she demanded abruptly, "Why on earth are you looking at me like that?"

She had half expected him to utter a denial. Instead he said, "I was wondering what you would do if I kissed you."

"K-kissed me?" she stammered. Without warning, a heat wave flashed through her entire body. Her heart began pounding, and a loud roaring filled her ears. Desperately she searched for something witty and sophisticated to say, but all she could come up with was, "Why don't you try it and find out?"

He didn't wait for a second invitation. Or for her to change her mind and say she'd been joking. His long legs erased the distance between them in one step, then his hand was on her neck, his thumb was tipping her head up, and before she was ready, his mouth was on hers.

Kate had been kissed before, but never like this. Every sense she possessed flared to life at the first touch of his lips, and without realizing what she was doing, she pressed against him. In a daze, she felt the splay of his fingers in her hair and at the side of her face; she felt the fervor of his body even through their clothes. It was the most wonderful sensation she had ever experienced.

Without questioning the impulse, she lifted her hands to his face. His lean cheeks were warm and smooth beneath her palms, and when she ran her fingers through his hair, the strands were silky to the touch. The scent of his after-shave was in her nostrils, but she detected another scent, as well—the musky fragrance of a man. Desire rose so swiftly and savagely inside her that it frightened her, and she tried to pull away.

"Nick—" she gasped.

"Shh," he murmured, his lips on hers. He put his other arm around her waist and slowly pulled her toward him until their bodies touched once more.

She was electrified. A thrill raced through her at the contact; she could feel the telltale bulge of his arousal and pressed against him again. His breathing changed, and she felt him tremble. As he pulled her even more tightly into him, she wrapped her arms around his neck. She felt his probing tongue and opened her mouth to take him inside her—as she wanted to take *all* of him inside her.

Their kiss deepened. Kate's pulse was pounding; she felt as if she might drown in sensation. Passion flooded through her; every nerve tingled. In another second, she'd pull him to the floor and beg him to make love to her right there in the kitchen.

She didn't know where she found the strength of will, but somewhere inside her, she knew it was now or never. In another few seconds, she wouldn't be able to stop. If he didn't reach for her clothes and tear them off her body, she would.

She put her hands on his broad chest and pushed. Gasping, she said, "Stop! We have to stop!"

He lifted his head at once. His dark eyes glazed, he

shook himself as though to clear his senses. He stepped back, putting some slight distance between them.

"Lord," he muttered, breathing hard. He still looked dazed. "What just happened?"

She wasn't sure. Whatever it was, it had never happened to her before. Thoroughly shaken, she grabbed the counter. It took her a few seconds to feel its solidity beneath her trembling hands. Even so, she had to wait for the floor to stop rolling beneath her.

She raised a hand to her head. Her heartbeat was returning to normal, but it took a few more seconds for the dizziness to clear. She dared a look at Nick.

"Well," she said. "I guess we found out."

"I guess we did." He shoved his long fingers through his disheveled hair. "Now what? Do you want me to leave?"

Kate knew that she should tell Nick Santos to leave now and never come near her again. She knew she should tell him to go far away and not come back. He was dangerous—dangerous to the order of her carefully planned life, dangerous to her emotional equilibrium...just dangerous.

Yet as she looked at him, filling her kitchen with his sultry good looks, gazing at her with the same endearing befuddlement she felt, she wanted to throw herself back into his embrace and feel his strong arms around her. More than anything, she yearned again for the touch of his lips.

When she didn't answer, Nick reached for the jacket he'd tossed on one of the kitchen chairs. "Maybe this wasn't such a good idea, after all. I think I should leave."

She had wanted just that—a moment ago. But now she put her hand out. "No. Don't...go. We have to talk about this. I...I don't know about you, but this is happening too fast for me. I thought we were going to just be...friends.''

"Is that all you want to be—just friends?"

No, she thought. She wanted to be much more than that. But she said, "I need a little space, Nick."

"How much space?"

She smiled shakily. "Not much."

He smiled back. "Good."

The crisis had passed, and she felt calmer, more sure of herself—more *like* herself. Even so, before she could change her mind and do what Roz would have done— ravish him right there—she handed him his coat and said, "I think we should go to Erin's party now, don't you?"

It was clear what he thought, but he didn't argue. Taking the coat from her, he kissed her lightly on the lips, almost destroying her resolve right there.

"Whatever you say," he said. And then added, "For now."

CHAPTER SEVEN

VIGNOBLE WINERY was an hour or so away. After what had happened between them in her apartment, Kate wasn't sure how they would handle the long drive. It was just the two of them, alone in the car, with *that kiss* still hanging over them.

But after some initial awkwardness, she found that being alone with Nick wasn't hard at all. On the infrequent occasions she'd been out with men these past few years, she'd felt the need to fill up the quiet spaces with chatter. She didn't feel that way with Nick. If she didn't want to talk, she didn't; if she felt like pointing out something of interest as they drove along, she did.

So they spoke of inconsequential things as they headed north on 101, but when they left the freeway and entered the famous wine region, things changed between them again. Kate wasn't sure why; perhaps it was because the setting suddenly seemed more intimate than the impersonal highway.

On either side of the car the land rolled away in gentle slopes. Everything had been green with the winter rains, but now the once-lush grass was turning to gold under the hot sun. Sheep slept under ancient oak trees; cattle and horses grazed in quiet meadows. It was a lovely, pastoral sight that reminded Kate of England.

They drove past the vineyards, row upon row of military-straight vines, which in some cases stretched far away across the hills. Clusters of tiny grapes could be seen among the brilliant leaves, and Kate was admiring the beauty around her when Nick spoke.

"This area reminds me of some of the places I saw in France," Nick said.

The words were out before Kate could stop them. "When you were trailing my sister, Megan, you mean?"

Even under his dark skin, Nick flushed. "I wasn't *trailing* her," he said impatiently. "It was part of my job to talk to every member of your family."

Kate didn't want to quarrel with him—not on such a beautiful day. "You're right," she said. She turned to look out the window again. "It reminds me of France, too. I've never been a wine connoisseur, but when I see the vineyards in full bloom like this, it almost makes me a convert." She looked at him again. "You've traveled quite a bit in this job for my father, haven't you?"

"It's been a way to see the world, all right," Nick agreed. He smiled ironically. "Though sometimes with all the frenetic zipping from one place to the next, I think there should be a better way to organize things. But it's been my experience that clues don't just line up one after the other in logical order. I have to check out each one as it comes."

"And what have you found out so far?"

He sighed. "Where to start?"

"Why don't you begin with the tiara that showed up in New York?" she said. She rested her head against the seat. "I hate to admit it, but I've been so busy that I haven't paid much attention to all the goings on."

"It's a good thing. Otherwise, you'd only be confused, like I have been. But to answer your question, I traced the tiara to an American buyer in Australia—"

"How did you like Australia? I've never been there."

"It's an interesting country. It's so big that ranchers measure their land in square miles rather than in acres. It's understandable why your great-uncle Dirk emigrated. Even if he hadn't changed his name, he could easily have gotten lost in all that space."

"Are you sure that Dirk—or Derrick—really stole the jewels? What about the persistent rumor that someone in the Villeneuve family did it? When I first talked to Megan about this, she reminded me that those pieces were promised to our great-aunt Marie-Claire upon her marriage to Armand Villeneuve. When she called off her engagement to Armand, there was a lot of bitterness between the Villeneuves and the DeWildes. Perhaps they stole the jewels for revenge."

"True. Except we know now that the tiara was in the possession of Maggie Cutter, who sold it to finance her son's wildlife preserve in northern Australia. So that essentially eliminates the Villeneuves."

"I guess so. But it's still amazing that you traced Dirk to Australia."

He feigned offense. "Amazing? Not a matter of talent?"

Kate was embarrassed. "I didn't mean—"

"Never mind. I did trace him, but I had assistance. Everyone in your family has been very helpful."

"Tell me about the mysterious woman who accompanied Dirk to Australia. Maybe he stole the jewels for her."

Nick shot her a glance. "I thought you hadn't paid any attention to all this."

Kate waved a hand. "I haven't, really. But for some reason, my sister feels it's her duty to keep me informed. Though, much of what she tells me goes in one ear and out the other. But I do have to admit to a certain fascination about Dirk's mystery lady. It sounds rather romantic, don't you think? Two star-crossed lovers running away to start a new life.''

"Yeah, one a thief, the other a married woman," Nick said. "Real romantic."

It was the first time during the drive that he had sounded cynical. Kate glanced over at him, but he was paying attention to his driving—or appeared to be. Even so, she felt the change in him and tried to think what she had said to offend him. Had he really been affronted by her whimsical remark about two lovers?

When she tentatively put a hand on his arm, it felt like granite beneath her fingers. "Nick? Did I say something wrong?"

He shifted away from her. "It wasn't you."

"Are you sure?"

He drummed his fingers on the wheel, thinking. Finally, he spoke. "What you said about the two lovers running away reminded me of my so-called parents. My father—and I use the term loosely—left when my mother was eight months pregnant with me. I was about five, I guess, when *she* ran off with some biker type. Of course, by then, my grandmother and I hardly noticed. Mother was always off somewhere, trying to score to support her habit."

"Oh, Nick, I'm so sorry. I had no idea."

He shrugged. "That's life."

Kate had trained herself to listen to nuances when she talked with patients. She had learned to give as much weight to what they didn't say as to what they did. Often a critical diagnosis depended upon her being able to read between the lines.

But even if she hadn't been able to read people as well as she did, she would have known by Nick's too-casual response just how much he had been hurt by the actions of his parents. And though he would vehemently deny it, it was obvious he was still affected by their abandonment.

Now wasn't the time to talk about it. To her dismay, the gates to Vignoble Winery were straight ahead. She started to say, "Nick, I—"

"Forget it. It doesn't matter."

"But it does matter," she insisted. "You shared something very important with me. I can't just go into that party and pretend that—"

"Yes, you can," he said, reverting to his hard-edged self once more. He didn't speak until after he'd found a place to park, then he turned to her with a set expression. "I told you, it was long ago—far into the past. It doesn't have anything to do with what's going on today."

"But—"

He was already out of the car, coming around to her side to open the door. When she saw his face, she sighed and reached for the gaily wrapped birthday present she'd brought for Erin. If he didn't want to talk about his personal life right now, she couldn't force him to do it. As it was, she was surprised that he'd revealed as much of himself as he had.

They were heading up the long walk to the elegant stone mansion when Nick stopped. "Wait," he said. "There's something I have to tell you."

Hopeful that he'd changed his mind after all, she turned to him. "What is it?"

He hesitated before he said, "I think Marguerite Kauffman is the woman Dirk ran off with when he went to Australia."

"*What?* But...that's what Mother wondered!"

Right before her eyes, he changed again. Without

warning, he looked alert, watchful...suspicious. She was staring at him in dismay when he said, "And why did she think that?"

His expression had sharpened his features and made him seem vaguely menacing. Uneasily, Kate stepped back. "I'm not...sure. Why is it important?"

With a visible effort, he tried to relax. "It's not," he said. "Because I'm going to be sure before I leave here."

"What do you mean?"

He looked around quickly, then pulled her off the path into the shadow of some shrubbery near the door. "In order to find out, I'm going to need your help."

"What? But how can I help you?"

"Will you do it?"

Her alarm was growing by leaps and bounds. "I don't know. It depends on what you want me to do."

"I want you to stand guard."

"Stand *guard?* Just what do you intend to do?"

"I'm going to search the house."

"What?" She looked at him incredulously before casting a furtive glance around her. "Are you out of your mind? You can't do that!"

"Yes, I can," he said calmly. "I've done it before."

She regarded him as though he'd suddenly metamorphosed into a monster. Then she became angry. "Well, you're not going to do it here!" she declared. "Marguerite Kauffman is the grandmother of one of my friends. I'm not going to allow you to go in there and...and *search* her house! In addition to the fact that I'm sure it's a criminal act, it's...it's rude!"

It was a ridiculous thing to say, but she was so upset she hardly knew what she was saying. As she glared at him in total indignation, he said, "All right, fine. Pretend you don't know."

"But I *do* know! Oh, I don't believe this! You must be mad—or think that I am!"

"Look," he said impatiently. "I'm just trying to do my job."

"And that includes rooting around in people's private things?"

"If necessary, yes."

She stared at him, nonplussed. Then she tried a different tack. "But what can you possibly hope to find? Marguerite is a lovely woman."

"Who abandoned her husband and ran off with another man."

"Even if it's true, that was years ago!"

"And that makes it all right?"

He had her there. "No, of course not," she had to say. "But you don't know the circumstances. She could have—"

"It doesn't matter," he said flatly. "The point is, I think she has the jewels, or at least knows where they are."

"No, you're wrong! She's just a—"

Nick's expression hardened. "What? A sweet little old lady? Well, let me tell you, one of the most vicious killers I ever tracked had exquisite manners and a baby face that made women weep. So don't tell me about trusting appearances!"

"All right. So you know more about criminals than I do. But that still doesn't mean that Marguerite has the DeWilde jewels or that she knows anything about them!"

"Fine. Then let me prove it."

Angrily, she turned away. "You're not being fair,

Nick. You've boxed me into a corner, and I don't know what to do."

He put a hand on her arm, turning her to face him again. "I do," he said. "Let me do my job, and we'll get out of here."

She made the mistake of looking up at him. The heat of his gaze seemed to bore right into her soul, and incredibly, she found herself wondering what harm it would do if he just…looked. After all, what could he possibly hope to find? If Marguerite *did* have the jewels—and Kate couldn't imagine anything more unlikely—the woman would hardly be so foolish as to leave them lying around.

"All right," she said finally. But to show she meant business, she gave him a warning look. "But if you *dare* put me in the embarrassing situation of having to explain why you're skulking around the house of our hostess—"

Smiling, he tucked her hand through his arm. With breezy confidence, he assured her, "Don't worry. As long as you're watching out, Marguerite won't know a thing."

"You'd better be right," she muttered. Annoyed and upset, she disengaged her arm and quickly preceded him up the steps.

She felt so guilty about agreeing to be a sentry for Nick that she was overly effusive when they went inside and were greeted by Marguerite and her granddaughter. As soon as the pleasantries and introductions were finished, Erin pulled her aside.

"Are you all right?" Erin whispered.

Kate looked at her a little too brightly. "Of course, why do you ask?"

"Because you seem…I don't know—maybe *hyper-*

active would be a good word. It's almost as if you're on something.''

"Don't be silly." To avoid her friend's all-too-sharp glance, Kate gave her a hug. "If I'm a little... enthusiastic, it must be because I haven't had a day off in so long."

"I'm flattered that you chose to spend it here, but—"

"No buts about it," Kate said firmly. To her relief, several other guests arrived just then, and she gestured toward them. "More people to see you, birthday girl. I'll talk to you later."

Erin still looked doubtful. "You're sure you're okay?"

"I couldn't be better. Now, go see to your guests."

Erin glanced at Nick, who, Kate suddenly realized with a sharp pang of nerves, was still talking to Marguerite. "By the way," Erin added with a grin, her blue eyes twinkling, "I like your date. Is it serious?"

"He's just a friend. Besides, you know I don't have time for a relationship."

"Maybe you should make time," Erin said with a wink.

"Now, Erin—"

"Okay, I'll tell you what. If you throw him over, toss him in my direction, will you?"

Kate forced a smile. "I don't think he's the kind to be tossed. But if it comes to that, I'll give it a try."

"Can't ask for more than that. Enjoy yourselves."

As quickly as she could, Kate rejoined Nick and Marguerite. To her relief, they were discussing how beautiful the wine country was in the spring. Marguerite abandoned the topic when Kate appeared at Nick's side. Greeting Kate with a smile of genuine pleasure, she held out her hands and Kate took them.

"It's so good to see you again, my dear," Marguerite said warmly. "But you'll forgive me if I say you look a little peaked."

Keenly aware of Nick by her side, Kate forced a laugh. "You sound like Mother," she said fondly. "But as I told her, it's an occupational hazard—at least for the present."

Marguerite shifted her bright-eyed gaze to Nick. "I'm charging you, young man, to see that Kate has a good time today. She works too hard. And since it's rare that she takes any time off, I want her to enjoy herself."

"I'll do my best, Mrs. Kauffman," Nick said gallantly.

"Oh, please call me Marguerite. We don't stand on ceremony here at Vignoble, especially on such a day as today. Now, I must attend to the other guests, so please, make yourself at home. My house is yours. I want you both to feel welcome."

Kate could hardly wait until the spry figure in dramatic fuchsia-colored silk moved away. As soon as she was sure Marguerite's attention was occupied, she grabbed Nick's hand and tugged him over to a huge, potted ficus near the living room.

"Now do you see what I meant about Marguerite?" she hissed. "You've met her, talked to her. Surely you can't believe she's actually hiding stolen jewels!"

Nick wasn't impressed by her impassioned defense. "There was a woman over in Sacramento a few years ago that everyone thought was a saint because she cared for senior citizens in her boarding house. Trouble is, the old guys kept disappearing. Police finally found most of them buried in her backyard. Turned out she'd poisoned them for their social security checks."

Exasperated, Kate said, "Why do you persist in thinking the worst of everyone?"

"Because I'm rarely disappointed that way."

She started to voice her disapproval, but he stopped her with that devastating half smile. "You misjudge me, Kate. I don't think the worst of *everyone*. I think highly of you for helping me today."

"And that's another thing," she snapped. "Now that I've had time to think about it, I don't want to be your lookout. In fact, I can't believe I even considered it."

"Hey, doc, don't chicken out on me now."

"Stop teasing. I mean it!"

"I wasn't teasing. But I'm sure *you* were. So let's go—"

"No, we have to talk about this—"

He took her arm. "Fine. Let's talk about it while we check out the second floor."

"Wait a minute!" she protested as he moved away, pulling her along with him. "I don't think—"

As though he didn't even hear, he took her up the magnificent curving staircase that led to the second floor. She finally managed to free herself when they reached the upper landing.

"Which room is the master bedroom?" he asked.

"I haven't the faintest idea! But in any case, you can't be serious. You're not going to rifle through Marguerite's bedroom!"

"Yes, I am," he said, preoccupied as he scanned the long corridor. There were eight rooms down its length, each with its door closed. Before she could stop him, he tried the doorknob of the one closest. It was a bathroom, decorated in shades of pale blue and gold.

"You stand here," he said, practically picking her up and setting her in front of the door. "That way, if anyone

comes, you can pretend you were looking for the ladies'
room.''

She didn't like being manhandled. ''And just what are
you going to do?''

He was already on his way down the hallway, moving
like a giant wraith. Despite herself, Kate was fascinated
by the sight of such a big man moving so swiftly and
silently. Opening each door in turn, he would slip in and
out and then head for the next one in line.

Kate inched farther down the hallway as he tried the
handle of the fifth door, opened it and slipped inside.
She waited for what seemed an interminable length of
time, but still he didn't come out.

''Where *is* he?'' she muttered.

Just then, she thought she heard voices on the stairs.
Galvanized, she whirled to look, then whipped around
again in the direction where Nick had disappeared.

No sign of him.

The voices were louder now. Whoever it was seemed
to be coming up the stairs and not just lingering below.
Springing into action at the thought of Nick getting
caught—and having to explain what *she* was doing up
here—Kate fled her post by the bathroom and sped down
the hall. Flinging open the door to the room she had last
seen him enter, she called in a low voice, ''Nick, where
are you? You have to get out of here—''

The room was the sitting room of the master suite,
and Nick emerged from a doorway to her right.

''I found a safe,'' he said. ''I just need two more
minutes to open it.''

Kate was horrified. ''You're not going to break into
Marguerite's safe!''

''How else am I going to see what's inside?''

She was so distraught that she nearly gave a hysterical

laugh. Clamping down on the panic rising inside her, she said, "Nick, we have to get out of here! People are coming!"

Instantly, his demeanor changed. His voice sharpened as he demanded, "Who is it? Is it Marguerite?"

"I don't know! Does it matter? Whoever it is, they're going to discover us if we don't—"

"Shh—" Like a swift, silent panther, he moved to the door, which she had left partially open. They could both hear voices coming down the hallway toward them.

"Oh, Nick! They're going to find us!"

"No, they're not." Before she knew what he was about to do, he grabbed her hand and pulled her into Marguerite's bedroom. She guessed his intention, and she was even more appalled.

"We can't hide in here! How will we ever explain—"

"You talk too much. Just get in the closet and don't make any noise."

"In the *closet?*" She would die of embarrassment if she was discovered hiding in a closet with Nick. Wildly, she shook her head. "No, I absolutely will not—"

The voices suddenly became louder. It was obvious that whoever it was had come into the sitting room of the suite. In two seconds, they might enter the bedroom. Before Kate could argue further, Nick clapped one hand over her mouth, put an arm around her waist and pulled her into the closet with him. He'd barely closed the louvered doors when Marguerite and Erin entered the bedroom.

Kate was never so glad of a hiding place in her life. As dreadful as this was, at least she was safe—for the moment. The doors had louvers, which were slanted down, and through the slats she could see the two women, who were sitting on the bed just a few feet away. She closed her eyes. If they were caught, she'd never be able to explain it.

Her heart was pounding so hard she was sure that Marguerite and Erin could hear it; her breath was a harsh rasp in her ears. She just knew that she'd make a noise and then the jig would be up. Furious with Nick for placing her in this embarrassing, humiliating, *mortifying* predicament, she glared at him over the hand he still held against her mouth. He had the audacity to grin back at her and silently mouth the word, *Quiet.*

Did he actually think she'd scream if he took his hand away from her mouth? Outraged, she jerked her head away and glared at him again. The last thing she wanted was to be found hiding in the closet with him. If Gabe or Megan ever heard about it, she'd never live it down.

Until now, Kate had been too irate to realize how small this space was. It was used for outdoor gear, and she and Nick were shoved up against a half-dozen coats and jackets with no room to move. Nick still had an arm around her waist, and as much as she wanted to fling it away to show him how angry she was with him, she didn't dare move. All Marguerite and Erin needed to hear was the rattle of a coat hanger to realize they weren't alone.

Despite the harrowing circumstances, Nick's nearness was beginning to affect her. With one arm wrapped around her and his breath gently fanning her cheek, she was more than acutely aware of him. Memories of that kiss they'd shared tantalized her and she could feel herself weakening, wanting to lean back into him, longing to turn her face up to his and feel his lips on hers again.

Fiercely, she told herself to get a grip. She couldn't let him have this effect on her. The only explanation must be that all her senses were heightened by the danger of discovery. Dim light filtered in from the bedroom, casting shadowy lines across Nick's handsome, dark face, and for a few desperate moments, she could almost believe that she'd been transported to some awful B movie. She wished with all her might that Marguerite and Erin would go so she could burst free from this damned closet and be in control of herself again.

But Marguerite seemed to be in no hurry to leave the bedroom. In fact, as Kate frantically focused on her in an attempt to forget her teeming fantasies about the man standing behind her, Marguerite was just giving Erin her birthday present. When Kate saw what it was, her eyes widened. The present was the "cat on the moon" pin.

"I can't accept this, Grandmother," Erin protested when she saw what it was. "I know how much you love this pin."

"I do," Marguerite said with a smile. "That's why I want you to have it."

"But you've had it so long. You said it was an heirloom."

"That's exactly why I want you to have it. Someone I…loved long ago gave it to me, and it's very special."

Kate stiffened. She was certain Marguerite meant that *Dirk* had given her that pin. Quickly, she looked at Nick. In the dim light, all she could see were his eyes, but what she saw alarmed her. What would he do if he couldn't prove that Marguerite knew where to find the missing jewels?

Erin was still staring down at the pin in her hand. She looked at her grandmother. Quietly, she said, "A man gave you this, didn't he?"

Marguerite's expression softened. "Yes. In many ways, he was a remarkable man. One of the greatest tragedies of his life was that he didn't believe it."

"It wasn't Grandfather, was it?"

Marguerite didn't answer for a moment. Then she sighed and said, "No. But it no longer matters. Suffice it to say that knowing this man changed my life. And I'm not sure it was for the better."

Erin put a hand on her grandmother's arm. "I'm sorry," she said.

Marguerite smiled sadly. "Things have a way of working out in the end. We all pay for our actions, both good and bad. And now I have just one thing left to do to make peace with the past."

"What's that, Grandmother?"

Before Marguerite could answer, excited voices sounded in the hallway and a merry group of Erin's guests burst into the bedroom. "We've been looking all over for you, Erin!" someone called gaily. "And you, Mrs. Kauffman! Come on, you two. It's time to cut the cake!"

Kate waited until everyone had departed in a flurry. When she was absolutely certain that the suite was empty, she opened the closet door and stumbled outside. Nick followed.

"Whew," he said. "That was close."

"*Close?*" She looked at him incredulously. "Is that all you can say?"

Nick must have seen the storm signals whirling up in Kate's green eyes. In an obvious attempt to forestall the blast he guessed was coming, he made the mistake of joking, "No, I was about to say that maybe we should go back to the party."

Kate didn't laugh. Icily, she said, "The only reason I'm going back downstairs is to make our excuses and say that I've been called away on an emergency."

"Oh, now, Kate. We just got here—"

"Don't you 'now, Kate' me! I have never been so embarrassed in my life! To think that I would have to hide in a closet to avoid being caught snooping around a close friend's house! I'm never going to forget this, and it's all your fault!"

If he'd been a lesser man, the look she gave him would have turned him to stone. As it was, he winced as she swept by him, her head held high. A few moments later, after she had gracefully tendered her apologies to her hostess and her friend for having to leave early, she led the way to the car. She and Nick didn't speak during the entire drive back to the city. And when he pulled up to her apartment complex, she got out without a word and pointedly slammed the car door shut.

IT WAS EARLY EVENING by the time the last of the party guests departed Vignoble. Erin left with friends in the final car, and as Marguerite waved them down the long drive and then closed the door, she was exhausted but pleased. The birthday celebration for her adopted granddaughter had gone well; everyone seemed to have had a good time.

Except for Kate and her handsome young man, Marguerite thought suddenly. It was a shame that Kate had had an emergency call and had to leave so early, but Marguerite supposed that was the way things were with doctors: their lives weren't their own.

As hers hadn't been for so many years.

The thought came out of nowhere, and she winced. She didn't like to think of that phase of her life when she'd returned to New York to care for her first husband. It had been the proper thing to do, but she had paid a high price for finally doing what was right.

And she wasn't the only one who had made sacrifices,

she thought with a heavy sigh. Everyone who was connected with that time had suffered. She'd wanted to make it right for years, but she hadn't known how.

Or maybe she'd just been too frightened to try.

She thought of Kate again, and of Kate's mother, Grace DeWilde. Perhaps through them, the means for her redemption might be at hand.

CHAPTER EIGHT

KATE WAS STILL FUMING about what had happened at Vignoble when the phone rang. Involuntarily, she glanced at the clock. It was almost eleven. She knew it wasn't the hospital or the clinic, because her beeper hadn't gone off. Maybe it was Nick.

Dismissing the little lurch of her heart at the thought, she turned away angrily. Hadn't she told herself a dozen times since Nick had dropped her off that she never wanted to speak to him again?

The phone rang again. She couldn't stand it. Snatching the receiver up, she barked a hello.

"Kate?"

"Mother?" Not sure if she was relieved or disappointed, she dropped into a chair, only to bolt upright again. "What's wrong? Why are you calling so late?"

"Is it late?" Grace said. "Oh, dear, I guess it is. I'm sorry, darling. I'm working and must have completely lost track of time. I hope I didn't wake you up."

"No, no, it's all right."

"I'm glad to finally reach you. You're never home. I must have tried to call you half-a-dozen times in the past few days."

Kate glanced at her answering machine. Because she always carried the beeper, she'd developed the bad habit of not checking her messages. To her relief, no incriminating red light was blinking.

"Why didn't you leave a message?" she asked.

"I know how busy you are. I didn't want you to have to call me back. It wasn't really important."

Kate tried to control her exasperation. "That doesn't matter, Mother. And you know I'm glad to return any of your calls. Er...what did you want?"

Grace laughed fondly. "That's my Katie—always direct and to the point. I didn't really *want* anything. I merely wondered how you enjoyed the birthday party at Marguerite's."

"Oh...it was very nice," Kate hedged, and knew as soon as she said it that her mother would pick up on her hesitation.

She was right. Quickly, Grace asked, "What is it? You sound—I don't know. Did something happen at the party?"

Kate couldn't confess. In fact, she cringed at the thought. But then she realized that it would be worse if she let something slip out later on. Better to get it over with now, she decided.

"Yes, something happened," she said, beginning to get angry all over again. "As you know, I made the mistake of asking Nick Santos to come with me, and he—" She stopped, indignation almost choking her. "He wanted to search the house!" she blurted out.

Even over the phone, Kate could hear her mother draw a sharp breath. "He thinks Marguerite has the jewels!" Grace gasped.

Kate had been sure that Grace would be appalled at the thought of Nick rooting around in someone's home—especially the home of someone she knew. The fact that her mother seemed more concerned about Marguerite and the jewels threw her. "Aren't you missing the point, Mother?" she asked tersely. "I invited him there. I feel responsible for his behavior. When he told me he wanted me to stand guard while he looked around, I should have—''

"He asked you to be his...his lookout?"

As her mother's voice rose in disbelief, Kate cursed herself for revealing so much. "Yes, he did," she admitted. "That's why I'm so upset. Erin is a friend of mine. And her grandmother is, too. But he treated her like a...a common criminal!"

"Don't you think you're being a little melodramatic? I realize you're upset—''

"Yes, I am upset! If anyone ever found out I had to hide in a closet with that man, I'd—''

"You hid in Marguerite's *closet?*"

Kate winced. "I know it sounds bad—''

"*Bad?* For heaven's sake, what in the world were you thinking of?"

Wondering that herself, Kate put a hand to her forehead. "I don't know, Mother. It's such a blur. All I can say is that it seemed...the only thing to do at the time."

"Oh, Kate!"

"I know, I know. I can't believe it myself. The only redeeming factor is that we didn't get caught. If we had, I don't know how I would have explained it. Although," she added grimly, "I'm sure Mr. Santos would have come up with a way to rationalize everything."

"I just can't picture Nick Santos skulking about Marguerite's house. What do you think he hoped to find? Even if Marguerite has the jewels, I'm sure she wouldn't leave them lying around."

"Who knows what people will do?" Kate said, exasperated. She couldn't understand why her mother was worried about the jewels at a time like this. "And who knows what Nick would do? He's a private investigator, isn't he? He's obviously accustomed to using under-handed tactics to get what he wants."

"Oh, now, Kate, I'm sure that Nick is an honorable man."

"Honorable! If he'd had time, he would have broken into Marguerite's bedroom safe!"

"Now, Kate, you can't possibly know that."

"Why are you defending him? You don't know what he'd do! In fact, he was looking for a safe, and he found one. If Marguerite and Erin hadn't come along when they had, he would have tried to open it."

"But that's breaking the law!"

"You see what I mean?"

Grace was silent a moment. Then she said, "You know, perhaps I should speak to your father about this. It sounds to me as though Nick is going a little too far in this quest to find those jewels."

Despite what she'd just said, Kate reacted with dismay. "You're going to tell Dad? Oh, Mother, maybe we should think about this."

"What is there to think about? You've just said that Nick's actions are bordering on the criminal. I think we have a duty to let your father know."

Kate closed her eyes. What had she done? As angry as she was with Nick for dragging her into this whole mess, she didn't want to be the cause of him losing his job. Nervously, she said, "Maybe I overreacted. Maybe Nick *was* only doing his job."

"By searching someone's home when he was a guest? I hardly think that's ethical, Kate."

"Even so—"

"You'll forgive me, darling, but now you sound upset with me."

Kate was weary of the whole thing. "I'm sorry,

Mother, I think I'm just tired. Could we talk about this again later?"

Grace hesitated. "I really think—"

"Please, Mother."

Grace relented. "All right, darling. But only if you promise to get some rest. You haven't been sounding like yourself lately. Are you sure you're just overtired?"

Kate wasn't sure of anything at the moment. Until Nick had flown into the clinic that night and wrestled Emilio Sanchez to the floor, her life had been going along in its orderly, predictable, exhausting fashion. Everything had been just as it should be. Now nothing was. She had never felt so confused, and she hated it.

Damn that man! she thought angrily. Why couldn't he have found those blasted jewels before he disrupted her entire life?

"I'll be fine, Mother," she said. "I'll talk to you in a few days, all right?"

"All right, dear. Good night."

Kate hung up the phone. Her mother was right. She hadn't been herself lately and it was all Nick Santos's fault. And so much for a restful day off; right now she was so exhausted she could sleep around the clock. She glanced at the time and made a face. In six hours she would have to get up for hospital rounds. Well, she was glad; that wouldn't give her any more time to dwell on this problem of her ambivalent feelings for Nick. Wearily, she got up and went to bed.

ACROSS TOWN, GRACE was too keyed up to sleep. She, too, glanced at the clock, calculated what time it would be in London, looked at the phone and hesitated. Perhaps she should, as Kate had suggested, stop to think about this. Did she really want to make trouble for Nick? She frowned. Maybe Nick had been doing his job.

She shook her head. No. His job was *not* to search the house of an older woman without her permission. Marguerite Kauffman had welcomed him into her home; she had treated him as a guest. To think that he'd rummaged through her things, that he'd found her safe—and worse, might have opened it if he'd had the chance—was outrageous. What kind of man had Jeffrey hired?

Spurred by the thought, she reached for the phone again, but dropped her hand a second time. She might try to fool others about the purity of her motives, but she couldn't fool herself.

The truth was, she wanted to talk to Jeffrey—under any pretext.

There. She'd admitted it. Now what?

Restless, she got up and went into the kitchen to pour herself a glass of wine. She didn't really feel like one, but perhaps it would help her to relax.

Then she realized that she didn't want to relax. She felt excited and alive, her mind buzzing with all Kate had told her. She had suspected that Marguerite was a key player in the mystery of the jewels, and Nick obviously believed the same thing. He'd been on the track for almost a year now, and he had gathered more information about what had happened than she might ever know.

And all paths seemed to lead to Marguerite Kauffman, who for some reason had decided to seek out Grace.

Grace leaned against the kitchen counter. Nick had come so far, she thought. He was right on the cusp of solving this mystery, which seemed to have preoccupied Jeffrey to the exclusion of everything else. But what if *she* got to the jewels before Nick did? What if *she* presented them to Jeffrey as a—

A what?

A fait accompli?

What would that accomplish?

Grace allowed herself a moment of pure fantasy, imagining Jeffrey's face when he found out that *she,* not the investigator he had hired, had found those jewels. It was so important to him, she thought. He had made their recovery a personal quest. What if she was the one who brought them back to him? Might that not be the first step toward—

Toward what?

Grace returned the wine bottle she was holding to the fridge and willed herself to slow down. She was getting ahead of herself. She and Jeffrey were divorced. There would be no shared future.

But there could be, she thought suddenly. And what better way to show Jeffrey that she still cared about him than to give him the one thing that had become so important to him? Wouldn't that be a beginning, at least?

Grace was well aware she was grasping at straws, but she had no choice. This divorce was all wrong. Both she and Jeffrey knew it, but once they'd become caught up in the process, embroiled in misunderstanding and wounded pride, the whole thing had steamrollered, with neither of them able to stop it. She would give anything to…go back.

Once again she thought of Marguerite. Should she tell Nick Santos what the woman had confided in her?

No, she decided. She shouldn't. Inexplicably, she felt she had a stake in this mystery, and as she saw it, she had this one opportunity to prove something to Jeffrey.

She walked across the kitchen and reached for the phone. It was time to make that overseas call.

BECAUSE IT WAS EARLY Sunday morning in London, Grace decided to call Jeffrey at their Chelsea flat—*his* flat, she amended silently. She held her breath until the phone was picked up on the fourth ring.

For a moment, Grace couldn't speak. She'd thought she was prepared to hear his voice, but as soon as he spoke, a lump formed in her throat and it was a few seconds before she could say anything.

"Hello?" Jeffrey said again. "Hello? Gabe? Meg? Is that you?"

Grace finally found her voice. "It's me, Jeffrey. How are you?"

Instantly, his tone became guarded. "I'm...fine, Grace. And you?"

"I'm well, thank you," Grace said. She knew how intuitive he could be, so she proceeded cautiously. She didn't want him to suspect the true motive behind her call. "I know how busy you are, so I'll get right to the point. Kate told me a disturbing story tonight about your investigator, Nick Santos. I thought you should know that in his zeal to recover the DeWilde jewels, he's come perilously close to breaking the law."

She could almost see him stiffen. "Oh?"

"Yes. Apparently Kate made the mistake of inviting him to a birthday party for one of her friends. While they were there, Nick searched the house."

"Searched the house?" he repeated.

This was the part where she had to be especially careful. "I don't have all the details, but Nick seems to believe the woman has some remote connection to Dirk. The point is, he dragged Kate into it—"

"Kate was involved?" Jeffrey interrupted sharply. "How?"

She took a deep breath. "He made her stand lookout for him while he skulked around."

To her satisfaction, Jeffrey was as shocked as she had been. "What? Is she all right? What's Kate doing with him, anyway? Were they caught?"

"Were they *caught?*" Her sense of triumph vanished. "Is that all you care about?"

"Of course not," he said hastily. "I meant...I mean...I'm astounded. I can't believe that Kate would engage in such...behavior."

"*Kate!*" Grace exclaimed. "What about your Mr. Santos?"

Jeffrey recovered himself quickly. "Whatever Nick has done, I'm sure it was within the context of his job," he said tersely.

"And that includes ransacking a private home?"

Instead of answering, he asked a question of his own. "Have you talked to Mr. Santos about this?"

"I certainly have not! I didn't see the need to discuss it with your investigator. Our daughter's word was good enough for me."

"You still haven't told me what Kate and Nick were doing together in the first place."

"Nick wangled an invitation from Kate to get into the house," Grace told him curtly. That wasn't quite the truth, of course, but she didn't want to stray too far from the main purpose of her call.

Jeffrey was silent for a moment. "What do you want me to do, Grace?"

"I want you to let him go, that's what I want," she said. "Now, I realize how important it is to you to resolve this matter of the jewels, but even so, I can't imagine that you would countenance such behavior—"

"You're right, Grace. Normally, I would not condone it. But these are special circumstances—"

This wasn't going at all the way she had planned. Incredulously, she said, "You can't be thinking of keeping him on after what I've just told you!"

"As a matter of fact, I am. At least, until I hear his part of the story."

"You don't believe our own daughter?"

"It's not a matter of believing one over the other, Grace. I merely said I wanted to talk to Nick before I come to any decision."

"And that's all you have to say about it?"

"At this point, yes."

Grace knew that tone. She was so outraged she couldn't even say goodbye, and had to content herself with slamming down the phone.

"So much," she said between clenched teeth, "for extending an olive branch to my ex-husband. After this, I don't care if he ever finds those jewels. In fact, I hope they're gone forever!"

She threw herself down and burst into tears.

CHAPTER NINE

NICK WAS SLOUCHED on the couch in his living room, staring gloomily at the wall, when his phone rang. He'd been in such a brown study that he almost jumped. Involuntarily, he looked at the offending instrument. Now that Kate knew he kept an apartment in the city, he had the irrational thought that it might be her calling. Then he realized how ridiculous that was, since she wasn't speaking to him.

What if she'd changed her mind?

Reaching for the receiver, he said hello.

"Hello, Nick." It was Jeffrey DeWilde. "I'm glad I caught you in. Is this a bad time, or can we talk for a moment or two?"

Nick groaned inwardly. He'd completely forgotten that this was the time he and Jeffrey had agreed upon to discuss the progress of the case. He wondered if he was imagining the cautious note in his employer's voice.

"No, this is fine," he said. "In fact, I'm glad you called. I needed to talk to you about something."

"Yes, you were going to give me an update."

"That's true. But I did fax you some information this morning—"

"Yes, you did. But you were, if I might say, somewhat obscure. You said you'd located the woman who ran away with Dirk—"

"Yes, her name is Marguerite Kauffman. Currently,

she lives in Napa on an estate called Vignoble. It was once a well-known winery—''

''Yes, yes,'' Jeffrey interrupted impatiently. ''But the point is—does she have the jewels? Or, failing that, does she know where they are?''

Nick winced at the eagerness in Jeffrey's voice. ''I'm not sure.''

There was a silence. Then Jeffrey said, ''I see. I thought you'd made contact with this woman.''

''I did. I attended a party there. With your daughter Kate, in fact.''

''Yes,'' Jeffrey said. ''So I heard. Grace called me. Apparently there was some problem at the party?''

Nick never made excuses; he wasn't going to do so now. Clearing his throat, he said, ''That's what I wanted to talk to you about. There could have been a problem, and it was completely my fault. I made a bad judgment call, and you should know about it.''

There was another silence. Then Jeffrey said, ''Why don't you tell me what happened?''

There was no point in evading the truth. ''When Kate invited me to the birthday party for Mrs. Kauffman's granddaughter, I accepted because...well, there were several reasons—'' He broke off. The last thing he wanted was to get into his feelings about Kate—whatever they were—with her father. Clearing his throat, he tried again. ''One of the reasons was that I thought it would be a good opportunity to case the house—''

''To case the house?''

''Yes. I wanted to do a quick once-over to see if there was anything obvious. I didn't think there would be—after all, if Mrs. Kauffman has the jewels, she wouldn't be fool enough to leave them lying around in plain sight.

But I was hoping I might find out something useful—something concrete to go on."

"So," Jeffrey said, "you simply wanted to look around, as it were—is that correct?"

"Yes. But since Kate was with me—and since she knows about the case—I didn't see how I could just disappear for a while without arousing her suspicions. So I made the mistake of telling her what I intended to do. Naturally, she objected."

Jeffrey chuckled. "Strenuously, I'm sure."

"To say the least."

"What did you do?"

Nick swallowed. "I did the only thing I could think to do at the time...I asked her to stand guard for me."

He waited for the explosion he was sure would come—the one he so richly deserved. But to his surprise, Jeffrey actually laughed.

"I can just see her face," Jeffrey said. "Perhaps that's why you nearly got caught."

Nick couldn't believe that Jeffrey found this amusing. He'd been prepared for a thorough chewing-out, and now that it didn't seem to be forthcoming, he felt off balance. All he could think of was to go back to his main point.

"As I told you," he said, "it was completely my fault. I want you to know—it won't happen again."

"I should think not," Jeffrey said. "But as far as I can tell, no harm was done. I admit that my...that Grace was a little upset at the thought that you had involved our daughter in your search, but Kate is a grown woman, capable of making her own decisions. And knowing Kate, she probably enjoyed the excitement."

"I'm not so sure of that," Nick said. He clearly recalled the murderous look in Kate's eyes when they escaped from the closet. There was no doubt in his mind that if she could have smitten him down without making any noise, she would have done exactly that.

Jeffrey laughed again. "*I'm* sure. You don't know Kate as well as I do."

"I won't argue with that," Nick said. "And after what happened, I can assure you I'm not going to get to know her any better."

"Well, now, let's not get ahead of ourselves, shall we?" Jeffrey soothed. "As I said, I know my daughter. Kate has always been the most hotheaded of my offspring, but in the end, she's scrupulously fair. She'll realize that if—and I stress the word *if*—there's any blame in this, she shares it equally."

Nick didn't believe that for a minute, and he knew Kate wouldn't, either. But he said, "I hope you're right."

"I am, you'll see," Jeffrey said confidently. "Now, in the meantime, I'd like to address this other matter. What do you think about this Kauffman woman? Does she have the jewels, do you think?"

Nick had to be honest. "I'm not sure yet. But I promise you, I'll find out."

"I hope so. We've come a long way, and I feel we're very close to solving this mystery once and for all."

"I think so, too."

"Good," Jeffrey said with satisfaction. "Keep me posted, now."

"You'll learn everything as soon as I do."

Nick hung up the phone, cursing himself. He felt like a fool. He should be focusing his energy on closing this case, and all he could think about was Kate DeWilde.

Why had he said he'd stay away from her? Who was he kidding? She wouldn't leave his mind. Right now, despite the fact that she had made it crystal clear she never wanted to see him again, he couldn't stop thinking about her.

Disgusted with himself, he grabbed his jacket. He was glad now that he'd made another date to meet Max downtown; seeing her tonight would be just the distraction he needed.

THE BAR WHERE NICK had arranged to meet Max was as crowded and noisy as the time before. He supposed they could have chosen a quieter spot, but this had been one of their favorite watering holes when they were partners.

"Hi, handsome," Max said as he sat down beside her. She gave him a thorough once-over before she tossed back the last of her highball. "If you don't mind my saying so, you look a little ragged around the edges. Hit a snag in the case?"

"Things could be better," he said, gesturing to the bartender. He ordered Max another drink, plus a beer for himself.

His former partner waited until the bartender had returned with their drinks. Then she picked up her glass, gestured for Nick to bring his, and led the way to a minuscule table near the back of the bar, where they could at least have a conversation without having to shout at each other.

For the next hour Max filled Nick in on all the latest changes at the SFPD. There were still a lot of people there that Nick had worked with and he liked to keep in touch. He never knew when he might have to call in a favor.

"All right, Nick," Max said suddenly. "Tell me

what's wrong. If I have to talk any more I'll be hoarse tomorrow."

"Sorry to be such lousy company, Max." Nick stared down into his beer. "It's a long story."

Crossing her arms, Max sat back. "I've got all night."

Nick sighed. He knew Max wouldn't let it go, so he said, "I did something really stupid. I involved my client's daughter in a search I made of someone's house the other day."

Max looked at him in real surprise. "That's not like you."

"I know. I don't know what happened."

She studied him for a minute, then she smiled. "Who was it? No, don't tell me. It was your doctor friend, right?"

He glowered at her. "I knew it was a mistake to see you tonight. You always did know too much."

"So, what are you going to do about her?"

"Nothing. She's already said she never wants to see me again."

Max smirked. "And that's going to stop you? It wouldn't have put a crimp in your style before."

"That was before. Besides, even if I wanted to, I'm hardly going to force myself on a woman who hates me."

"As they say in court, that hasn't been proved yet. But let's take this in order. Maybe you should decide first if you want to see her."

"I don't know." He turned away from Max's knowing glance and focused on a neon sign over the bar. "It's complicated."

"Why?"

He turned back to her. "Come on, Max, you know how it is. People in our line of work don't do very well in relationships. It's always the job that takes precedence.''

''So it's better not to get involved, is that it?''

''Yes.''

''You don't mean that.''

''Yes, I do. I've tried it before—with disastrous results.'' He glared at her, daring her to contradict him. ''And so have you.''

She shrugged. ''That doesn't mean I've stopped looking. I just haven't been as fortunate as you yet.''

''What do you mean?''

She chucked him under the chin. ''I haven't found my man. But it looks to me like you've found the woman for you.''

''How can you say that? I hardly know her!''

Max's eyes were wise. ''Ah, but you'd like to, wouldn't you? So what are you waiting for?''

They'd been friends longer than they had been partners, and Max knew Nick better than anyone. She laughed and gave his bulky frame a push.

''Go on, you. I know you're dying to get out of here. And as much as I love your ugly mug, it belongs somewhere else.''

Nick had to grin. ''You always were a pushy broad.''

She grinned back. ''True. But you gotta admit, I do get results.''

He started to get up, only to sit down again. ''We've forgotten one thing.''

''What's that?''

''Kate's told me she never wants to see me again.''

Max waved a dismissive hand. ''It's my experience that whenever a woman says that, she means just the opposite.''

He looked at her in exasperation. "It's no wonder men are so confused about what women want."

Max's reply was serene. "You wouldn't be confused if you would all just pay attention."

Suddenly eager to get going, Nick got up again. "Thanks, Max," he said.

She had the last word. "Don't thank me," she said with a laugh. "It's Kate you still have to convince."

TWENTY MINUTES LATER, Nick was still sitting outside Kate's apartment house. Incredibly, he was nervous. When he realized he was tapping his fingers against the steering wheel, he clenched his hand. He couldn't remember being this apprehensive even when he'd been a rookie cop.

Get out of the car and go inside, he told himself. *What's the worst she can do? Slam the door in your face? That's no big deal. You've had doors slammed on you before.*

But not by Dr. Kate DeWilde.

Before he could think about it any longer, he opened the car door and walked into her building. It didn't occur to him until he was actually standing outside her door that she might not be alone. Maybe she wasn't even home.

There was only one way to find out. Lifting his hand, he knocked.

"Who is it?" Kate called from within.

"It's me...Nick," he said.

There was silence. When she didn't open the door, he wasn't sure whether to knock again or just to walk away. He was standing there like an idiot when he heard the rattle of a chain. She opened the door six inches and looked at him.

"What do you want?" she asked.

It wasn't an auspicious welcome. He tried a smile, but when she stared at him stone-faced, he said, "I know you're angry, Kate—"

"Angry? I'm not *angry*," she said, her eyes flashing. "I'm way beyond that. But let's not talk about me. What are you doing here? I thought I told you I didn't want to talk to you again."

Aware she might close the door on him, he put his hand on it, sure that she'd never slam it shut on his fingers.

"I know I'm always doing this," he said, "but I came to apologize—again."

She stared at him a moment, her face expressionless. "All right, I accept your apology. Now, if there's nothing else—"

He could only go so far. *Thanks a lot, Max*, he thought. He'd tried, but it wasn't going to work. He wouldn't beg.

"No," he said, "there's nothing else. Good night, Doctor. I'm sorry I bothered you."

He turned and started down the hall. He'd gone half a dozen steps when she called, "Wait!"

He stopped and looked back. Kate had come out into the hallway. His heart began to pound. He had always thought she was a beautiful woman, but dressed in jeans and a T-shirt, her feet bare and her hair pulled back in one of those ridiculous scrunchy things women used to hold their hair back, she had never looked more lovely to him. He had to search to find his voice.

"What?" he said.

For a minute, when he saw the struggle going on in her expressive face, he thought she was going to say that she'd forgotten to tell him to go to hell. She stood there, shifting from one foot to the other; he stood there, too.

"Don't go," she finally said.

"But I thought—"

Her cheeks turned pink. "I've been thinking about it, and I've realized that I wasn't exactly fair to you the other day about...about what happened at Marguerite's. I can't blame you for everything. After all, the decision was mine, too."

Nick thought of what Jeffrey had said about Kate and her sense of fair play. He hadn't believed the man then, but it seemed Jeffrey was right. He looked at Kate again; when she smiled tentatively, he felt encouraged enough to walk back to her again.

"Are you sure?" he said.

"Yes, I'm sure." She gazed up at him, tendrils of hair clinging to her cheeks. He had to clench his hands to stop himself from reaching out and brushing the hair back. Her skin looked so soft, her mouth so inviting...

"Would you like to come in?" she asked.

Now that they'd come this far, he didn't want to press his luck. "It's a little late—"

"No, it's not. I just got home, and it takes a while for me to unwind. In fact, I was just making myself a cup of tea—but I could fix you something stronger, if you like."

Nick despised tea, but he said, "That would be great."

She smiled again. "Then, come in."

He'd been in her apartment before, but when he followed her inside tonight, he saw it with different eyes. In his work, first as a police officer and then a private investigator, he'd trained himself to be especially observant of the way people lived. So often, clues that would

otherwise be missed about their habits or their person-
alities could be found in the way they kept their homes.
Years of experience had made him an expert on things
that seemed odd or out of place, and he couldn't help
looking around as Kate shut the door.

"This is really nice," he said.

She seemed surprised. "You've been here before."

"Yes, but it was a different time of day, then. Tonight,
it looks...comfortable and...soft."

Kate glanced around, then she laughed. "It just looks
messy to me. There's that pile of journals by the chair
that I keep promising myself I'm going to get to. And
over there is all the mail I still have to answer. And..."
She stopped. "Why are you looking at me like that?"

Embarrassed that he'd been caught staring, he said, "I
was just thinking how beautiful you are."

"Beautiful!" Blushing, she lifted a hand to her hair.
"I'm a mess!"

"Not to me."

And just like that, the atmosphere changed. He hadn't
meant it to, yet one second they were talking about mun-
dane things, and the next, there was a charge in the air
that made the hair at the nape of his neck stand on end.

Kate felt it, too. He saw her expression soften, her
eyes turn limpid. When she gazed up at him with be-
wilderment, he almost took her into his arms.

"I...I don't know what's happening here, Nick. I...I
never wanted to..."

He hadn't wanted this, either. But it seemed they had
no choice. Gently, he reached for her. Then, when he
felt her against him, he closed his eyes.

"Kate," he said.

"I didn't want this, Nick."

He looked down at her. Somberly, he said, "Neither did I."

She bit her lower lip. "I just can't seem to help myself."

His voice hoarse, he answered, "Neither can I."

As if in a dream, he pulled her closer, and she didn't resist. Holding her gaze, he reached for her hand and turned it palm up. He kissed her palm, and then the pulse at the inside of her wrist. Still holding her to him with one hand, he moved his mouth down to press his lips to the inside of her elbow. Then, before he realized what he was doing, he was trailing his lips up her arm, to the softness of her shoulder, the sweet indentation of her neck....

"Nick—" she whispered.

He put his mouth on hers and stopped her protest with a kiss.

He didn't know how they got into the bedroom. He only knew that as they walked down the hall, she felt so soft and pliable beside him that he became lost in the touch and scent of her. Suddenly, they were just inside the room, with the bed beckoning....

Gently, he turned her toward him, placing both hands on her waist and drawing her lower body to his. Already, his groin was throbbing, and his pulse quickened as she pressed tightly against him.

If he was going to stop, it had to be now. His eyes burning, he looked down at her. "Do you think we should—"

He broke off when she slipped a hand around the back of his neck. Her gaze like a dark, green pool, she looked up at him. Then she gently pulled his head down to hers.

The touch of her lips on his opened the floodgates of passion he'd been trying to keep shut. Without realizing it, knowing only that he wanted all of her, he crushed her to him and returned her kiss with a pulsing desire that rocked them both. They clung together, swaying.

At last, he lifted his head. He wanted to see her, he thought. He wanted to see this beautiful woman in the flesh. He looked down at her T-shirt. Suppressing the urge to rip it off her, he reached down and slowly lifted it over her head.

She wasn't wearing a bra. Her slim torso rose out of her low-slung jeans to perfect breasts, and he drew in a sharp breath.

"You're...magnificent," he said hoarsely. With a shaking hand, he reached out and cupped one of her breasts. The fullness of it in his hand was enough to send his head spinning; when he lowered his mouth and sucked on her nipple, her back arched in response, and the rush of blood to his head made him dizzy.

Lost in swirling desire, he reached for his belt, but she pushed his hand away. Her eyes on his face, she struggled with the belt until the buckle released. Then, still gazing deep into his soul, she pulled his slacks and shorts down over his hips. When she cupped him in her hand, he almost climaxed right then.

"Let's go to bed," she whispered.

His head spinning, he wasn't sure how they got rid of their remaining clothes, but by the time he lay down beside her, he was naked and his body felt on fire. He wanted to step back, to slow down and take his time, but he had no will of his own. Her touch raised an inferno inside him, and when he began hungrily running his fingers over her smooth, silky body, feeling the tautness of her muscles, the softness of her breasts and the wet, secret places inside her, he knew he couldn't last much longer.

"Oh, Kate," he murmured, his breath hot against her cheek. "I can't last…"

She put her arms around his back. The scar from the bullet he'd taken was there, and she carefully touched the place, her fingers expert and gentle. Then she ran her fingers down his back and up to his face again, placing a hand on either side of his jaw. "Now…" she whispered.

Hunger was their master, and Nick had never felt so strong and powerful as they came together. He couldn't get enough of her; his mouth was on her breasts, his tongue laved her sweet nipples, his hands moved lower and lower until she moaned for him to end this sweet agony. In one swift motion, she spread her legs for him and guided him inside her. There was a fierce rushing sound in his ears, and dimly Nick realized it was the pounding of his blood.

He knew she was ready; he could feel it in the most intimate part of her, her muscles tightening, her heat urging him on.

"Oh, Nick—" she groaned, clutching at his head, his hair, savagely pulling him up to kiss her so deeply he moaned.

Before they knew it, they were caught up in a timeless rhythm, hips moving together, breath rasping. A pinpoint of pleasure began to spread through him until it took him over, and he put his hands under her, lifting her up to him, grinding his hips into her, taking her with him to a height he'd never experienced before.

She was right there with him, crying his name over and over.

A long time later, he rolled away and put his arm under her waist, drawing her close and snuggling her against him.

"I thought you were asleep," she murmured.

"I was," he said, marveling. Always watchful, he never let down his guard like that. "I must have been crushing you."

"Never," she said with a drowsy smile.

Raising himself on one elbow, he looked down on her flushed face. The scrunchy thing that had been holding her hair back had come off at some point during their wild lovemaking, and her hair was tousled around her face on the pillow. With a smile, he twined a tendril around his finger.

"What did you do to me, woman?" he whispered. "I feel as though I've been through a wringer and come out flat on the other side."

She laughed softly. "How romantic."

"I can't help it. That's how I feel."

She sighed luxuriously. "I don't know how I feel. That was...wonderful."

He kissed the tip of her nose. "We could do it again."

She looked up at him with a teasing arch of her brow. "So soon?" she asked.

"That's what you do to me. Do you want me to prove it?"

He gave her no time to protest, even if she'd been planning to. Smiling, he reached for her again, and without effort lifted her on top of him. But passion was no longer such a hard master, and this time he took his time. Instead of kissing her, he began to whisper of the sensations she caused in him and the ways he wanted her. With every word, he put his hands and mouth over her body, gently at first, then with increasing desire as she responded to him with caresses of her own.

But he wouldn't be rushed this time. Deliberately prolonging anticipation, he spoke of how soft her breasts were—and kissed them. He whispered about how smooth her skin felt under his lips—and ran his tongue down her torso. He caressed her until they were both trembling, but even then, he delayed.

He kissed her eyelids and her nose, her cheek and her chin, telling her how lovely she was. He didn't know where the words came from, but suddenly, there they were, springing up from a well of feeling inside him, and with every kiss, every caress, every whispered word, their desire reached a fever pitch that could no longer be denied.

He hadn't thought it could be better the second time, but it was.... And when the climax finally thundered down upon them, he almost shouted in heedless abandon. Seconds later, her cry echoed his as they joined together in the ultimate pleasure.

When his racing heart had finally calmed, Kate was lying beside him, one arm flung across her face. "What happened?" he murmured.

She smiled without opening her eyes. "You tell me. You're the one who said you had something to prove."

He felt as though a ton of bricks had fallen on him. "And did I?"

She snuggled against him. "You have to ask?"

The last thing he remembered was putting an arm around her and drawing her close. Then, a satisfied smile on his face, he fell into a dreamless, exhausted sleep and didn't wake up until the early morning hours.

CHAPTER TEN

MARGUERITE HAD BEEN sitting on the striped lavender-and-ivory sofa in the living room at Vignoble for twenty minutes now, staring at the phone.

What was the matter with her? Hadn't she decided that Grace was someone she could trust? And if she couldn't trust Grace, what was she to do? Go to the police? Turn herself in? The jewels had been on her conscience all these years. She couldn't go to her grave with this burden.

She looked down at the letter in her lap. The embossed heading listed the prestigious legal firm of Brown, Anderson and Grown, with offices in Sydney, Australia. The date of the letter was June 1995. Below the formal greeting to her were the words, "We regret to inform you..."

Marguerite had no need to read further because she knew the contents by heart.

By heart.

Tears stung her eyes and she got up abruptly and went to one of the living room windows that overlooked the vineyard for which Vignoble had once been so famed. The vines were still being tended—one did not allow a vineyard that had produced such excellent chardonnay and cabernet grapes for over fifty years to lie fallow. But in the past five years since her husband had died, she

had leased most of the vineyard to another wine-making
family named Cavanaugh, who lived over the hill.

She still felt a deep possessive pride as she looked out
at the seemingly endless rows. Dark green leaves flut-
tered gracefully in the gentle breeze, and she could see
the rich clusters of grapes ripening in the sun, bursting
with pregnant promise.

She had always found the sight of the vineyards calming; even in the depth of winter, when the vines were
bare and empty branches poked disconsolately toward
the cold, gray sky, she had been able to derive comfort
from their barren beauty.

She sighed. She was delaying the inevitable. Resolutely, she turned back to the phone. The letter she had
dropped when she got up caught her eye, and she retrieved it. Gently, she smoothed the single page. She'd
read and reread it and folded it and unfolded it so many
times that the once-stiff parchment was almost limp.

But as she went to fold it yet again, Dirk's name
caught her eye.

"We regret to inform you that our client, Derrick
Freeman (né Dirk DeWilde) passed away on this date.
As per his instructions to this firm, we are writing to
advise you of his death...."

Oh, Dirk! she thought sadly as she finished folding
the letter and placing it in her pocket. Even though he
had led a full life before he died—and at his death had
left a widow, daughter and granddaughter in New Zea-
land—Marguerite still pictured Dirk as the dashing
young man who had stolen her heart all those years ago.
How handsome he'd been. She had been ready to throw
everything away for him—and she had. But had it been
worth it? Sometimes, she wondered.

At the thought, her smile faded. Somberly she took

another letter from her pocket, this one more worn than the other. Although she had no need to reread it to know what it said, she opened it even more carefully. She could picture his handwriting in her mind, but today she needed to see it with her own eyes. After all, she thought, Dirk was a big part of this decision, too.

"Dearest heart..." the letter began.

After all these years, she still felt a pang at the sight of his bold, careless writing. It was a moment before she could continue reading.

Dearest heart,

I stand before you a broken man bowed down by the weight of promises I could not keep. If only events had turned out differently....

But I will not offer excuses you would not, and should not, accept. I leave you with a pain too profound to express. I would beg you to reconsider, but as you have made clear, your duties, and your heart, lie elsewhere. I try to be grateful for the all-too-brief time we had together, but when I ponder a future without you, desolation swamps me.

My darling, the only course available to me now is to leave with you the objects that I believe drove us apart. Do with them what you will. They're yours to keep, to sell...to return, as you insisted I do too many times to count.

But if you choose the latter course, my only love, the one thing I ask is that you keep my whereabouts a secret. Whatever lies between my family and me is an issue for another time.

So goodbye, my precious dear. Please keep the promise I ask, until I die. But know that whatever you decide, you will forever live in my mind, my soul...and my heart....

When Marguerite came to Dirk's signature, she brushed renewed tears away. Once again, she blessed her darling, wonderful Edward, who had known about Dirk and hadn't cared. She had never told Edward about the jewels, though many times she had longed to share the terrible burden she was carrying. But she hadn't wanted to involve her husband in something that could have been considered criminal. If anyone had ever found the jewels…

She shuddered. Edward had loved her despite her past, and for that she would always be grateful. They'd had a good marriage, and right now she missed him more than she could ever say.

Wearily she stood and crossed the room to the safe. After placing the letters inside, she began to close the door, then hesitated. On impulse, she pulled forth a rectangular jewelry case from one of the safe's drawers. The case was so old that its purple velvet covering had faded to a dusty violet. She held it in her hands for a moment, then she reached for the key, which she had placed in another of the safe's compartments. She inserted the key and the lid of the box opened with a tiny *click!*

Nestled in the box were four pieces of jewelry of breathtaking beauty. Tentatively, Marguerite reached for one of the pieces. It was the Empress Catherine tiara, the most magnificent of the four. The large, shell-cut emerald set in the center of the gold circlet was worth more than a million dollars on its own, and surrounding it was a dazzling array of precious rubies, diamonds and emeralds. *Spectacular* didn't even begin to describe it.

Next Marguerite removed the so-called Dancing Waters necklace, two intertwining strands of white diamonds interspersed with the blue brilliance of sapphires. As she held it up before her, the faceted stones caught the light and shot rainbows toward the ceiling. For a few seconds, the room seemed to pulsate with color, as though she were holding a cascade of shimmering sunlight and water.

Reverently, she put the necklace back into the box. The brooch she removed next was one of the loveliest pieces she had ever seen—a confluence of precious gems that sparkled with the blazing flame of rubies, the brilliance of diamonds, the cool green of emeralds and the midnight fantasies of black onyx.

The fourth and final piece were earrings composed of diamonds and Burmese rubies, which contained some of the deepest and richest crimson colors in the world.

Across the room an ornate mirror hung over the fireplace. Unable to resist, Marguerite held the earrings up to her ears and turned toward the mirror. Even from across the room, the diamonds flashed their icy brilliance, while the rubies glowed against her skin.

Almost reluctantly, she put the earrings back. But she couldn't bear to lock them out of sight again, so she held the box in her hand. She had delayed long enough. It was time to make her call.

She went back to the sofa and sat down. Before she could change her mind again, she put the jewelry case on the coffee table and reached for the phone. She had already memorized the numbers for the store and for Grace's apartment, and since it was still afternoon, she decided to call the store first.

Grace answered her private line on the second ring, sounding preoccupied.

"Grace, this is Marguerite Kauffman. I'm sorry to

bother you at work. Are you very busy, or do you have a few minutes to talk?''

As soon as she heard Marguerite's voice, Grace's tone warmed. ''Of course I have time. It's so nice of you to call.''

Daring to hope that this would be easier than she had anticipated, Marguerite said, ''I have something very important that I'd like to talk to you about.''

''Oh? What is it?''

''I'd really rather not discuss it over the phone.''

''It sounds quite mysterious.''

Marguerite realized that it did, and she laughed nervously. ''I don't intend for it to be. But it does have to do with—'' She paused, doubt flashing through her mind once more. She thought of Dirk and sent up a silent apology to him. She had to do it; if she didn't, she would never rest. And neither would he.

''Yes?'' Grace prodded.

Marguerite took a deep breath. It was now or never, she told herself. ''It has to do with the missing DeWilde jewels, Grace.''

She heard Grace draw in a sharp breath. ''The missing jewels? You know something about them, Marguerite?''

''Yes,'' Marguerite said, and with that single word felt the heavy burden she'd carried all these years begin to lift. Her voice stronger, she repeated, ''Yes, I know something about them, Grace. And I'd like to tell you what I know.''

''When?'' Grace asked immediately. ''Where? I'll meet you any place you say, Marguerite. Any time.'' She paused, then whispered, ''Oh, Marguerite, do you *have* the jewels?''

Marguerite was about to answer when she happened to look out the front window. Her heart almost stopped.

Coming up the walk toward the front door was Nick Santos.

"Marguerite?" Grace asked.

Marguerite watched as he came closer. What was he doing here? He was Kate's friend. What would he want with her?

Suddenly—probably because she felt so guilty—his presence seemed sinister. Kate had said he was a private investigator, but surely he could have nothing to do with... Her heart began to pound wildly, and she wondered if she were having a heart attack. She put a hand to her chest. *Not now!* she told herself fiercely. Not when she was so close to unburdening her conscience. After all these years, she finally had a chance to redeem herself—and Dirk—and she wasn't going to lose it.

"I'll explain everything when we meet, Grace," she said hurriedly. "Unfortunately, I...I have some unexpected company. I'm sorry, but I have to hang up now."

"Marguerite, wait! Why don't we set a date and a time now?"

But with Nick Santos about to ring the bell, Marguerite couldn't think. "I'll call you soon, I promise."

"But—"

She was about to answer when the open jewelry box she had carelessly left out caught her eye. The doorbell chimed, and she could hear Lorene, one of the maids, walking toward the front door to answer. She jumped up. She couldn't let Nick Santos see this box! She had to get it out of sight before Lorene let him in.

"I'm sorry, Grace, I'll...call you," she said abruptly, slamming down the phone.

Her heart racing, she grabbed the box from the coffee table and snapped the lid shut. With frantic haste, she shoved it into the safe. Slamming the door, she spun the dial, replaced the picture that covered it and managed to get back to the sofa before Lorene ushered in her visitor.

"Why, Mr. Santos," she said, hoping he wouldn't be suspicious about the sight of an old woman panting slightly and holding a hand to her chest. "How nice to see you. To what do I owe the honor of this visit?"

It seemed that very little missed the private investigator's sharp eyes. To Marguerite's dismay, he stared at her until she was nervously forced to drop her hand from her chest. Then he said, very politely, "I'm sorry I didn't call first, Mrs. Kauffman, but time is of the essence, and I'm here on a matter of some importance. I came to talk to you about the missing DeWilde jewels."

The time had come, Marguerite realized with a sinking heart. She knew from the look on that handsome dark face that it would be futile to say she had no idea what he was talking about. It was obvious that Nick Santos wouldn't have made the trip to Napa if he didn't have a good reason—a very good reason.

"I see," she said. "In that case, Mr. Santos, why don't you sit down? I'll order some tea, and then we can have a nice, long chat."

"KATE? OH, KATIE," Grace said excitedly, "I'm so glad you're home! You'll never guess what just happened!"

Kate swam up out of a deep, dreamless sleep. She hadn't realized she'd answered the phone until the receiver was at her ear and she heard her mother's voice. Groggily, she sat up.

"Mother? What time is it?"

"The time? Oh, I don't know, Kate—it's late afternoon, I guess. Does it matter? Oh, dear, did I wake you?"

"It's okay, I guess it's time to get up, anyway," Kate said. She pushed her tangled hair out of her eyes. "I had an early shift at the hospital, and I thought I'd take a short nap before I went to the clinic."

"I'm sorry, Kate. I know you don't get much rest. I shouldn't have called."

"No, it's all right," Kate insisted. She stifled a yawn, wondering what her mother would think if she knew the reason *why* she hadn't gotten much rest last night. After that glorious session of lovemaking with Nick, she'd had to drag herself out of bed this morning for hospital rounds.

"You said something had happened, Mother. What is it?"

"Marguerite Kauffman called me," Grace said, sounding even more excited than she had before. "She said—" Grace paused dramatically "—she said she had something to tell me about the missing DeWilde jewels!"

At that, Kate snapped awake. "What did she tell you?"

"She didn't tell me anything—yet. But—" Grace's voice rose again. "But she promised to tell me the whole story when we meet!"

Thinking of Nick again, and how hard he'd worked on this case, Kate was cautious. "And when is that?" she asked.

"I don't know," Grace admitted. "Some unexpected company arrived before we were able to set a time. But I'm going to make sure it's soon. Oh, Kate, suppose she *does* have the jewels? If I can persuade her to give them to me, I—"

"Why would you do that?"

"What?"

"Why do you want the jewels, Mother? I thought you didn't care anything about them."

"I don't—I mean, I didn't. Oh, Kate, it's too complicated to explain right now. It's just important to me. Please don't ask me why."

But Kate couldn't get Nick out of her mind. "But if she gives them to you, what about Nick?"

"What about him?"

Kate sat up straight. "What *about* him? He's been searching for the damned things all year! Imagine how it will look if you just—"

"I'll work it out," Grace assured her vaguely. "But we're getting ahead of ourselves here, aren't we? We don't know if Marguerite actually *has* the jewels."

"Mother," Kate said slowly, "why are you so obsessed about this? Does it have something to do with Dad?"

Grace didn't answer for a moment. "In a way, yes," she said at last. "You know how intense he's been about this. It's so important to him to retrieve those jewels."

Kate sat back against the headboard. She was beginning to see what was going on here—or at least she thought she did. But what about Nick?

Kate suddenly felt torn between her mother's obvious intentions and concern about how they would affect Nick.

"Well," she said finally, weakly. "I wish you luck."

"Thank you, darling," Grace said cheerily. "I'll keep you posted."

"Please, do that."

Kate sat there for a moment after they'd hung up, hugging her drawn-up knees, wondering what she would say to Nick about this. She decided she wouldn't say anything. After all, no one, not even Nick, knew for certain that Marguerite had the jewels. Maybe, as her mother was wont to say, this was all a tempest in a teapot.

Hoping she was right, but sensing deep inside herself that she wasn't, Kate went to take a shower. Before he left last night—or rather, before he left early this morning, Nick had told her he'd be out of touch until later this afternoon. He had promised to call her before she left for the clinic, so after she was ready, she paced restlessly throughout the apartment until the phone rang. On pins and needles, she snatched it up, hoping it was Nick.

She was not disappointed.

"Hi," he said.

After last night, just the sound of his voice was enough to make her feel weak. But now was not the time to conjure up tantalizing images of their lovemaking. She had to keep herself on track.

"Hi," she said. "Where have you been?"

He seemed taken aback by her question. "I thought I told you I had business to take care of today—"

"You did. I just wondered what it was."

"It had to do with the case," he said. Suddenly cautious, he asked, "Why? Has something happened I should know about?"

Her mother hadn't made her promise to keep the conversation to herself, but Kate knew that Grace wouldn't want Nick to know that Marguerite had called her. Beginning to feel miffed with both of them for putting her in such an awkward position, she said, "No, nothing *happened*. I just wondered. If you don't want to tell me—"

"No, no, it's all right. I was going to tell you later, when I picked you up from the clinic. But I can tell you

now, it's no big secret. I went to see Marguerite Kauffman today, and—''

''Oh, Nick, you didn't!''

''Yes, I did,'' he said, clearly surprised at her dis-
mayed tone. ''Is something wrong with that?''

Kate glanced at the clock. She had to leave now or
she'd be late in relieving the doctor at the clinic. Hurriedly, she said, ''What did she say? No, don't tell me.
We don't have time to talk about it now.''

''Talk about what? Kate, what happened?''

She told him, after all. ''My mother called a while
ago. Marguerite Kauffman phoned her today about the
missing jewels.''

''And?''

When his tone went from guarded to downright suspicious, Kate wished that she hadn't mentioned it. But
it was too late now. ''And...nothing,'' she said weakly.

Nick was silent. Then he asked coldly, ''Why is your
mother suddenly so interested? I thought she couldn't
care less about this.''

Miserably, Kate said, ''I don't know, Nick. But she
obviously has her reasons.''

''So it seems.''

Aware of the minutes ticking away, she said, ''We
really don't have time to discuss this now, Nick. Can we
talk about it tonight?''

''Oh, you still want me to pick you up at the clinic?''

''Don't be that way,'' she said quietly. ''If you think
about it, you'll appreciate how difficult a situation this
puts me in. If this jewel business has suddenly become
important to my mother, I have to respect that. It has
nothing to do with my feelings for you.''

He was silent for so long that she said, ''Nick?''

She was sorry she'd asked. Uncompromisingly, he said, "I'll think about it."

"Thank you. You—"

Kate could tell Nick wasn't happy about what she'd told him. "All right," he agreed, "we'll talk about it later. But I want you to know right now that I've never left a job unfinished in my life. I'm not inclined to start now."

"I'm not asking you to—"

"You said you didn't have time to discuss this now. We'll talk later."

As dissatisfying as that was, Kate knew she had no choice. But as she took a cab to the clinic because her car had broken down again, she began to feel more and more hostile. Why couldn't Nick see how torn she was between her growing attraction to him and her loyalty to her mother?

And what about her father's part in all this? He would think that Nick had done his job simply by *finding* the jewels; he wouldn't consider it necessary for Nick to hand them over personally. The important thing was that they had been located after all these years.

Kate couldn't forget the lilt in her mother's voice when Grace had talked about being the one to give Jeffrey the family heirlooms. She hadn't heard her mother sound so happy since... she couldn't remember when.

Damn, she thought as she stormed into the clinic door. When she'd chosen to go into medicine, she'd hoped she would be distancing herself as far as she could from the family business. Yet here she was, tangled up with family jewels and family scandal—and the man her father had hired to sort it all out.

CHAPTER ELEVEN

THANKFULLY, IT WAS A BUSY night at the clinic. Kate and Mary, the nurse-receptionist who was on duty, were so preoccupied with the stream of patients who came in that they had no time for chitchat. As Kate took temperatures and stitched up cuts and dispensed medications, she was glad that she didn't have a chance to dwell on the twin problems of Nick Santos and her mother. The only thing she could think about as she gently mopped up the tears of toddlers after she'd given them a shot or lectured pregnant women on the importance of nutrition was that she wished she'd never heard of the DeWilde collection.

As time passed, she became less sure that she wanted Nick to pick her up tonight. She couldn't deny that *physically* she wanted to see him so badly she ached. But once she saw him, she'd have to decide whether or not to continue their argument about how Grace wanted to handle this issue of Marguerite. What made it even more difficult was that Kate wasn't sure why this had suddenly become so important to her mother. What reason could she give to Nick to ask him to back off?

No reason, she told herself glumly. And she knew how that was going to sit with him. He'd told her that he prided himself on finishing every job to the end. That was something she could understand herself. She knew how she would feel if their positions were reversed.

Assaulted with doubt all over again, she was glad when Emilio and a few of his friends dropped in about ten. At least, she thought it was Emilio. When she saw the group standing in the reception area as she came out of one of the back rooms, she stopped in her tracks. She knew she was staring, but she couldn't help herself.

In the center of the large room were half a dozen Hispanic teenagers, four boys and two girls. All were dressed identically in clean, pressed jeans and tucked-in crisp white shirts with the long sleeves rolled up to their forearms. Each teen was wearing a blue beret cocked jauntily over one eye. At the center of the group was Emilio Sanchez.

"Emilio!" she exclaimed. "What's all this?"

Emilio tried to maintain a macho pose, but at Kate's surprised and pleased expression, he reverted momentarily to the sixteen-year-old he really was. Grinning boyishly, he said, "You like it, Doctor?"

Admiringly, Kate came forward to inspect the group. "I like it very much. But what—"

Emilio gestured. "These are my *vatos*—and my *vatas*," he added, when the two girls poked him in the back. "We just formed a new gang."

Kate wasn't sure she liked the sound of that. Cautiously, she repeated, "A new gang? Are you sure we need another one in this neighborhood?"

Emilio grinned again. "We need this one. Have you heard of the Guardian Angels?"

"Sure I have," Kate said. "They started in New York—patroling the subways and streets to keep them safe."

"Exactly," Emilio said. He touched his blue beret. "We decided we needed something to make *our* streets safer, so we formed our own group. Do you want to know what it's called?''

Kate smiled. ''Let me guess. The Blue Berets?''

''Too obvious,'' Emilio scoffed. But his dark eyes gleamed. *''Con su permiso,* we're gonna call ourselves Dr. Kate's Angels.''

Kate thought he was kidding, and she almost laughed. But then she saw his eager face and those of his companions and realized they were all waiting anxiously for her reaction. So touched that they were serious, she found she could hardly speak.

''I think...I think that's...wonderful,'' she said. To her embarrassment, tears filled her eyes, and she had to stop before she began bawling.

Emilio put an arm around her shoulders. ''It's okay, Dr. Kate,'' he said. Then he briefly became that earnest teenager again. ''Do you really like it?''

''Like it?'' Her shaky smile included the entire group. ''I love it. It's the most beautiful compliment I've ever received in my entire life.''

To a man—and woman—Dr. Kate's Angels shuffled their feet awkwardly. Kate wanted to hug them all, but she knew that the gesture would embarrass them. After all, these were gang members—*former* gang members, she corrected herself, still marveling. She turned to Emilio.

''I think it's wonderful,'' she said again. ''But I don't understand. What brought all this about?''

Emilio straightened. ''I don't know. I just been thinkin' about things, you know? I decided that no one was going to help us if we didn't help ourselves. This is our place, you know?''

''I do, indeed,'' Kate said.

He looked down at his feet. ''Then, there was you.''

"Me?"

He glanced up again. "Well, yeah. I figured I owed you."

"Owed me?"

"Yeah. You could have turned me in that night I came at you with the knife. But you didn't. I owe you for that. I could have been sent away for a long time because of that knife, but you gave me a second chance."

"I knew you didn't mean it that night," Kate said. She almost told him that she knew how scared he'd been, but she decided against it. It would weaken him in the eyes of his friends, and she didn't want that. So she added, "You deserved that chance, Emilio. And I didn't do anything that anyone else wouldn't have done."

"No? I don't think so. That cop—he would have put me away in two seconds flat."

Kate didn't know what to say. "Yes, well, he didn't understand...."

His dark eyes glimmered. "Oh, he understood, all right."

Kate didn't want to get into that. Still marveling at this transformation, she said, "But how did you decide to form a neighborhood group like the Guardian Angels?"

He shrugged. "I knew we had to do somethin'. This place is gettin' so bad with the druggies and the winos and all that. You can't walk down the street anymore without holdin' on to a weapon. And as my *abuela* says—" his eyes glinted again "—you and the other docs are workin' to help us, so we should give somethin' back, too."

"That's wonderful, Emilio."

His grin widened. "Besides, it gives me and the homies somethin' to do, other than just stand around on the street corner and look tough. Now we got a *reason* to be tough.''

He laughed, and Kate laughed with him. Everyone came forward then and she met and shook hands with each of them in turn. They were all about the same age, but Emilio was clearly the leader. Mary came over, and she and Kate both told the kids how proud they were of them.

Kate was still talking with the group when Nick walked in. He did the same double take as Kate had, and she rushed over to him. Excited, she introduced him to every one of the Angels, ending with Emilio.

"You remember Emilio Sanchez, don't you, Nick?" she asked.

Nick looked down at Emilio, who promptly puffed his chest out. Seeing that, Nick smiled sardonically.

"I remember," Nick said. He turned to Emilio. "I see you and your friends have decided to do something useful for a change."

Emilio looked at him suspiciously. "Hey, man, are you makin' fun?"

"Me? Make fun? No, but I'll wait to see how long this lasts."

Kate was appalled. Grabbing Nick's arm, she hissed, "What are you saying? Of course it will last! Can't you see how committed they are?"

Nick looked down at her. "Because of the matching hats, you mean?"

Emilio bristled. "These aren't just *hats,* man! These are *berets.* And they mean somethin'!"

Nick shrugged. "Prove it, then."

One of the girls pushed forward. "We will, you'll see. We're gonna take back this neighborhood."

Nick gazed calmly down at her. "How?"

Her eyes flashed, and she put her hands on her hips. Full of bravado, she declared, "We'll find a way! You just wait!"

"I hope you're right," Nick said. He flicked another glance at Emilio. "You do have a plan, don't you?"

Taking up an aggressive stance, Emilio glared at Nick. "What's with you, man?" He looked Nick up and down. "You think just 'cause you're wearin' a fancy suit and livin' away from the barrio, you're better'n us? Well, you're not, and we're gonna prove—"

Before Emilio could finish the sentence, he was interrupted by the sound of breaking glass. Startled, they all turned toward the front of the clinic. Before their eyes, the front window shattered. The glass seemed to crack into a million pieces and blow inward, and instinctively, everyone jumped in different directions.

All was noise and confusion. The boys were yelling something; the girls were screaming. Kate thought she heard Mary shouting something into the phone, and she turned to look, but Nick grabbed her and pushed her behind him. He held her there with one arm; with his other hand, he reached for something under his jacket, at his back. His attention was focused on the front of the clinic.

Kate looked that way, too, and gasped. Two young men were coming in the front door. She knew by the colors they wore that they were gang members—rivals of Emilio and his crew. Both were carrying guns that looked bigger than cannons.

She couldn't stop staring at those weapons. The guns seemed to grow before her very eyes, becoming so huge they filled her entire field of vision. She had never felt such terror. Sure they were all going to be killed, she grabbed for Nick. She didn't realize until then that a gun had materialized in his hand, too.

"Get down!" Nick shouted. "Everyone get down!"

Kate couldn't move; she was frozen with horror. But as Nick turned toward the menace at the door and started to bring his gun up, she reacted by grabbing his arm.

"No!" she shouted.

She didn't have time to say more. A series of crackling and popping sounds erupted and something hit her—hard—right in the shoulder. The force of the blow knocked her backward. She flailed for balance, but to her astonishment, her left arm wouldn't work. She looked down. A crimson stain was already spreading over the surface of her lab coat where she'd felt the blow.

At first, she was too surprised to comprehend what had happened. But then, as she watched the widening blot of red, she realized dimly that she'd been shot. She was wondering why she didn't feel anything, when the pain started. It began somewhere below her neck and fanned out so swiftly and brutally that she felt as if her entire body had suddenly been dipped in fire.

Gasping, she tried to speak, to say something, to call out for help, but nothing came out of her mouth. In addition to that fiery pain, she felt as though a terrible weight had fallen onto her chest. She couldn't breathe; every time she tried, the agony increased.

Was this how it felt to be shot? she wondered vaguely. None of her experience as a physician had prepared her for this. Why hadn't anyone told her it hurt so much?

She realized she was going into shock. She felt lightheaded and could almost sense her blood pressure drop. There was a rushing sound in her ears and she knew she was about to faint. Panicked, she looked around, trying to find Nick. She saw him, and, in an agony of pain, she called out to him.

"Nick—"

He turned toward her as if in a slow-motion movie, fear and anger blazing in his eyes. She saw his glance drop to the blood on her lab coat. His eyes widened, and he reached for her. He said something—yelled something—but she couldn't hear it. The roaring in her ears drowned out all other noise, and she felt her legs buckle. She knew she was going to fall.

"Nick!" she cried again. Or thought she did. Her mouth opened, but since she heard nothing, she couldn't be sure that any words came out.

Her legs would no longer hold her. She started to go down, but Nick caught her and carefully lowered her to the floor. He started to say something again, but she grabbed his wrist. She knew she didn't have much time; the edges of her vision were blurring, and she could tell she was about to pass out. Panicked, she gripped him even harder.

"Don't let..." She stopped and gasped as a fierce spasm of pain swept through her.

Nick leaned over her. His dark eyes frantic with worry, he said hurriedly, "Don't worry about anything, Kate. Someone's calling an ambulance and—"

She couldn't give up. Summoning the last of her strength, she said, "Don't let Emilio...and the others get hurt. Promise."

"Kate—"

She looked up into his anxious face. "Promise!" she hissed through a new wall of pain. She had to focus; this was so important to her. "They've come so far. If they go after these kids...who knows what will happen. Nick, promise!"

She wouldn't give up until he gave his word. Hurriedly, he said, "All right, I promise! But lie still now, Kate, please. You're bleeding badly. You need help...."

That was all she heard. With her eyes still on his face, her vision darkened, and she spiraled down into a black hole from which she wasn't sure she would ever return.

NICK ALMOST DECKED one of the paramedics who tried to tell him that he couldn't ride to the hospital in the ambulance with Kate. He was so fierce that the man backed off and promised to let him inside. Before they left, Emilio pulled Nick aside.

Hoarsely, the teenager asked, "Is she gonna to be all right?"

Nick ran a hand through his hair. Kate was still inside the clinic, being tended by Mary and the paramedics. He shook his head. "I don't know. I think so. But she was shot, and you know—"

Emilio's eyes darkened. He'd seen people shot before, too. "I know. But you tell her, we'll get those guys—"

Nick shot out a hand and grabbed him so tightly that Emilio cringed. "No," Nick rasped. "That's the last thing she'd want."

Emilio tried to squirm away from him. "You know we're not going to let this go. That's why I started the Angels, to take care of things like this."

"Then do it right," Nick said. "If you go after them, people are going to get hurt. Maybe one of them—"

"Damn right!"

"But maybe one of you. Your buddies there—" Nick jerked his head toward the little group huddled outside the door to the clinic. "Maybe one of the girls." He brought his hard glance back to Emilio. "Things will escalate, no matter what happens. And then everything you tried to do by starting Dr. Kate's Angels will be lost. Is that what you want?''

Before Emilio could answer, he added harshly, ''I know that's not what Dr. Kate would want.''

Emilio's face crumpled with anger and indecision. ''But we can't just let it go! They came into our territory! They hit one of our own! They have to pay!''

''And they will—if you let the cops handle it.''

The teenager recoiled. ''You want us to give to the cops? You know what they'll do. Nothing!'' To emphasize his point, he spat on the sidewalk.

The ambulance was almost ready to go; Nick knew he didn't have much time if he wanted to go with it. He pulled the kid around so that they were facing each other.

''Listen to me,'' he said. ''Once I was like you—I didn't trust the cops, either. But then I became one, and when I did, I learned that things aren't always what they seem—from either side. But I also saw that someone has to take the first step, or nothing will change.''

Emilio looked at him bitterly. ''Why are *we* always the ones who are expected to take that step?''

Nick held his eyes. ''I don't know,'' he said. ''Sometimes, that's just the way things are.''

Emilio said nothing at first. Glancing away from Nick's steely expression, he muttered, ''I don't know, man. I'll have to think about it.''

The paramedic who was going to ride in the back with Kate was gesturing to Nick. If he didn't go now, the ambulance would leave without him.

''You do what you have to, Emilio,'' he said. ''But if you go to the cops, know this—I'll go with you. I'm on your side, whether you want to believe it or not.''

Emilio didn't look at him; he just nodded. Nick stared

at him for a moment, then he gave the boy's shoulder a squeeze and jumped aboard the ambulance. Seconds later, lights flashing and sirens screaming, they were on the way to the hospital.

GRACE WAS READING IN BED when the phone rang. The sound startled her, and she glanced quickly at the clock. It was almost midnight; who could be phoning at this hour?

In her experience, calls so late in the night rarely boded well. Her heart beginning to race, she reached over and picked up the receiver. Hoping it was a wrong number, she said a cautious hello.

"Mrs. DeWilde, this is Nick Santos," Nick said without preamble. "I've got some bad news. Kate was shot tonight."

"Shot!" Grace bolted upright in bed. Her voice shook as she forced herself to ask, "She isn't—"

"She's in surgery here at San Francisco Golden Gate Hospital. I don't know how long it'll take, but maybe you should get down here. Do you want me to call Mr. DeWilde?"

Grace put a hand to her head. She was so shaken, she couldn't even think. "No...no, I'll call him," she said. "I'll be there as soon as possible."

"I'll be here."

She tried to thank him, but her voice faltered, and she stopped before she began to sob. Breaking the connection, she started to dial Jeffrey's number, but was so distraught that she forgot it halfway through and had to begin again. It seemed to ring forever at the other end, and all the while she was listening to that ringing tone, her mind was chanting *Oh, Kate...oh, Kate...oh, Kate.*

Jeffrey finally answered. She barely gave him a

chance to say hello before she said, "It's me, Jeffrey. I've got some bad news. Kate..." She stopped, her throat tightening. "Kate's been...shot. She's all right, I think. At least, she's in surgery...." Her voice wavered as she gave in to her rising fear. "Oh, Jeffrey, will you come?"

He didn't ask any questions. He didn't waste time. To her eternal gratitude, all he said was, "I'll take the Concorde. I can be there in less than twenty-four hours. Will you be all right until I get there?"

Wondering if she would ever be all right again, Grace sobbed, "As long as you come, I'll be all right... I'll be waiting at the hospital. It's the San Francisco Golden Gate Hospital. Oh, Jeffrey, please hurry!"

ONCE KATE WAS OUT of surgery, she was moved to intensive care. Grace hadn't left her side for a second; Nick, too, hovered like a huge shadow in the background. Vaguely, Grace noticed a group of young people haunting the corridors; all were dressed in neatly pressed jeans and white shirts with identical blue berets. She didn't know who they were; she didn't care. She was too preoccupied with Kate to think about anyone or anything but her daughter.

While Dr. Sheila McIntyre watched over the operation, another surgeon named Dr. Landry had successfully removed the bullet. Kate had been lucky: the bullet had lodged next to the collarbone instead of careering around inside her body, causing more serious harm. When the surgeon had assured Grace that Kate's recovery would be painful and require physical therapy, but no permanent damage had been done, Grace was nearly incoherent with her relief and gratitude.

But her relief was short-lived. Every time she looked

at Kate's lovely face on the pillow, so pale that even her
bright hair seemed faded as it spread out on the pillow-
case, she had to cover her mouth to stop from sobbing.
The doctor had told her that Kate had been heavily se-
dated, and that she wasn't to worry if she slept for a
long time, but as the hours passed, Grace couldn't help
willing Kate to open her eyes, even for a few seconds.
She needed to see her daughter actually look at her, recognize her, to know that Kate would be all right.

But Kate slept on while Grace sat, rigid and strained
beside the bed. Behind her stood Nick, and out in the
hallway, the blue-bereted teenagers maintained their
vigil.

Just when Grace was sure she couldn't bear to hear
another muted *beep* of the heart monitor or listen to another *swoosh* of some machine without going completely
insane, Nick touched her on the shoulder. She was so
tense that she nearly screamed.

Stiffly, she turned to him. He gestured, and when she
turned to look where he was pointing, she immediately
shot to her feet. Coming down the hallway was Jeffrey.
She had never been so glad to see him in her life.

"Oh, Jeffrey!" she cried as she ran to him and his
arms closed around her. "She's going to be all right. Or
so they tell me. She's out of surgery, out of danger.
But...but..."

She couldn't go on. She looked up at him mutely and
saw his own strained expression.

"I'm here, Grace," he said hoarsely, gathering her
even closer. "Together, we won't let anything happen
to her."

Those were the words she had longed to hear. And as
soon as she heard them, she forgot all the hurtful words
and quarrels of the past year that had finally led them to

divorce. As she stood there with Jeffrey's arms blessedly around her, it was as though nothing had changed between them.

She looked up at him, tears glimmering on her lashes. She had always loved him, but in that moment, she had never loved him more.

CHAPTER TWELVE

THE FIRST THING KATE SAW when she opened her eyes was Nick. He was sitting in a chair by the bed, his head and arm resting on the bed rail. His face was turned away from her and he appeared to be asleep, though his fingers still gripped the aluminum rail. It seemed as if, even in sleep, he remained alert.

Kate watched him for a moment, trying not to move, to breathe...even to think. She was afraid that if she did any of those things, the nightmare she had experienced in the clinic would come flooding back, and she would be inundated with terrible memories of noise and confusion and...pain. At the moment, she didn't feel a thing. She seemed almost to be floating above the bed; it was a wonderful feeling, and she wanted it to last.

She became aware of the hissing and beeping of the various machines surrounding her. She listened to the different noises they made, then she looked up. From what she could see, the readings were relatively normal. She relaxed a fraction and felt an answering twinge in her shoulder. She tensed instinctively, fearing the resurgence of that burning agony.

To distract herself, she tried to remember how long she'd been here. It had to be at least a couple of days; she could remember people coming in and out of the room, but it had taken too much energy to stay awake, and had been much easier to drift into that dreamless sleep. She had not felt afraid, because she was aware of Nick's presence in the room. Even now, the sight of him at the side of the bed, half asleep, comforted her more than she could have imagined. She knew she was safe when he was here.

And he'd been here the entire time, she thought. She knew they had talked, but she was so fuzzy she couldn't remember what they'd said.

In fact, everything was a vague blur. Or maybe, she thought, she just didn't want to remember. She knew her mother was here, but had she really seen her father? She wasn't certain. Her memories were so confused, as though she were trying to see through a curtain of gauze.

She had to check if Nick was really here now, or if she was imagining him. Slowly, carefully, moving her arm a fraction of an inch at a time, she lifted her hand and rested it on his hair.

He was real, all right. The instant he felt her touch, he jerked his head up. All traces of sleep vanished from his eyes when he saw she was awake. Relief flooded his face.

"Kate!" he exclaimed softly, reaching for her hand. Holding it gingerly, as though it might break, he asked, "How do you feel?"

She tried to smile, but winced instead. "Like a truck ran over me," she said in a hoarse whisper. "I can't imagine that I look much better."

Carefully, he kissed her fingers. "You look beautiful. I can't tell you how glad I am that you're back."

"How long have I been out this time?"

"A while."

She tried to sit up, only to fall back with a grimace. The quick stab of pain took her breath away. She knew she had asked it before, but she had to know again. "The others...was anyone else hurt?"

"No." His expression turned bleak. "You were the only one."

"Thank God," she said. She thought of something else. "Emilio—"

"He and the Angels have been haunting the halls."

"No, I meant... Emilio didn't go after those two thugs, did he?"

Nick shook his head. "It was touch and go for a while, but he agreed to let the cops handle it."

"I'm glad."

"It took a little arm-twisting, I admit. But in the end, he saw the wisdom of allowing the authorities to take over."

"Thank you, Nick. He's come so far. I'd hate to see him throw it all away because of a little thing like this."

"A little thing?" Surprised anger flashed across his handsome face. "Being shot isn't a *little thing*, Kate!"

"No, no, I know it's not. I just meant that I'd hate to see him throw away his future because of this."

"His future is his concern," Nick said uncompromisingly. "Your safety is more important. I warned you that you'd get hurt at that stupid clinic."

She wasn't going to argue with him about Emilio. "I know. You were right. But this was an accident."

"This was no accident! Those two *pachucos* were out to hurt someone, and they did. God only knows what would have happened if I hadn't been there."

Kate shuddered at the thought, but she couldn't think about the clinic now. It was too frightening. Quickly, she said, "You know I'm grateful, Nick. But you sound so angry."

"I am angry. You could have been killed!"

"But I wasn't. So can we talk about this reasonably?"

"I don't know. I don't think so. I was hoping that an experience like this would open your eyes, but I see that it hasn't. You still haven't learned that things in the barrio will never change. You just don't understand—" He broke off. "Oh, the hell with it. If a gunshot wound won't change your mind, nothing will."

"I don't want to talk about it, Nick—"

Silence hung between them until he stood. "I think I'd better go. You need your rest."

Kate didn't argue; the conversation had exhausted her. But she didn't want him to leave on such an angry note. "We need to talk about us, Nick."

He looked down at her, his face closed, his eyes cold and black. "I don't think so, Kate. It's obvious that we'll always be at odds about this. You think that if you just try to understand those losers, everything will work out. Well, I know better. And all the blue berets in the world won't change that."

She couldn't believe he would leave her when he was so sorry. She tried one last time. "Nick, please don't go."

"I have to. As it happens, I have to fly back to Australia to tend to one last detail for your father. I was supposed to go before this, but I waited to make sure you were all right."

She wanted to say that she *wasn't* all right, that she would never be all right, not until they worked this out. But the thought that business in Australia was more important to him than being with her stiffened her pride and kept her mouth shut. She turned her head away, muttering, "Go ahead, then."

She could feel him staring down at her, but she refused to look at him. Her mouth a tight line, she told herself that she would not beg. *Fine*, she thought resentfully. *Go. Do what you have to. But don't expect me to be waiting here when you get back.*

Finally, when she wasn't sure she could keep up her pose any longer, he turned and left. The door had barely closed behind him before Kate was trying to sit up. The stand holding her intravenous bottle rattled and clattered as she grabbed the rail and attempted to pull herself up. All she could think of was how wrong this was. She wanted to go after him and tell him she was sorry, but a stab of pain lanced through her and knocked her flat. Gasping, she lay back.

"Nick..." she whispered weakly, staring at the door. "Oh, Nick, don't go...not like this...."

But the door remained closed, and after a few minutes, she let go of the rail and closed her eyes. She was so devastated by what had just happened that she couldn't even cry.

KATE LEFT THE HOSPITAL a few days later, pale and withdrawn. Physically she was healing, but emotionally...that was a different story.

She knew that those who cared about her were worried, but she couldn't seem to make it matter to her. Nothing seemed to matter to her anymore. She, who had once viewed life with such joy, had lost all zest. She, who had always been the optimist, eagerly anticipating each day, now felt as though she viewed everything through a gray cloud that never seemed to lift.

As the days passed, she did what was expected of her and nothing else. When the physical therapist came, she performed the exercises with dull determination because she knew she must. When food was put in front of her, she ate it—most of it, anyway—but none of it had much taste.

As a physician, she knew that in time the ache in her shoulder would go away; what she wasn't so sure of was whether the pain in her heart would ever vanish.

Or the fear.

At first, she'd been terrified by a recurring nightmare in which two monsters burst into her room with exploding firearms aimed straight at her. When that happened, she'd jerk awake, drenched with sweat and shaking with fright. She no longer had that dream, but sometimes, during the day, she would get a flash of those two cruel faces and cringe. Would she never be free of those terrible images?

She tried to occupy herself with reading, but the medical journals she had once avidly devoured just gathered dust. She tried to watch television, only to realize after a while that she was staring dully at the flickering screen without taking note. She'd taken enough psychology courses to realize that she was suffering from something akin to post-traumatic stress syndrome, but that knowledge didn't seem to help.

What difference did it make? she asked herself dully.

She wouldn't allow herself to think of Nick, who had abandoned her. Instead, she tried to face her future without him—or the clinic. Because the one thing she had decided was that she was never going to go back to the clinic. Even the thought made her break out into a sweat. She was so terrified that she wasn't certain she could ever return to the hospital, either. As irrational as it was, she felt that the medical profession had let her down. She didn't want to have anything more to do with it.

She knew her parents were worried about her. In fact, her father was still here. He'd booked into a hotel, and he came every day to see Kate at Grace's apartment, where her mother had insisted Kate stay until she recovered.

That was another thing that worried everyone. The old Kate would have refused to stay anywhere but at her own place while she recuperated. But she was different now, and she hadn't argued when her mother insisted that she come home with her. So she was staying here—for how long, she didn't know. Right now, her life seemed to be on hold.

Consequently, she was sitting in her mother's living room one bright morning, staring blankly out the window at the boats skimming the waters of the Bay, when Grace entered the room. Kate could feel her mother staring at her; she knew without turning around that Grace's expression would be a mixture of affection and concern. Kate wanted to say something to reassure her, but she couldn't summon the energy or the will. She could only sit there, wondering why she didn't feel anything, not even gratitude that she was alive.

Grace sighed before she joined Kate on the couch. "Katie, darling," she said, "it's such a beautiful morning. Why don't I take the day off and we'll do something fun. Whatever will please you. Would you like that?"

Kate knew her mother was doing her best to drag her out of this pit she seemed to have fallen into; with a great effort, she turned to Grace and tried to smile.

"Thanks," she said, "but I'm really not feeling up to anything today. Do you mind?"

Grace gazed at her sadly for a long moment, then she reached for her hand. Quietly, she asked, "What is it, Katie? Please, tell me what's wrong. Are you still in pain? Is that it? Because if you are, we'll find a doctor who—"

"I'm not in pain, Mother," Kate said, and thought, *At least, not the kind you mean.* "It's just... I don't know...." Her voice trailed away, and she turned to look out the window again. "You go ahead and go to work. I'll be all right here alone."

Grace tried again. "Your father is coming over in a while. You and he could do something together. He hasn't seen much of the city on this visit. Maybe you could show him around."

Kate felt exhausted just at the thought. Disinterestedly, she said, "What is there to see? It's the same old Golden Gate Bridge, the same old trollies. Besides, Dad doesn't really want me to play tour guide. He's got to get back to work himself."

"He's not going to leave until we're both sure you're all right, darling. Now, please, let us in. We want to help."

With an effort, Kate tried to rouse herself. "I'm all right, Mother, I promise. I...I guess this is just going to take time."

Grace continued to look at her worriedly. "But you won't even see anyone."

The last thing Kate wanted at this low point in her life was to have to see people and make an attempt to be cheerful, especially when the one person she did want to see...

"That's not true," she said. "I saw Emilio and the other kids when they came to the hospital, and Sheila has visited. So has Mary. The only person who hasn't come to see me is—"

She broke off, biting her bottom lip.

Nick's name hung unmentioned in the air, and Grace said quietly, "He was there night and day when you were in intensive care—"

Kate couldn't keep the bitterness from her voice. "That's right, but he's not here now...."

"He cares for you, Kate—"

"Oh, really?" She waved a weary hand. "Do you mind if we don't talk about this anymore? I'm so tired. I think I'll go lie down for a while."

Grace didn't say anything when Kate dragged herself up from the couch and walked slowly out of the room without looking back. As her youngest disappeared down the hallway toward the guest room, she sighed deeply.

"Oh, Katie," she murmured. "What are we going to do?"

She had no answer; in fact, everyone who knew or cared about Kate was stumped. Since the shooting, her personality seemed to have undergone a complete alteration. No one could understand her, not even her mother. Grace was so upset that she had visited a counselor who specialized in trauma disorders. The woman had been sympathetic, but basically—as far as Grace was concerned—unhelpful. The woman had said they all had to be patient. If Kate refused to come in for counseling herself, the only thing anyone could do was wait.

Grace didn't want to wait. She was frightened for her daughter, who had become a stranger right before her eyes. She didn't recognize this wan wraith who rarely spoke; she was accustomed to a vibrant, engaging daughter who changed the dynamics of a room just by walking into it. She wanted that girl back—the young woman who had devoted her life to helping people by becoming a warm, caring, dedicated doctor....

A doctor who had endangered her life by trying to help those less fortunate than she was, Grace thought in sudden anger. And look what had happened. She had been seriously injured for her pains, and her entire life had veered off course.

The doorbell rang, jolting Grace out of her bitter introspection. As she went to answer it, she realized that all of their lives had been changed by that gunshot. Things that had seemed so important before had been relegated to the background as inconsequential. Kate was uppermost in Grace's mind; everything else was secondary, including the store and finding those missing jewels.

In fact, she had forgotten all about the jewels until Marguerite called to offer sympathy. Erin had told her grandmother about the accident, and, considerately, Marguerite had assured Grace that they would meet at a more appropriate time.

Grace opened the door to find Jeffrey standing there. He immediately asked, as he did every day, "How is she?"

Grace felt a pang. In the two weeks he'd been here, Jeffrey had aged—as she had. His hair had more gray; his eyes looked lusterless and worried—like hers. She shook her head at the question.

"She's the same," she said, her voice low. "She's not interested in anything. I offered to take the day off and do something fun, but she didn't want that. I told her that you were coming over, and that maybe the two of you could tour the city. All she said was that she was tired and wanted to lie down." Despite herself, Grace couldn't hold back stinging tears. "I simply don't know what to do!"

Jeffrey came in and shut the door. "Has Nick called?"

"No, and I don't know why. What's the matter with him, Jeffrey? Have you spoken to him?"

Jeffrey hesitated. "Yes...but not about Kate."

She looked at him, angry and exasperated and feeling more helpless than she ever had in her life. "Why not?"

He hesitated again. Then he said reluctantly, "Because I believe that whatever might be between them is just that...between the two of them. It's none of my business."

"Oh, Jeffrey!"

"Now, Grace, let's not quarrel about this again."

She spun away from him. Bitterly, she said, "Our daughter is in a depressed state, and I'm sure it has something to do with Nick. You saw how he was at the hospital when Kate was in intensive care. He practically *haunted* the place. He was there day and night. He never left her side."

"He was worried—as we all were."

"Of course he was worried! But...listen to me, Jeffrey. I saw his face. I *know* how much he cares for Kate. So why isn't he here?"

"He went to Australia to finish up something for me."

"I know that! But why did he choose to go now? What could be more important than Kate?"

When Jeffrey merely stared at her helplessly, Grace cried, "Oh, men! You're so oblivious at times! How can he be gone at a time like this?"

"I don't know, Grace." Tentatively he took her arm. "But we'll get through this...somehow."

She looked up at him. "How?"

He shook his head. "I don't know."

Then he dropped his hand—too soon for Grace. His gesture had been so comforting that she'd wanted to put her own hand over his and just hold his palm to her face. He had not touched her since the night he'd arrived at the hospital.

She thrust the notion away. How selfish she was to be thinking of herself! Fiercely she brought her thoughts back to Kate. "We have to do something, Jeffrey," she said. "I want you to call Nick and tell him—"

"What? I told you, the man has his own problems."

"Whatever his problems are, they pale in comparison to what is happening to Kate!"

"I know. But I think, from what little he's said to me about it, that he feels responsible for what happened."

"Responsible!" Grace looked at him incredulously. "That's ridiculous!"

"I know. From the jumbled accounts I heard of the incident, he probably saved everyone. When those two gang members saw him with a gun, they thought better of whatever cretinous plan they'd hatched and ran for their lives."

Grace shuddered. "I never thought I'd ever say I was glad someone was carrying a gun. But in this instance..." She stopped. She'd had nightmares, imagining what had happened. Plaintively, she said, "I still don't understand why he feels responsible."

"I don't, either, Grace. On the surface of it, it *is* ridiculous. But as we both know, sometimes we can't control our feelings...."

His voice trailed away, and Grace knew he was thinking, as she was, just how true that was. If either of them had been able to control their feelings, they wouldn't be divorced. Grace liked to think that she would still be in England, happily married to her husband. Once, she couldn't have imagined any other life than living with Jeffrey, loving him, and working by his side. What a source of satisfaction and pleasure that had always been!

At the thought, she closed her eyes. She had to stop this, she told herself. All she was doing was torturing herself, and for what purpose? Jeffrey was here only because of Kate; together they had to work to help make their daughter well again.

"Anyway," Jeffrey said after a moment, "about Kate... I've been thinking—"

Avid for any solution, she turned to him. "Yes?"

As though he knew she wouldn't like the suggestion, he said hurriedly, "I've been thinking that maybe I should take Kate back to England with me."

"Take her back to England!" Grace was fiercely protective. "Why?"

"Well, it would be a change of scene, for one thing. And you know how worried Meg and Gabe have been. Meg could come over from Paris, and maybe seeing them would cheer Kate up again."

Men are so simple, Grace thought with a mixture of tenderness and exasperation. This wasn't a matter of "cheering Kate up." They were talking about a young woman whose entire future had been thrown off course, a woman who was suffering the after-effects of a trauma.

But she didn't want to hurt Jeffrey's feelings; he looked so anxious. Carefully, she said, "I know they're worried. One or the other calls practically every day. In fact, they both wanted to fly over here, but I asked them to wait. I told them it would be too much for Kate, but the truth is, I didn't want them to be hurt. You know how listless Kate is. If they came all this way and she wouldn't even see them..."

She didn't have to finish the thought. Nodding, Jeffrey said, "I agree. But perhaps things would be different if I took *her* to them. You know how much she's always loved Kemberly...."

Their eyes met, both of them thinking the same thing. Grace had always loved Kemberly, too. They'd had such wonderful times there—first, just her and Jeffrey; then after the children came, as a family.

But if she thought of Kemberly, Grace knew she would start weeping. Quickly, she glanced away. "I'm...I'm not sure I want her to go," she said. "Maybe it would be good for her, in a way. But I think she needs me right now, whether she knows it or not. And with the...the situation the way it is between us, I could hardly go with her."

Jeffrey put his hands on her shoulders. "That's not true," he said quietly. "You know you're always welcome at Kemberly."

The simple gesture was almost her undoing. Closing her eyes, Grace fought for control. She longed to lean against him, as she had so often in the past; she yearned for the comfort she'd always found in his embrace. Oh, to turn around and bury her face against his chest, to surrender to him the pain and worry that threatened to swamp her every day!

Grace had been trying so hard to control her roiling emotions that at first she didn't feel Jeffrey's fingers tightening on her shoulders, didn't realize that he was trembling, or hear the way his breathing had coarsened. When she finally recognized that he was as emotional as she, that Kate's situation brought as much pain to him as it did to her, she looked up at him. He had tears in his eyes.

"Oh, Jeffrey!" she whispered.

He couldn't answer. His face crumpling, he opened his arms, and without a thought, she went into them. They held each other tightly, united in their suffering over their youngest child.

At last, Jeffrey lifted his head and wiped his face. So private a man, always so self-contained, he was clearly embarrassed. Grace, who knew him so well, wisely ignored what had just taken place. Shakily, she said, "I think we both need a cup of coffee."

He pulled out a handkerchief and blew his nose. "Thank you, but no. I have an errand to run."

"An errand? Now?"

He put the handkerchief away. "I think it's time that Nick Santos and I had a little man-to-man chat."

CHAPTER THIRTEEN

EVEN BEFORE HE GOT BACK from Australia, Nick wasn't sleeping well. When he did manage to fall asleep, his dreams were of Kate. Again and again, he saw her lying on the floor of the clinic, her face absolutely white, her lab coat soaked with her own blood. Again and again, he saw those two gang members entering the clinic, guns in their hands. And, dreamlike, he saw himself turning in slow motion, trying to draw his own gun...and failing. When he'd finally jerk awake, he'd be drenched in sweat, and the sheets and blankets were on the floor.

One morning, he was just getting out of the shower when the phone rang. Wrapping a towel around his waist, he answered, hoping it wasn't Max. She'd been on his case about Kate, and he didn't feel up to another argument about why he hadn't gone to see her.

"Hello, Nick," Jeffrey DeWilde said. "Am I calling too early?"

"No, it's okay," he said cautiously. He mistrusted that breezy sound in his employer's voice. "What's up?"

"I'd like to meet this morning, if that's convenient for you. I've got something I want to discuss."

They'd already talked about Nick's trip; Nick had given Jeffrey a full report when he returned from down under. Even more wary now, he said, "Okay. Where and when?"

"How about the coffee shop at my hotel. In, say, half an hour? Unless it's too short a notice, that is."

Whatever it was, Nick just wanted to get it over with. "Half an hour is fine. I'll see you then."

THIRTY MINUTES LATER, Nick had just ordered his coffee when Jeffrey walked into the coffee shop. Although they'd talked over the phone, Nick hadn't seen his employer since Kate had been released from the hospital, and he was shocked by how drawn Jeffrey looked. His first thought was that something had happened to Kate; he barely allowed Jeffrey to sit down before he asked, "How's Kate?"

"Funny you should ask that, Nick," Jeffrey said, signaling the waiter to bring him a cup of coffee.

Nick stiffened. "What the hell does that mean?"

Jeffrey gave him one of those cool, aristocratic stares. "Well, you have to admit, we haven't heard too much from you lately."

"I've kept you up to date on the case," Nick said. "And with Kate trying to recover, I didn't feel I should intrude on what should be a family time."

"Don't you think you're carrying that a little too far?"

Try as he might, Nick couldn't hold that gaze. "I don't know what you mean. I thought you wanted to meet me to talk about the case."

"We can do that later," Jeffrey said, as if the theft hardly mattered, when it had been uppermost in his mind these past months. "Right now, other things are more important."

"Kate, you mean."

"Yes."

Nick sat back. "I don't know what you want from me, Mr. DeWilde."

Until then, Jeffrey's posture had been ramrod straight. But now, before Nick's eyes, he slumped. Gone in an instant was the self-confident, almost arrogant demeanor of a man who ran a multimillion-dollar international company; in his place was a father, terribly concerned about his child.

Jeffrey started to say something, then gave up. His coffee had arrived, and as though his hands were suddenly cold, he wrapped his long fingers around the cup. He looked as miserable as Nick felt.

"I don't know what I want from you, either, Nick," he said, his voice low. "It's not my custom to drag others into my family's private affairs. I did make an exception when I hired you, and I haven't been sorry. You've done a wonderful job for me. But right now, I'm too worried about my daughter to stand on ceremony. If there's anything I can do for Kate—anything at all—I'll do it. But the truth of the matter is that Grace and I simply don't know what to do. We've never seen Kate like this. She's so...withdrawn."

"That's common after a trauma like this. I know, because I felt that way after I got shot."

Jeffrey leaned forward. "I know it's a great imposition, Nick—and undoubtedly a terrible invasion of your privacy—but could you tell me about that time? Your feelings, I mean. How you dealt with it."

Nick tried to think of that episode as little as possible. It was a painful time in his life, and had led to his retirement from the police force, a job he'd hoped to have until they had to carry him out.

But he couldn't ignore the pleading look on Jeffrey's face, so he forced himself to say, "I...didn't deal with it well, I have to tell you. And remember, I was a police officer at the time. We never really expect to get shot, but it's always there at the back of our minds. Kate didn't have that buffer.''

The hope in Jeffrey's eyes almost broke Nick's heart. It was even worse when Jeffrey asked plaintively, ''So you think that she'll get over this?''

''I'm not qualified to answer that,'' Nick said. He couldn't hold out false assurances. ''I'm not a counselor or a psychiatrist. Maybe you should seek professional help.''

''We've tried. But Kate refuses. She insists there's nothing wrong with her.''

''Maybe she just needs more time.''

Jeffrey hesitated. Finally, he voiced his deepest fear. ''Both Grace and I are afraid that this...incident has shaken Kate to the extent that she might give up medicine.''

Nick was so shocked he didn't know what to say. The idea that Kate would abandon her medical career seemed inconceivable to him. He couldn't imagine it; she was too dedicated.

''You can't let that happen,'' he said.

''I don't see how we can prevent it.''

Nick didn't give himself a chance to consider what he was about to say; he knew that if he did, he might not go through with it. Whatever his feelings were—and at the moment, he wasn't sure *how* he felt—the only thing that mattered was Kate.

''Maybe,'' he said, ''I can talk to her.''

''Would you?''

Jeffrey looked at him, a strange expression in his eyes. For a moment, Nick thought that it was a sly look of satisfaction, but then he decided he was wrong. He hadn't promised anything. In fact, if he knew Kate, she probably wouldn't even let him in.

And who could blame her? he asked himself grimly. He'd been a coward and a jerk.

He stood abruptly. Tossing a couple of bills down on the tabletop, he said, "I can't guarantee she'll even talk to me, but I'll give it a try."

"That's good enough for me."

THEY TOOK TWO CARS, Jeffrey leading the way. When he and Nick appeared at the apartment door, Grace looked startled.

"What is it?" she asked.

Jeffrey didn't waste words. "Where's Kate?"

Grace looked from one to the other. "In her room, where she always is. Why?"

"Will you please ask her to come out? Nick wants to—"

Since Nick wasn't exactly sure what he was going to say to Kate, he didn't want to say it in front of an audience. Quickly, he said, "Never mind, Mrs. DeWilde. I think it's best if I talk to Kate privately."

Grace seemed uncertain. "If you wish. But I have to warn you, Kate—"

"I know," he said. "Now, will you both excuse me?"

He left them standing in the living room after Grace had dubiously gestured toward the hall and told him Kate's bedroom was the second door on the right. He headed in that direction, but when he was standing in front of the firmly closed door, he wondered what the hell he was doing. What right had he to go in there and tell Kate how she should act?

Before he lost courage, he knocked briefly—three

hard taps. When she answered listlessly, he opened the door and went in.

Kate was sitting by the window when Nick entered. When she saw him, she stared dully at him for a moment, then turned away.

"What are you doing here?" she asked.

The instant he saw her, Nick forgot all the confusion and emotional disarray this woman had caused him. The sight of her pale face made him long to take her into his arms and protect her from all the ugliness in the world. But he couldn't do that, so he said, "I came to find out when you're going to stop feeling sorry for yourself and get back to work."

She turned to look at him again. "What?"

"You heard me." She was wearing a robe and slippers. When he saw that, he went to the closet and jerked the door open. Grabbing the first clothes he saw, he threw them on the bed. "Get dressed. I'll drive you to the hospital, or the clinic, whichever you want to see first. But know this, Kate—one way or the other, you're getting out of this apartment."

She stared at him blankly. Then she shook her head. "You can't come in here and order me around. You lost that right—if you ever had it—when you...when you walked out on me."

He felt a dull red creeping up his neck. He couldn't argue that, so he didn't try. "You're right. I did walk out. I have no excuse. It was cowardly and stupid. But I thought it was the best thing at the time."

She turned away. "Yeah, right. Go away, Nick. I have nothing to say to you."

"But I have something to say to you. Someone has to say it." He steeled himself against reacting to her paler-than-pale face and the weight loss that was obvious beneath the thick robe she wore. He couldn't weaken now; he wouldn't allow himself to think about how shadowed her eyes were, or how lifeless. If he did, he wouldn't be able to do this.

Her mouth turned down. "Well, it won't be you."

He crossed the room in two strides. Being careful not to hurt her, he pulled her up out of the chair. Hating himself, he said, "Yes, it will be me. No one else has the guts to tell you the truth, so I will."

"I don't want to hear anything you have to say."

"Too bad. You're going to hear it, anyway. You're the one who insisted that this little 'incident,' as you called it, was just one of those things. If that's true, there's no reason for you to be hiding behind your mother's skirts."

That got to her. A faint flush stained her cheeks as she denied, "I'm not hiding."

He couldn't let up. "What do you call it, then?"

She was so pale that when her flush deepened, her face was still only a pallid pink. "I'm not hiding," she repeated, trying to twist away. "And anyway, what do you know about it?"

He wouldn't let her go. "You know what I know about it. I had the same experience."

"It's not the same thing."

"Why not? Because I was shot in the line of duty, and you were just an innocent bystander? Well, let me tell you one thing, honey, it hurts just the same. But you've got to get over it. Life goes on, whether you want it to or not."

She dropped her head. He could hardly hear her when she muttered, "What if I don't want it to?"

With her head down, her hair had parted at the nape; for some reason, the exposed skin made her seem so vulnerable that he longed to rest his hand on the slender column of her neck before sliding his fingers under her jaw and turning her face up to him. He clenched his hands instead.

"You don't have any choice," he said harshly. "Especially you. People depend on you, Kate. All those sick and hurting people out there, waiting for Dr. Kate DeWilde to heal them, or at least make them feel better. Are you going to abandon them?"

The picture of misery, she wrapped her arms around her. "There are other doctors."

"That's true. But there's only one you."

"Only one me," she repeated. Her lip curled in self-loathing. "Maybe that's a good thing. That way, there's only one fool in the world."

He was beginning to feel scared. The Kate he knew would have reacted strongly long before now, probably throwing him out on his ear after berating him for daring to say any of these things to her—even if they were true. This Kate was a shadow of herself; he couldn't get a response out of her no matter what he said. It was like confronting a zombie.

He took a different tack. "You surprise me, Kate. I never thought you were the kind of person who lacked the strength of her own convictions."

She didn't react to that, either. "Well, now you know."

Trying to hide his growing desperation, he said, "Then I guess it's a good thing you're not going back. You'll never be any kind of doctor at all if you cave in at the first sign of trouble."

"I didn't cave in," she muttered. "I was shot."

He was beginning to wonder if anything would move her. Scornfully, he said, "So what? Half the people in that neighborhood where the clinic's located have been shot. But maybe, as you said yourself, it's no big deal. So let's look at it this way. Now you all have something in common. As you bleeding hearts are so fond of saying, now you can feel their pain."

That did it. She jerked her head up and stared straight at him. Her voice choked with tears, she cried, "What do you want from me, Nick? You told me that working at the clinic was too dangerous, and you were right, it was! I shouldn't have been there in the first place. And if I have any doubts, all I have to do is remember what happened. Unfortunately for me, I had to get shot before I realized what a fool I was to think that I could possibly make a difference!"

She was reacting, all right—but not in the way he'd intended. Alarmed, he tried to say, "But you did—"

She whirled around, wincing with pain at the sudden movement. "Get real, Nick! I mean, who did I think I was? Some hotshot doctor who was magnanimously giving of my time to people less fortunate than I am. Well, they showed me, didn't they? You tried to tell me I wasn't wanted down there, and they proved your point."

"Not *they*." He regarded her even more uneasily. Before, her glance had been empty, faraway. Now she looked... He didn't know how to describe it. Desperate, maybe? Frantic, certainly. Wondering if he should call her parents, he started to say, "It wasn't everyone, Kate. It was two gang members—"

"Oh, who cares?" she cried. "Two, ten, what does it matter? What's important is that I finally got the point. I don't belong there and I never did!"

"That's not true. I've been there since, Kate, and everyone asked about you. They wanted to know when you were returning."

"They think I'm going back?" She looked at him wildly. "I'm never going back! Haven't you been listening to me? What have I been saying to you all this time?"

Nick didn't know what to do. She looked close to a breakdown and he wondered again if he should call her parents. He didn't know how to handle this; he hoped to hell they might have an idea. He was turning toward the door when she reached for him. Abject terror had tightened her features.

"Oh, Nick," she said, choking. Her eyes were tortured, agonized. Her voice cracking, she said, "I think I'm losing my mind! Please, help me!"

Without a word, he took her into his arms. His eyes closed, he held her tightly, as if by his very will he could hold the world at bay. As she trembled against him, he stroked her hair and whispered, over and over, "Shh, it's all right...it's all right...I'm here. Nothing can hurt you...."

Clinging to him, she finally burst into the tears that would help to heal her. Her face against his chest, she wept. "I was so afraid, Nick. All the time I worked at the clinic, I was terrified. Every time someone came in, I wondered if this was the one who..." For a moment she couldn't go on. "I wanted to do good—I did. But...but..." She shuddered. "Then when you accused me...when you left..."

He held her even more tightly. "I was wrong about what I said, Kate. So wrong. And I never should have left you, not like that."

"Oh, Nick!"

He didn't say anything more; he just held her. She cried until she couldn't cry any longer, until her tears finally stopped. Still, he pressed her to him. When at last she looked up at him, he released her just enough so that he could look into her reddened eyes. She had never appeared more beautiful to him than she did at that moment, her cheeks wet, her beautiful skin red and blotched. Gently, he smoothed back her sweat-drenched hair. He knew she was going to hate him—he knew he'd hate himself—but he had to say it. Before they could talk about their own problems, she had to face the biggest one on her own.

Quietly, he said, "You know you have to go back—" She shook her head. "No, no, I can't!"

He took her trembling hands in his. "Yes, you can. You must."

She tried to pull away from him. "No!"

He held her eyes. "Yes," he said. "You'll never get over this if you don't. You know it. I know it, too."

Her face crumpled. "I can't!" she wailed.

"Yes, you can," he insisted.

She tried to protest again, but when he continued to stare at her, she stopped. Shaking from head to foot, she finally said, "Will you go with me?"

That's when he knew for certain that she had turned the corner. Hiding his relief in a smile, he said, "You bet."

CLEOPATRA ENTERING ROME couldn't have competed with Dr. Kate DeWilde's return to the San Francisco City Free Clinic. Kate didn't know that Nick had made a quick call to Emilio before they left; she was amazed to see that, long before they pulled up to the clinic door, people were out on the streets waving and calling her name to welcome her back.

Sitting across the seat from him in the car, holding

tightly to his free hand, Kate smiled tremulously at Nick as they drove slowly down the street.

"I feel like Sally Field," she said. "They like me. They really like me."

Nick smiled, too, and gestured. They had turned the corner onto the street where the clinic was located. When she looked in the direction he pointed, she gasped.

The Free Clinic was situated in the center of the block. On either side, up and down the street, were Dr. Kate's Angels. Dressed in their identical uniforms—jeans with crisp creases, stark white dress shirts with the sleeves rolled up, and, of course, their badge of honor, the blue berets—the Angels stood at attention, their eyes hard front, their hands clasped behind their backs.

"Oh, Nick," she whispered when she saw the proud display. She was too overcome to say more. Nick squeezed her hand as they pulled up in front.

Applause erupted when he helped Kate to get out of the car. As she looked around, tears of gratitude in her eyes, Nick leaned down.

"Better wave, doc," he said with a grin. "Because as far as I know, those cheers are all yours."

CHAPTER FOURTEEN

WHEN KATE MOVED BACK to her own place, Nick was there to help. He carried her suitcase down to the car while she checked inside to make sure she hadn't forgotten anything. He was stowing it in the trunk when he realized that Grace had followed him out to the street.

"Oh...Mrs. DeWilde," he said, slamming the trunk lid down. "Did Kate forget something?"

"No, but I did," she said. She gave him one of those dazzling smiles that reminded him so much of Kate. She held out her hand. "I wanted to thank you, Nick. I don't know what you said or did, but whatever it was, you brought Kate back to us. Jeffrey and I are more grateful than we can express."

Her gratitude embarrassed him. "I can't take credit. Kate was ready to get back to her life. She just didn't know how to do it."

"But you knew how to help her. We didn't."

"All I did was push her a little. It wasn't any more than my partner did for me after I was shot."

Grace looked at him in mild exasperation. "Nick, I'm trying to thank you, and you're making it awfully difficult."

He smiled uncomfortably. "Sorry. But as I said, there's no need for thanks. I was glad to do it. I'm...fond of Kate."

"As she is of you," Grace said, her expression carefully neutral. "I know it's difficult sometimes to tell. Kate can be...prickly at times."

"At times?"

"All right. *most* of the time," Grace said with a laugh. Her smile faded. "That's why her father and I were so worried when she became withdrawn. It wasn't like her."

"Well, she had a lot to deal with. Not only the physical pain, but the psychological. It's a sobering thing to be forced to confront your mortality."

Grace was doing her best to understand. "Yes, but in her capacity as a physician, Kate does face death and dying all the time."

"In other people, yes. It's different when its your own mortality you're forced to recognize. But it's over now. She'll be all right, I think."

"She said everything went well at the clinic, but...did it?"

He was still marveling at the memory. "I have to admit, I've never seen anything like it. All those people clapping and cheering to welcome her back...it was something to see. And those kids—"

"You mean Dr. Kate's Angels? I met them all at the hospital. At first, I thought they were...you know... tough. It must have been quite a sight to see them lined up and down the block like that for her."

"I saw it, and I'm still not sure I believe it myself," Nick said. His voice hardened. "I grew up with kids like that, in a neighborhood very similar. It remains to be seen whether their sudden community spirit will last."

"Kate said that you seemed cynical about their efforts."

He shrugged. "Like I said, I'm withholding judgment."

"For Kate's sake, and for those kids', I hope you're wrong, Nick."

"I do, too."

Kate emerged just then on the arm of her father. As she embraced her mother before getting carefully into the car, the glances of the two men met. Nick was glad to see that the tension had left Jeffrey's face. His eyes were still shadowed and marked with some lingering pain, but he seemed to have regained his characteristic vigor. His grip was strong when he shook Nick's hand.

"Thank you," he said simply. His eyes went to Grace and his daughter, who were going through the female ritual of the endless goodbye—telling each other "just one more thing," as though they hadn't said enough inside. He turned back to Nick. "We'll talk later."

Nick nodded and walked around to the other side of the car and climbed in. After much waving and many goodbyes from Kate and her mother, they were finally off. As they drove away, Kate looked back at her parents, standing side by side on the curb, and sighed.

"It's so good to see them together like that," she said.

Nick glanced in the rearview mirror. He suspected what Kate might be leading up to, so his reply was a cautious, "They make a nice-looking couple."

"They belong together." Still stiff and sore, with a long road of physical therapy ahead of her, Kate faced forward again and tried to find a comfortable position. "And that brings us to our next topic of conversation, doesn't it."

He looked at her warily. "What do you mean?"

"Don't play dumb with me. You know what I mean. I want to know why you left me all alone in the hospital."

His hand tightened on the wheel. "I admit, it was stupid—"

"Oh, it was more than stupid! It was insensitive and callous and cruel, and…and… Oh, Nick, how could you do that to me?" she cried. "I thought we meant something to each other!"

"We did! We…do. It was just that I…"

He couldn't say it. His jaw tight, he stared straight ahead.

Kate watched him for a moment, trying to control both her temper and her tears. Finally, she said, "I see. Well, if that's all you can say, I guess we have nothing more to talk about."

"I don't know why you're acting like this now, Kate. Everything was fine when we were at the clinic—"

She turned to him, her body rigid. "Everything wasn't fine! It was a start, yes, and before you say it, I know I have you to thank for that. But—" she stopped, swallowing. "But now that I've faced that fear, I realize that I was using it to distract me from something that is equally—if not more—important."

"And that is?"

"You have to ask? It's you. But when you abandoned me, I realized—"

"I didn't *abandon* you—"

"What do you call it then?"

He knew what to call it, but he wasn't ready to admit it aloud. Turning back to his driving, he muttered, "I thought you needed time to heal. And I had a job to do."

"Oh, yes, a *job*. Well, do you know what? I hope Mother finds those jewels before you do. It would serve you right!"

"What does your mother have to do with this?"

"I see that's another thing you've forgotten," she said angrily. "We talked about this before, Nick. I told you, it's important to Mother to find those missing jewels herself. And because it's important to her, it's important to me."

A "so there" hung between them. Kate tightened her lips again and turned to face forward. "We're here. Stop the car."

They had reached the street where her apartment was located. Nick pulled up in front of the building and obediently cut the engine. But when Kate reached for her door handle, he put a hand on her arm.

"Wait—"

She turned to him with an icy expression. "For what? I don't think there's anything more to say, do you?"

There was a lot more to say, and they both knew it. But pride kept Nick silent as he got out and went around the car to open Kate's door for her. She emerged stiffly, but ignored his proffered hand and didn't even wait until he got her suitcase from the trunk. She was struggling with the heavy front door by the time he reached her. He opened the door himself, but barred the way, forcing her to stop.

"I don't want to leave things like this, Kate," he said.

She refused to look at him. "Why not? You left it this way at the hospital, didn't you?"

He had reached the limit of his patience—and his guilt. Angry now himself, he said, "This might not mean much to you, Kate, but it's my *job* to find those jewels. Your father hired me to do it, and that's what I'm going to do."

"Fine," she said between clenched teeth. "Now, get out of my way. I should have known you'd be like this."

"Like what? Responsible? Determined to do the job

I set out to do?'' He was so angry he didn't consider his next words. ''You might think so little of your work that you could give it up without a thought, but not me. I—''

Her face turned red, then white, then red again. ''How *dare* you say that to me! You know how much being a doctor means to me!''

''You could have fooled me. As I recall, you were only too eager to give it all up.''

''I can't believe you would throw that in my face! When I said that, I was…distraught. In fact, I hardly knew what I was saying. It's not fair for you to hold that up to me!''

''You talk about fair, yet you expect me to back off on my search for these damned jewels just because your mother has a whim? Well, let me tell you something, princess. I was right about you all along. I had you pegged the first time we ever met.''

She stiffened. ''And just what do you mean by that?''

''You think you're the great humanitarian, the one who's going to show us the right path. You're full of good, kind deeds—as long as everything goes your way. But you know what? I saw through you right off, and everything you've said to me today proves it. You're nothing but a spoiled rich kid who runs at the first sign of trouble!''

Kate's face was crimson. ''That's not true!''

''Oh, yes, it is,'' he said relentlessly. ''You're just like all the other ''Patties'' I've known. You go down to the barrio knowing nothing about those people or their lives, but thinking that you do just because you're educated and rich and white. You convince yourself that you're helping them, but all the time it's just an ego trip. And you know what? You can come home at the end of the day to your posh little apartment and forget about them until the next day. But the people you left behind can't leave. They're stuck.''

Kate couldn't have looked more stricken if he'd dealt her a physical blow. "Why are you doing this? I was only trying to help—"

He couldn't stop himself. He wanted to hurt her so badly she would never want to have anything to do with him again. He'd known this wasn't going to work; they were too different. They couldn't agree about anything, not even those stupid jewels. Better to leave now, before...

"Who were you trying to help, Kate?" he asked contemptuously. "Them, or yourself? Never mind, I can answer that. It made you feel good, didn't it? Oh, yes it did—don't deny it. But that ended when one of them turned on you and showed you that you weren't as smart as you thought.''

He didn't give her a chance to reply. Intending to leave on that low note, he moved aside to let her walk by him into the building. But she didn't budge, her eyes as fiery as her red face.

"Just a minute," she said furiously. She jerked the door he held open out of his hand and slammed it with a bang. "We're not done yet.''

He could almost feel the heat of her anger. "Oh, no?" he said bravely. "What else is there to talk about?"

"Just one more thing." She backed him up against the door. "That was very dramatic just now, telling me what a fool I was because I wanted to help someone— but it won't wash. You wouldn't have forced me to go back to the clinic if you really felt that way. This isn't about differing ideologies. This is about you and me!''

"Don't make more of this than there is, Kate—"

"Are you actually going to tell me you don't feel

anything for me, Nick? Are you going to try and say that what we had together didn't mean anything at all?"

He had to force himself to look her in the eye. "Of course not. But I realize now that it was a mistake. You know it, too. We don't belong together and never will."

She took a step back. "You know," she said with deceptive calm, "you're right."

That threw him. "I am?"

"Yes, you are. I don't want to get involved with a...a coward."

"What?"

"I pictured you as a lot of things, Nick, but never that. And a coward is exactly what you are. You're so afraid of your feelings that you'd rather ignore them than act on them. It's a real pity." Her eyes met his, and he was almost frozen by that arctic glance. "I'm glad I found out when I did."

She reached past him and opened the door. Her face expressionless, she said, "I think you'd better go now. You were right. We have said all we need to say to each other, so this is goodbye."

He was too numb to say anything in response, so he left without looking back. As he got in the car and started the engine with a roar, he was still trying to convince himself that this had all happened for the best. It wasn't until he got in the car and turned the corner, out of sight, that he felt a sting behind his lids.

It had been years since he'd shed a tear; the last time he could remember, he'd been a child, the night he realized his mother wasn't coming back. He'd believed that he could never feel such desolation again in his life. But today he felt it again, wave upon wave of sheer pain at what he could have had and just lost. Pulling over to the curb, he put his head against the steering wheel and

covered his eyes. He didn't cry, though he almost wished
he could. At least tears would have been a release.

There was no release for him this day. After a long
time, he lifted his head, started up the car again and
slowly drove away.

CHAPTER FIFTEEN

WITH KATE SETTLED in her own apartment again, Grace was finally able to make the trip to Vignoble. As soon as she saw the estate, she was reminded of Kemberly. The house and grounds had the same stately air as her beloved former home in England, and when she arrived, she sat a moment in the car, overcome by nostalgia.

But soon she was in the living room, seated opposite a clearly delighted Marguerite Kauffman, and when she happened to mention how much Vignoble reminded her of the DeWilde family estate, Marguerite surprised her by nodding.

"Oh, yes, Kemberly," Marguerite said. "Dirk told me so much about it."

"I'm surprised," Grace said carefully. The older woman's mention of Dirk had given her the opening she needed, but she didn't want to rush Marguerite.

"Oh? Why is that?"

Grace put down the cup of tea Marguerite had given her. With a shrug, she said, "I never knew much about Dirk—or Derrick, as he was known in Australia. But it always seemed to me that he did everything he could to distance himself from the DeWildes. I wouldn't have thought he'd mention anything to do with the family."

Marguerite's gaze was steady. "You mean," she said, "he wouldn't mention his family to his married lover from New York—the woman who ran away with him to Australia.''

Try as she might, Grace could not suppress her shock at the older woman's bluntness. Marguerite saw her struggle and smiled.

"I shouldn't have put it so baldly, I suppose," she said. "But I decided it was past time to drop all pretense, especially when you—and, of course, the very clever Mr. Santos—know that I'm Derrick's mystery woman."

Grace reached for her tea again. "You're right," she said. "It seems silly to keep all these secrets, especially when they reach so far into the past."

Marguerite smiled again. "Except for those missing jewels. They're very much in the present, aren't they. And they will be, until they're disposed of properly."

"Disposed of?" Grace repeated. "Do you mean that you really do have them?"

Marguerite considered her a moment. "What would you do if I did?"

"Are you asking if I would go to the police?"

"I suppose I am."

Grace had thought about this long ago. She shook her head. "No, I don't think this is something that the authorities should be involved in. But then, the jewels don't belong to me. I suppose in the end it should be Jeffrey's decision."

Marguerite sighed. "I know you're right. I'm only glad I finally have someone to share my secret with. Oh, Grace, you don't know how difficult it's been to keep this all to myself for so many years."

"I can imagine," Grace murmured.

"I told Dirk at the time that it was wrong, wrong, *wrong* for him to have taken those precious pieces, but he insisted that his family owed him the compensation.

'Nobody is going to miss them,' he told me. But of course, I knew better. He convinced me that even if the theft was discovered, by that time we would be far away, and no one would be able to trace us.''

''And he changed his name to cover his tracks even more thoroughly,'' Grace said. She glanced at the other woman with sudden compassion. She knew she wouldn't have felt this way last year, but all the changes in her own life had made her see things differently. She reached for Marguerite's hand. ''It must have been very difficult for you.''

''It was. I'd like to tell you the whole story, if I might. I know it won't excuse either Dirk or myself, but at least it might explain a few things. As I told Nick Santos a while ago—''

''Nick was here? When?''

''It was just before Kate had her accident. I didn't know at first that he was working for Mr. DeWilde, but I suspected.''

''Why?''

Marguerite laughed ironically. ''When you've been on the 'lam' for as long as I have, you learn to spot someone in authority a mile away. And Nick Santos has...that look.''

Grace had to smile, too. ''I know what you mean. But he earned that presence. He was once a police officer.''

''So he told me. I should have suspected him long before that. Kate had told me he was a private investigator, but I thought he was simply her friend.''

Grace knew she could never tell Marguerite that Nick and Kate had been forced to hide in the bedroom closet to avoid detection while Nick had been searching the house. Instead she asked, ''What happened when he met with you, then?''

Marguerite's eyes took on a sparkle. "Not much. You know, part of Mr. Santos's problem is that he's much too polite and considerate—of little old ladies, at least. I know I frustrated him immensely when I wouldn't answer his carefully constructed questions, but I couldn't help it. I wanted to talk to you first about this business of the jewels, so I played the confused old woman to put him off, though I know I didn't fool him for a minute. But now—"

She hesitated, and Grace's heart seemed to stop. "Now?" she said.

"Now," Marguerite repeated, "I won't have to put him off. He called me this morning and told me that while he knew I had the jewels, he wasn't going to report it."

"He did?" Grace didn't know what to make of that. "But... why?"

Marguerite's eyes gleamed again. "All he would say was that this was important to you—and to Kate. He told me that he would call you about it later."

Grace shook her head in confusion. "I'm afraid I don't understand," she said.

"I don't, either. But I suppose it will all come clear when you talk to him. In the meantime, do you want me to tell you about Dirk?"

Grace decided that she'd have time to ponder Nick's strange behavior later. Eagerly, she said, "Oh, yes. From what you've said, it must have been a grand love affair."

"Oh, it was." Marguerite looked down at her clasped hands for a moment. Her gaze was wistful when she glanced up again. "I told you before, I thought Dirk was the most mesmerizing man I had ever met. He was so charming, so erudite. And though I know it doesn't count for much these days, he had the most exquisite manners.''

Grace thought back to her own past. "I know what you mean,'' she said. "I felt the same way about Jeffrey when we first met.''

Marguerite sighed. "I've never been sure to this day what would have happened if I'd been happily married. Maybe I would have had the strength to resist Dirk, but perhaps not. And it doesn't really matter, I suppose. The point is, Dirk and I embarked on an affair. He was like a drug to me. I couldn't get enough of him. I knew what would happen if we were caught, but I didn't care. I was so in love with him that I would have done anything for him, and I did—sneaking out to meet him, making up stories about where I was going and what I was doing, even forcing some of my friends to lie for me.'' She shook her head. "It sounds so sordid now....''

"You were a woman in love.''

"I was a woman with responsibilities to her husband,'' Marguerite said. "Responsibilities I completely abandoned when I found out that I was pregnant with Dirk's child.''

"You must have been beside yourself.''

"I was. I didn't know what to do, for it would have been obvious—at least to my husband—that the baby wasn't his. We hadn't been intimate in quite a while, you see. And even though I had been unfaithful to him and treated him badly in every way, I couldn't add to my sins by seducing him and then pretending some time later that the baby had arrived early....''

Marguerite shook her head. "I saw no option but to tell Dirk, and when he immediately proposed that we run away to Australia and start a new life together, I seized the chance. I was desperate, and I saw that as my salvation. In fact, I was so frantic to get away that I didn't think it through. I didn't question how we would live, until we arrived and Dirk showed me the jewels."

"Is that why he took them? To finance your new life together?"

"That was one of the reasons. The other...who knows? But it was a moot point, because by then, my guilt was so overwhelming that I wouldn't allow him to sell them. I'd committed many sins by that time, but one thing I couldn't do was live on stolen money."

"How did you live, then?"

Marguerite laughed bitterly. "Not well. Oh, we had many quarrels over those jewels! There we were, sitting on a fortune and living like destitutes. Then Dirk learned of a new opal field where men were reaping millions. He left me in a rundown boarding house while he went out to dig opals."

"And did he find his bonanza?"

"No, he barely made enough money for us to live on until after our...our daughter, Maggie, was born. But long before then, I'm ashamed to say, I was so homesick and disillusioned that I'd begun writing to a dear, trusted friend back home. When she sent me a telegram that my husband had been badly injured in a suicide attempt and wasn't expected to live very long, I was so stricken that I begged her to send me the fare so I could fly home. I vowed that in reparation for my failings, I'd stay with my husband until he died. It was the least I could do."

Grace hated to ask. "But what about the baby?"

Marguerite bowed her head. "Yes, the baby," she whispered, wiping her eyes. "My beautiful, beautiful Maggie. I left her with Dirk, of course, since I couldn't arrive home with my love child in my arms. I intended to go back as soon as my husband didn't need me anymore. But even though he was confined to a wheelchair for the rest of his life, he lived a very long time. We weathered the inevitable whispers about my absence by saying that I'd gone to care for my aging parents in Quebec.''

Marguerite looked up at Grace with haunted eyes. "Dirk left me alone for a while, but when I refused to answer his letters or take his calls, he finally came to New York to get me. In doing so, he left Maggie in Australia." Her lips tightened. "But he did bring all the jewels, except for two, which he left behind in Australia. He begged me to go 'home' with him, but I couldn't abandon my husband a second time. He needed me, and since it was my fault that all this had happened, I couldn't leave him. I told Dirk that I would send for Maggie when the time was right, but..."

Marguerite faltered a moment before continuing. "In the end," she said sadly, "I never did go back. And I never saw Maggie again. The people Dirk had left her with when he came to New York disappeared, taking her with them. Losing her was my punishment, something I have lived with all of my life, a decision that will haunt me forever, long after I die."

Grace was silent, debating whether or not to tell her what she knew of Maggie Cutter, who had a Bible inscribed with the names of her parents—Marguerite DuBois and Dirk DeWilde. She decided that before she said anything, she would contact Maggie to ask how she felt about meeting her birth mother after all these years.

"Dirk left four of the jewels with me as a sign of his devotion," Marguerite said. "He knew how I felt about them, so before he went back to Australia, he told me that I could do whatever I liked with them. If I wanted to return them, I could do so—but on one condition. I must not reveal where he was, or what had happened.''

''But you're telling me the story now,'' Grace said.

''That's because now it no longer matters. Last year, his attorney traced me to tell me that...that Dirk had died. With his passing, I finally felt free to do what I should have done long ago—return the jewels to their rightful owner.''

As painful as this was, Grace knew she had to ask. ''But if you felt that way, Marguerite, why didn't you just contact Jeffrey? Or DeWilde's in London?''

Marguerite made a weary gesture. ''It wasn't that simple. Those jewels are worth a lot of money, and even now I'm too much of a coward to face criminal prosecution. But then, when I read that you were coming to San Francisco, I thought...''

Without finishing the sentence, Marguerite got up from the couch and retrieved a worn velvet case from the sideboard. She sat down again and handed Grace the box.

''Go ahead,'' she said. ''Open it.''

Her heart beating fast, Grace obeyed. With a click of the clasp, the lid sprang open. Inside, nestled against the worn velvet were the four missing pieces of jewelry. Diamonds blazed up at her, emeralds flashed green. Pearls glimmered among the deep blue sapphires, and rich rubies burned.

Grace could hardly speak. ''They're beautiful,'' she whispered. Dazzled, she looked up to see that Marguerite was watching her.

Marguerite smiled. Very simply, she said, ''They're yours.''

CHAPTER SIXTEEN

DAYS AFTER THAT LAST furious argument with Nick, Kate was still seething. How dare he? she thought angrily, for what must have been the hundredth time. How could he have called her a bleeding heart—a spoiled rich kid who thought she knew best! There was nothing wrong with believing that everyone deserved a chance to prove themselves. She knew she was right. The evidence was in Emilio and all the Angels, who *had* turned themselves around.

And furthermore, she thought irately, she had been right to accuse Nick of being a cynical loner who didn't want to see the good in anyone.

Was it any wonder they couldn't agree about anything?

"What is the *problem?*" she muttered as she paced her apartment, still trying to work this out. She had known that their differing ideologies made a relationship impossible—he'd known it, too. She should be glad they'd quarreled. Now they could simply walk away from something that had become much too complicated.

But if that were so, why was she having such a hard time putting it—and him—out of her mind? Why did she have to keep going over and over everything, until she felt she could scream?

She wanted to feel angry—or at least relieved—that it was over. Instead, she felt miserable. Against all reason, she wanted Nick Santos. No matter what he'd said, she couldn't just put him out of her life.

The phone rang and she stopped midstep. Should she answer it? No, she decided grimly. Whoever it was, she didn't want to talk to them. She had never felt so miserable in her entire life.

But what if the caller was Nick?

Before she knew it, she was grabbing the phone. "Hello?"

"Kate," her mother said warmly. "How are you?"

Kate shut her eyes. Why had she answered? Her mother would know how she felt right away. She'd see through any excuses Kate might try to make.

"Oh, fine," she said vaguely. "How about you?"

"I'm wonderful," Grace said. "I had the most interesting visit with Marguerite Kauffman. We talked about the missing jewels, and I wanted to tell you all about it."

At that moment, Kate didn't care if Marguerite had confessed to stealing the *crown* jewels and hocking them for a baseball mitt. Dully, she said, "Go ahead."

Grace ignored her lack of enthusiasm because she was so enthused herself. "You'll never guess what happened, Kate." She paused dramatically. "Marguerite gave me the jewels!"

That penetrated Kate's dark mood. "She did! Then she did have them all this time."

"Dirk DeWilde gave them to her years ago, and she gave them to me. Can you believe it?"

No, Kate couldn't believe it. She knew she should be happy for her mother, but perversely her thoughts flashed to Nick. He wasn't going to be pleased about this. Then she scoffed, So what? Did she care?

Frowning, she shoved Nick out of her mind. "That's... wonderful, Mother. You must be delighted."

"Oh, I am. And your father will be so pleased. Imagine, after all this time, those jewels will be coming home again."

"That's great."

Grace finally realized that Kate wasn't as excited as she was. "Is something wrong, darling?" she asked. "You don't sound very pleased."

For her mother's sake, Kate tried to muster some verve. "Oh, no, I am—really. I know how important it was to you to recover those missing pieces." She paused. "I'm just not sure why."

Grace laughed. "Do you know what? I wasn't sure myself until I actually had them in my hands. But now—"

"Now?" Kate said cautiously.

"Now," Grace said with renewed drama, "I have a plan!"

"And that is?" Kate asked even more warily.

"All in good time, darling," Grace said. "First, I have to speak to Nick."

"Oh?"

Grace laughed again. "Don't sound so suspicious, dear. I promise I won't do anything that will affect his reputation."

"Then you're going to let him return the jewels to Dad?"

Grace hesitated. "Well, not exactly."

Kate couldn't keep her impatience from her voice. "What, then?"

"Just let me speak to Nick first, will you, Kate? If nothing else, I do have him to thank."

"For what?" Kate was having trouble keeping track of the conversation.

"Because he called Marguerite and told her that he knew she had the jewels—but he was going to let her decide what to do with them."

Kate straightened. "Nick said that?"

Grace laughed delightedly. "He did, indeed. So, Marguerite decided to give them to me."

"I don't understand."

"I don't, either, darling. After all, you told me that it was of the utmost importance to Nick to get his hands on these jewels." Grace paused. "Can you think of a reason why he might have volunteered to stand back? I mean, he's worked very hard tracking the pieces down. I would have thought he'd want to present them to Jeffrey himself—a job well done."

Kate sank into a chair. "Yes," she said slowly. "I believed that, too." She thought of something and straightened again. "When did he call Mrs. Kauffman to tell her that? Do you know?"

"Why, I'm not sure, dear. Is it important?"

Kate put a hand to her head. "I don't know," she said slowly. "Maybe."

"Well, let me see..." Grace thought a moment. "It was after you went back to your own apartment—I'm sure it was, because Marguerite asked about you, and Nick said that you'd been to the clinic, and everything was all right. Does that help?"

It helped more than her mother could possibly have known. Kate's quick mind was racing ahead, seizing on and discarding possibilities, arguments, rationalizations. There was only one answer, she thought excitedly. She was right. She knew she was.

Hastily, she said, "I'm very happy for you, Mother,

but I have to get off the phone right now. There's something I have to do.''

Grace didn't argue. ''All right, darling,'' she said serenely. ''I'll talk to you later. And if you do see Nick, will you thank him for me until I can tell him myself?''

''Yes, yes, I'll do that. Goodbye, Mother.''

''Goodbye, Katie—and good luck.''

Kate didn't realize what her mother had said until she was in the car and on the way down to the clinic. *Good luck?* she thought. She shook her head with a mixture of exasperation and tenderness. Her mother knew her too well. Grace must have guessed what this would mean to her. The real purpose of her call had been to tell Kate what Nick had done.

She started to smile, then frowned again. *Good luck,* her mother had said. Well, if things were going to work out the way she wanted them to, she'd need all the luck she could get. Before this day was over, she and the man she loved had a lot of talking to do.

EMILIO AND TWO OF THE Angels were standing outside the clinic when she pulled up. As soon as they saw her, they sauntered over, and Emilio said, ''Hey, doc. What're you doing back here again so soon?''

''I had some things to do,'' Kate said. ''How about you?''

He grinned, showing those beautiful white teeth. ''Things're goin' okay. We had two more Angels sign up, and I'm working on a third—a real blowhard who thinks it's cool to be bad. But he'll come around.''

''I'm sure he will,'' Kate said with a smile. ''With you as leader, anything is possible. Look what you've done already.''

''Hey,'' said Sylphide, one of the female Angels, as

she came up behind Emilio. She pushed his shoulder. "Don't you go talkin' like that to him, doc. You'll give him a bigger swelled head than he's already got."

"*Callate!*" he muttered to her, though he wasn't serious. "You know I don't like no back talk."

Sylphide pushed her beret farther down over one eye and thumbed her nose at him. Saucily, she said, "This is what I think of you."

Ignoring her, Emilio turned to Kate again. "So, doc, you got anything we can do?"

"As a matter of fact, I do need a favor, Emilio."

"What's that?"

"Have you seen Nick Santos?"

"Sure, he came down here a coupla days ago, to see how things were hang...to see how things were." Emilio squinted at her. "Why, can't you find him?"

She knew she had to be honest with him if she were to ask his help. "To tell you the truth, we had a...a disagreement. But now when I want to talk to him, I can't find him. I called his apartment and the office he has here in town, but he's not there. I don't know where to look."

Emilio grinned again. "No problem. We'll find him for you."

Suiting action to words, Emilio put two fingers to his mouth and let out a piercing whistle. Blue-bereted teens came running from all directions, and about two seconds later, a small crowd surrounded him. Emilio explained what he wanted, and they all scattered. Kate grabbed him before he ran off himself.

"What are you going to do?" she asked.

Emilio smiled cockily at her. "Hey, I don't give out no secrets. Don't worry, we'll find him."

To her amazement, they did. Or at least, they found out about a place where he might go.

"Sometimes he goes to a bar near Market called the Olive Pit," Emilio said when he returned to the clinic less than an hour later. "Do you want us to stake it out?"

Kate shook her head in amazement. "How on earth did you find that out?"

"We're on the side of the angels now, remember?" he said cockily. "We can find anything out." Then he shrugged. "Besides, it wasn't so difficult. He's from the neighborhood, you know. A guy that size is pretty hard to miss."

"Thanks, Emilio," she said gratefully. "I owe you one."

He thought she was going to get emotional on him, so he quickly backed away. "Hey, this is what we're here for, remember? So, go get him. Besides, he isn't so bad—once you get to know him."

Kate smiled. "I agree."

"Do you want us to go check out the bar? We can stand watch around the clock, but there's no guarantee he'll show up."

Kate knew there was no guarantee Nick was even in the city. She'd left messages on his answering machines, and Nick knew *her* number. If he had wanted to, he could have called her. Maybe she was wrong, she thought. Maybe she had misinterpreted...

No. She wouldn't allow herself to think like that. If she did, she'd be defeated long before she found him and they talked. Realizing that Emilio was still waiting for an answer, she said, "Thanks, but you've done your bit. There's no need for you to watch the bar. I have an idea I hope will work."

Emilio looked disappointed that he and the Angels wouldn't be needed for a surveillance job, but he nodded. "It's your call. But will you let us know what happens?"

"You bet I will," she said, giving his arm a squeeze. "And, thanks again."

He touched two fingers to the beret in salute. *"De nada."*

Kate watched him saunter jauntily down the street. Then she went into the clinic to use the phone. Waving at Mary, who had visited her several times in the hospital, she headed to the tiny office in back and sat down at the battered desk. Both calls she had to make were important, but she chose to call Sheila first.

Dr. Sheila McIntyre answered the page so quickly that Kate knew she'd been waiting for the call. Sheila had phoned Kate this morning, asking if she'd made a decision about the proposition Sheila had put before her months ago. Kate hadn't been able to give her an answer then. Now she could.

"Dr. McIntyre here."

"Hi, Sheila."

"Hey," the neurosurgeon said. "Have you decided yet?"

"Yes, I have." Kate took a deep breath. "The answer is… yes."

"Good." There was real pleasure in Sheila's voice. "I'm so— "

"On one condition."

Sheila groaned. "I should have known. But never mind. I'm too delighted that you've finally seen the light. So, what's the condition?"

"I really want to do this new surgical residency, Sheila," Kate said. "I know how lucky I am that you chose me to work with you. But I can't stop working at the clinic."

"I understand," Sheila said with a sigh. "And to be honest, I knew you were going to say that. I've given up trying to talk you out of it."

"Good."

"I have to admire the work you do there, Kate. But—"

"I'm glad you do," Kate said with a wicked smile. "Because I wanted to ask you something."

"What's that?" Sheila said warily.

"Well, you know that so many of the people who come to the clinic haven't much money, never mind insurance—"

"And?" Sheila asked even more cautiously.

Kate laughed at her friend's tone. It was obvious that Sheila had guessed what was coming. "Now, Sheila, you'll feel better if you offer your surgical services to the clinic. You'll be performing a community service, and even more important, you'll be helping people who really need you." She paused, trying not to laugh again. "I promise you, it really won't hurt."

Sheila sighed. "You drive a hard bargain, Dr. De-Wilde."

"Then you'll do it?"

"To get you into a neurological surgery residency, where I always said you belonged? Yes, I will. But only if, on those *rare* occasions when we're offering our services for free, you'll be there to assist me."

"I'd be honored, Dr. McIntyre," Kate said. She paused, then said gratefully, "And, Sheila, thanks."

"Don't thank me. You've got a long road ahead of you, Doctor. But it will be worth it. Just tell me one thing—"

"What's that?"

"What made you change your mind?"

"Oh, it's a long story," Kate said. "Sometime I'll tell you about it. For now, I guess you could say that getting shot made me see things a little differently."

"In what way?"

She'd never told this to another soul. In fact, she hadn't realized it herself until this morning. Taking a deep breath, she said, "Well, I guess I thought I had to make up for the advantages I've had all my life by denying myself something that really mattered. I know, I know—you don't have to tell me how silly that is."

"I don't think it's silly," Sheila said quietly. "We all have our demons."

"True. But that particular one is in the past now—thankfully. I've realized that I can have both things—a hospital practice and another kind of satisfying work down here."

"I'm glad you made the decision, Kate. And I'll be glad to help out down there whenever I can. I guess you've made me see things a little differently, too."

Kate hung up with a smile. She hesitated, then dialed another number. Nick had told her about his former partner, and Max was her last hope. When the desk sergeant down at police headquarters answered, she asked for Detective Maxine Roybal and held her breath while he put her on hold. What would she do if the detective wasn't in?

It took so long for someone to get back to her that Kate was beginning to fear that Maxine didn't want to talk to her. And if that were so, she thought glumly, she didn't have a backup plan. What would she do then?

Finally, when Kate was about to accept that everyone had forgotten about her, or that she'd been disconnected, the line clicked and a woman's voice said, "Detective Roybal."

Kate took a deep breath. "Detective, this is Kate DeWilde. You don't know me, but—"

"You're the doctor, right?"

"Why, yes," Kate said, surprised. "I mean, I am a doctor. How did you know?"

The woman laughed. "Are you kidding?" Max said. "Nick's told me all about you."

"He has?" Kate began to feel hopeful. "Well, Nick is the reason I'm calling. We had a serious disagreement, and now I can't get in touch with him. I was wondering if you might have any idea where I can find him."

"Me? I suppose you've already called his office and his apartment."

"I have."

"Let me check around. If I find him, what do you want me to do?"

Kate already knew. "I understand that he sometimes goes to a bar near Market called the Olive Pit."

"That's true. We've met there several times since he's been back in town."

"Great. I know it's asking a lot of you, since we've never met, I mean, but would you do something else for me?"

"Sure," Max agreed easily. "What is it?"

"I appreciate this, Max, really I do," Kate said. "Now, here's my plan..."

THE OLIVE PIT WAS CROWDED, as usual. Nick stood in the doorway to let his eyes adjust. He hadn't wanted to meet Max here—not tonight, when he felt so low. But she had insisted it would do him good, so he'd agreed.

He'd learned a long time ago it was easier to give in to Max than to try and fight her.

Why hadn't he learned that with Kate?

He didn't want to think about Kate. He was here. Where was Max? He couldn't see her in the throng of people, and was about to begin the trek toward the bar when the same hooker who had tried to come on to him that first night came up to him again. This time she was wearing a top—he couldn't call it a blouse—of clear vinyl, and pants so tight he wondered if they'd been glued on.

"Hey, handsome," she purred over the noise. "Want to buy me a drink?"

He started to answer, but someone elbowed in front of him, making the decision for him. "Sorry, lady," Kate said. "This one is mine."

The hooker looked at her; Kate DeWilde stared back. Then the woman tossed her head. Pouting, she moved off. Kate immediately turned to Nick.

"Hi," she said, as though they were meeting in a park.

He didn't know what to say. For one thing, he couldn't imagine how she had found him. He stood there staring at her, and then heard himself say stupidly, "I was supposed to meet Max here."

"I know," Kate said. "But she and I had a talk this afternoon, and we decided that I should take her place. Do you mind?"

His voice wouldn't work to form an answer. He thought he'd made up his mind that he was never going to see Kate DeWilde again, yet here she was, and all he could think of was that he wanted to take her into his arms and tell her both how sorry he was and how stupid he'd been.

"I...no," he said. He couldn't stop staring at her.

"How about a drink?" Kate said. "We have a lot to talk about."

He looked into her eyes—those eyes that made him feel like he was falling into a well—and told himself again, for about the thousandth time, that he couldn't go through it all over again. He'd agonized over the decision not to see her anymore, telling himself that this was for the best. But now, seeing her here, feeling her hand on his arm, he knew that he was dangerously close to forgetting all his resolutions.

He stepped back. "I don't think—"

"I do," she said firmly, grabbing his hand. "Come on, I've got a table over there—" She started off, towing him behind her, only to stop so suddenly that he almost bumped into her. "Oh, no!" she said. "Someone took it!"

At any other time he would have laughed at the dismay in her voice. Now he was just relieved. "Good," he said. "This isn't the place for you, anyway."

"You know, you're right," she said. "Let's go outside. What I have to say won't take long."

She led the way out the door before he could answer, giving the hooker another glare as they went by. Once out on the sidewalk, she took his arm again and said, "Let's walk."

Despite his conflicting emotions, he was concerned about her physical condition. "Do you think you should?"

She gave him a tart look. "I'm not so feeble that I can't walk a block or two while we work this out."

He still couldn't seem to gather his thoughts. Trying to stall, he said, "Work what out?"

She took his arm again and started off without answering. Left with no choice, he went with her.

"I've been thinking about what you said," she began. "And you were absolutely right."

That was the last thing he'd expected her to say. "I was?"

"Yes, you were. You were right about everything, Nick. I didn't belong at the clinic. I wasn't doing any good there. The whole time, I was just fooling myself."

He frowned. He'd had time to do some thinking himself, and he knew that his harsh condemnation of Kate had been partly a self-preservation technique—a way to convince himself that they were from two different worlds with no hope of ever bridging the gap. "Now, wait a minute—" he began.

"No, no, it's true," she insisted. "You said that one person could never make a difference, and you were right. Look what happened. I got shot for my trouble."

He didn't like where this was leading. Uneasily, he said, "That's not true. You did make a difference—"

She stopped and turned to him. "But you said—"

"I was wrong," he admitted. "How many times do I have to say it? And as proof of just how wrong I was, all we have to do is look at the Angels. They never would have come into existence if it hadn't been for you. You're responsible for that, Kate. Only you."

"You're very kind, Nick, but we both know that was just a coincidence."

"No, it wasn't. You forget, I grew up in that neighborhood. I hung around with kids just like Emilio. I *know* what it takes to turn someone around. You believed in those kids, Kate. You helped them. By your example, you showed them that there was another way—"

Slowly, she smiled. "In that case, so did you."

He jerked back. "Me? I didn't do anything."

"Yes, you did. Emilio told me how you helped them go to the cops and identify those two thugs with the guns. If it hadn't been for you, another gang war would have erupted. So you see, you made a difference, too."

"Yes, but that—"

He stopped at the look in her eyes. Reluctantly, he said, "I guess you're right."

"In that case, maybe we can move on to the issue that's really bothering you."

"There is no issue. I told you—"

"I know what you *told* me, Nick, but don't you think it's time we both told the truth?"

"I'm not sure I know what you mean."

"Then let me start off by saying that you were right when you accused me of being a spoiled little princess who ran at the first sign of trouble."

He could feel his face burn. "I shouldn't have said that."

"Yes, you should have. You were right. I thought that I was protected somehow, because of who I was. Being shot taught me that was far from the truth. It also taught me that I wasn't looking at things clearly. But then, neither were you. What you've said tonight proves it. We were both running from our backgrounds—and from each other. And for all the wrong reasons."

"We'll never agree, Kate—"

"I know. But who said we had to?" She smiled wickedly. "Besides, I think it will be more in'eresting this way, don't you?"

He didn't know what to think. "Kate—"

"There's just one thing I need to know," she said.

He didn't want to ask. "What's that?"

She looked up at him. "Why did you leave me in the hospital, Nick? I need to know."

Ashamed, he glanced away from her, but she put a hand on his arm and made him look at her again.

"Nick? Tell me. If nothing else, I think I have a right to know."

He knew she was right. But the reason he'd walked away—*ran away*—sounded so juvenile that it took all his courage to tell her. Forcing himself to hold her eyes, he said, "I left because I loved you too much, Kate. When you got shot, I thought my world was about to end. I...I've never allowed myself to feel that way about anyone. To tell you the truth, it scared the hell out of me."

Her hand tightened on his arm. Her eyes huge and oh-so-green under the street lights, she looked up at him and said, "Oh, Nick..."

Now that he had started, he knew he had to tell it all. "Growing up the way I did, I learned not to trust that people would be there for me, Kate. I never knew my father, and my mother—I told you about her. The only person I ever let myself love was my grandmother—and maybe Max. The others... I knew they would never be permanent fixtures in my life, so I didn't let them get too close. It was easier to be alone. That way, you didn't get hurt."

"But then?" she asked quietly.

He looked down into her lovely face. Lifting his hand, he tenderly touched her cheek. "But then I met you," he said. "And suddenly, I couldn't stand apart, as I always had. I found myself falling in love with you, and...and I didn't know how to handle it." He paused again and then added, the pain evident in his voice, "I'm sorry, Kate. I never thought I was a coward until I fell in love with you."

She reached for his hand. "Oh, Nick," she said. "You're not a coward. We all feel that way—at least, I do. Being in love is a scary thing. I feel it, too."

"You do?"

She smiled, a spark of fire leaping to those incredible eyes. "Yes, I do. But it's not going to stop me. And—" her expression turned wicked again "—I'm not going to let it stop you."

She knew she had reached him when she saw the hard, tense lines of his face relax, and his eyes soften with the love he'd been holding back.

"How can you be so sure about this?" he asked hoarsely, pulling her to him.

She looked up at him. "I don't know," she said honestly. "I just am. More than I've ever been about anything else in my life." She paused. "What about you?"

He gazed into her face, her eyes, her heart. After what seemed an eternity to her, he finally sighed. It was as though he'd come home when he said, "I'm sure, too."

She relaxed against him. "So," she murmured, "what are we going to do about it?"

Suddenly, he knew. All the doubts were gone, and he took a deep breath before he said, "I know one way—"

She trembled against him. She knew one, too. But she wanted to hear it from him. "And what's that?" she asked.

He reached down and tipped her head up toward him so he could see her face. "Will you marry me, Kate?"

She started to answer, but before she could say anything, a cheer went up and about a dozen Angels, led by a swaggering, grinning Emilio, appeared from out of the shadows and surrounded them, applauding all the while.

Emilio clapped Nick on the back. "Way to go, man," he said, his own dark eyes gleaming. "It's about time you got smart."

Nick felt a little dazed. He glanced around at the small crowd surrounding them, then at Kate, who was looking dazed herself. With a laugh, he said, "Not so quick, *mi vatos*. The lady hasn't answered yet."

All eyes turned to Kate. Emilio gave her a grin and a thumbs-up, and his cousin Eladio and the two girls, Sylphide and Amelianna, nodded vigorously, along with everyone else. Trying not to smile, Kate brought her eyes back to Nick's anxious face.

"The lady," she said softly, "says yes."

EPILOGUE

KATE AND NICK WERE married a week later. The arrangements were put together so quickly that Grace didn't have time to order the right flowers, much less the right gown. Kate couldn't decide on anything the store had in stock, but to Grace's dismay, it didn't seem to matter to her daughter.

"But, Kate," Grace said, as gently as possible. "If you could just wait—"

"I don't want to wait," Kate said blithely. "I'm starting my surgical residency next week, and after everything that's happened, Nick and I want to get away for a few days, at least. If we delay the wedding, we won't be able to do that. Besides," she added, her face luminous with joy, "I've got him now. I don't want him to get away."

"I doubt there's any chance of that," Grace said dryly. "If ever a man was in love, it's Nick."

Kate hugged her. "I love him, too. I know you're disappointed that it won't be a big, lavish wedding, Mother."

"No, no," Grace denied with a sigh. "After Gabe and Megan, and now you, I'm resigned that this branch of the DeWildes, at least, isn't destined to take advantage of the wonderful opportunities we give to others."

Kate laughed. "It is ironic, isn't it? Here we are in

the business of weddings, and yet all three of your children have frustrated you."

"That's all right. Your father and I are delighted that you're marrying Nick. He's going to make a wonderful husband for you."

"And a good son-in-law for you," Kate said. "Oh, I can't wait!"

Grace smiled. "I do appreciate how he's handled the...er...problem of your father and Marguerite and the jewels."

Kate gave her mother a hug. "I hope it works out, Mother. But now it's up to you. After I got through thanking him for his magnanimous gesture—" despite herself, Kate blushed furiously at the memory "—he said he'd send a message to Dad that he'd found the jewels and was sending them by a special courier."

Grace bit her lip. "You don't think that your father will suspect?"

Kate gave her another hug. "Don't worry! Nick has it all set up. And believe me—" she blushed again "—he knows what he's doing."

Grace had to smile at that. "I'm sure he does. But just in case I don't get a chance to thank him again, will you make sure—"

Kate's eyes sparkled. "Oh, I'll make sure he knows how much he's appreciated. Don't worry about that!"

"I won't," Grace agreed, laughing with her daughter. "But first of all, we have a wedding to attend to!"

THE CEREMONY WAS HELD on a beautiful, warm Saturday in July. Despite the rush, Grace and Rita had managed to decorate the little church with flowers. Kate's sister, Megan, flew over from Paris with her husband, Phillip, to be matron of honor. And when the bride

walked down the aisle, she didn't wear surgical greens—
as she had teased her mother she'd do—but was glorious
in a gown of satin and Chantilly lace. Gabe's wife,
Lianne, who couldn't travel because of her advanced
pregnancy, had nevertheless designed a magnificent
headpiece for the occasion, a twisted rope of pearls that
held back Kate's auburn hair and ended in a deep V in
the center of her forehead. Kate had never looked more
beautiful.

One of the proudest moments for the newly married
couple came after the ceremony as they passed through
an honor guard of Dr. Kate's Angels, who were dressed
for the occasion in their immaculate uniforms. Blue berets at a rakish angle, they stood at solemn attention, one
by each pew, as Kate and Nick walked by. Then, falling
into formation, they followed the newlyweds outside,
saving their cheers and the tossing of their berets into
the air until they were safely out of the church.

After numerous pictures, everyone went to the reception, which was catered by Kate's cousin Mallory.
Fueled by fabulous food, fine wine and high spirits, the
festivities lasted until well into the wee hours of the
morning.

GRACE WAS TIRED when she finally let herself into her
apartment somewhere around 2:30 a.m. Glad that she
didn't have to go to the store the next morning—or
rather, in a few hours—she went into the bedroom to
get ready for bed. Setting her beaded purse and gloves
on the dressing table, she went to the closet to get her
robe. She was just taking it off the hanger, when she
paused.

The floor safe she'd had installed beckoned to her,
and, kicking off her heels, she sat on the carpet to work

the combination. The door sprang open, and she took out the worn velvet box Marguerite had given her. A touch of the lock made the top pop up, and she stared down at the fabulous, glowing contents.

Slowly, she lifted the Dancing Waters necklace from the box. As she turned it this way and that, the many facets of the diamonds flashed all colors of the rainbow. The piece was so beautiful, she couldn't put it back.

As she sat there, she thought of Jeffrey, who had already left for England tonight. Feeling he'd been away too long, he wanted to get back to the London store, and as the day went on, he had seemed more and more nervous. Grace had wished him well, but the tension that had sprung up between them had prevented more than a superficial conversation as they took part in the bride's dance. Now that everything was resolved with Kate, it was as if the strain of their divorce had reestablished itself.

Because of that, Grace had almost been glad to see him leave. Several times she'd almost blurted out her plan, but somehow she had managed to hold her tongue. After all this, the last thing she wanted to do was ruin the surprise—or change her mind.

She was still holding the necklace up to the light. But as she continued to stare at it, to admire both the stones and the exquisite workmanship, she knew she wasn't going to cancel out. When she thought of Jeffrey earlier today, so tall and handsome in his tuxedo, so much the proud father as he walked with his daughter down the church aisle, she became more and more certain that this was the right thing to do.

Several times during the brief but eloquent ceremony, she had felt someone staring at her and, turning to look, saw that it was Jeffrey. Each time, his expression had been such a mix of emotions—happiness and pride for Kate, sadness and regret for their own plight—that Grace had had to turn away before tears sprang into her eyes.

Or had Jeffrey's reaction been just wishful thinking on her part, simply because she felt the same way herself? she wondered.

She looked at the necklace again, saw the deep fires glowing within, and knew she had to find out. Once and for all, it was time to learn what was on Jeffrey's mind. If their marriage was truly over, irrevocably gone, then they both had to acknowledge it and move on.

But if there was still a spark, an ember that could be fanned once more into flame... A union of thirty-two years shouldn't be allowed to meekly gasp its last breath—not without giving it one more chance.

She'd made her decision. Setting the velvet box aside, she got up and went to the phone in her bedroom. Nick had told her that if she couldn't do it, he'd take the jewels himself. Or hire another courier. Whatever she wanted.

And what *did* she want?

Her heart pounding with anticipation, she didn't dare pause to look up the number. Afraid that she wouldn't be able to follow through after all, she called the operator for assistance. A moment later she heard a click, and a pleasant male voice answered.

She could hang up now, with no one the wiser, she thought—and nearly did so. But she was still holding the necklace, and as she lifted it up, the gorgeous stones seemed to wink at her and whisper, *Go. Go to him one last time....*

She took a deep breath. Feeling excited and scared and apprehensive all at once, she said, "Reservations? I'd like to book a flight to London."

Weddings by DeWilde

continues with

I DO, AGAIN

by Jasmine Cresswell

The missing pieces of the famed DeWilde jewel collection were finally coming home to Jeffrey, and the courier was his ex-wife. Would the collection, his family and his marriage finally be whole again?

Available in March

Here's a preview!

I DO, AGAIN

To Jeffrey's absolute horror, Grace began to cry.

"Gracie! Don't! Please, don't cry! I didn't mean to upset you." He scrambled onto his knees and discovered that by stretching out his left hand, he could just manage to touch her cheeks. He tried to stem the flow of tears. "Gracie, please don't be sad. I can't bear it if I've hurt you again."

She took his hand and held it against his cheek. "You haven't hurt me." She sniffed. "Goodness, Jeffrey, have you forgotten so much about me already? I always cry when I'm happy."

She was happy! Relief left him limp. "You cry when you're sad, too. How is a mere man supposed to tell the difference?"

She reached for a tissue from the box on the bedside table. "I don't know. A woman would never be in the least bit confused, but men are so hopelessly inadequate—" She broke off. "Jeffrey, what are you doing?"

"Unlocking this damned handcuff," he said, freeing himself. He held up the key he'd stolen, dangling it just out of her reach.

She lunged for him. "Jeffrey DeWilde, stealing that key while pretending to console me was not the behavior of a gentleman."

He let her momentum topple him backward, so that

she lay straddled along the entire length of his body. "Gracie, darling, chaining me to the bedpost was not exactly the behavior of a perfect lady."

She wriggled, pretending she wanted to get away and actually making not the slightest effort to escape his grasp. He put his arms around her and rolled sideways, capturing her firmly beneath him. "Are you going to ravish me?" she asked.

He looked down at her, smiling. "Yes, I believe I am."

"Thank God." She linked her hands behind his head and pulled his mouth down to hers. "It's about time."

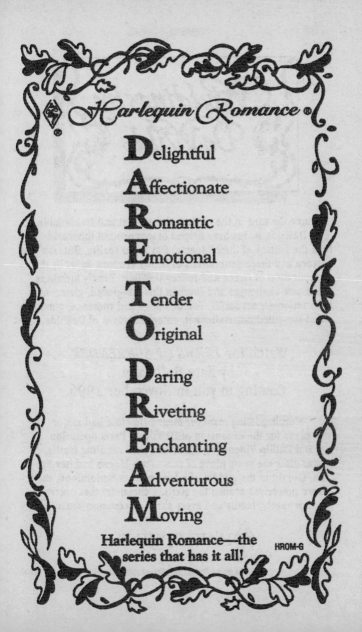

Harlequin Romance

Delightful

Affectionate

Romantic

Emotional

Tender

Original

Daring

Riveting

Enchanting

Adventurous

Moving

Harlequin Romance—the
series that has it all!

HROM-G

![Weddings by DeWilde]

Since the turn of the century the elegant and fashionable
DeWilde stores have helped brides around the world
turn the fantasy of their "Special Day" into reality. But now the
store and three generations of family are torn apart by the
separation of Grace and Jeffrey DeWilde. Family members
face new challenges and loves in this fast-paced, glamorous,
internationally set series. For weddings and romance, glamour
and fun-filled entertainment, enter the world of DeWilde...

Watch for *TERMS OF SURRENDER*,
by Kate Hoffmann
Coming to you in November 1996

Merchandising manager Megan DeWilde had major
plans for the expansion of DeWildes' Paris operation.
But Phillip Villeneuve, scion of a rival retailing family,
was after the same piece of real estate Megan had her eye
on. Caught in the middle of a feud neither understood, they
were powerless against the sizzling chemistry that overrode
property, family and every shred of common sense.

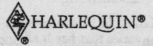

HARLEQUIN®

⬥ HARLEQUIN ®

Don't miss these Harlequin favorites by some of our
most distinguished authors! And now you can receive a
discount by ordering two or more titles!

HT#25657	PASSION AND SCANDAL by Candace Schuler	$3.25 U.S. $3.75 CAN.	☐ ☐
HP#11787	TO HAVE AND TO HOLD by Sally Wentworth	$3.25 U.S. $3.75 CAN.	☐ ☐
HR#03385	THE SISTER SECRET by Jessica Steele	$2.99 U.S. $3.50 CAN	☐ ☐
HS#70634	CRY UNCLE by Judith Arnold	$3.75 U.S. $4.25 CAN.	☐ ☐
HI#22346	THE DESPERADO by Patricia Rosemoor	$3.50 U.S. $3.99 CAN.	☐ ☐
HAR#16610	MERRY CHRISTMAS, MOMMY by Muriel Jensen	$3.50 U.S. $3.99 CAN.	☐ ☐
HH#28895	THE WELSHMAN'S WAY by Margaret Moore	$4.50 U.S. $4.99 CAN.	☐ ☐

(limited quantities available on certain titles)

AMOUNT	$
DEDUCT: 10% DISCOUNT FOR 2+ BOOKS	$
POSTAGE & HANDLING ($1.00 for one book, 50¢ for each additional)	$
APPLICABLE TAXES*	$_____
TOTAL PAYABLE	$_____
(check or money order—please do not send cash)	

To order, complete this form and send it, along with a check or money order
for the total above, payable to Harlequin Books, to: In the U.S.: 3010 Walden
Avenue, P.O. Box 9047, Buffalo, NY 14269-9047; In Canada: P.O. Box 613,
Fort Erie, Ontario, L2A 5X3.

Name: _____

Address: _____ City: _____

State/Prov.: _____ Zip/Postal Code: _____

*New York residents remit applicable sales taxes.
 Canadian residents remit applicable GST and provincial taxes.

Look us up on-line at: http://www.romance.net

HBACK-OD3

HARLEQUIN  PRESENTS®

HARLEQUIN PRESENTS
men you won't be able to resist falling in love with...

HARLEQUIN PRESENTS
women who have feelings just like your own...

HARLEQUIN PRESENTS
powerful passion in exotic international settings...

HARLEQUIN PRESENTS
intense, dramatic stories that will keep you turning
to the very last page...

HARLEQUIN PRESENTS
The world's bestselling romance series!

1997
Reader's Engagement Book
A calendar of important dates
and anniversaries for readers to use!

Informative and entertaining—with notable
dates and trivia highlighted throughout the year.

Handy, convenient, pocketbook size to help you
keep track of your own personal important dates.

Added bonus—contains $5.00 worth of coupons
for upcoming Harlequin and Silhouette books.
This calendar more than pays for itself!

 Available beginning in November at
your favorite retail outlet.

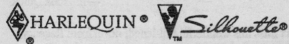

HARLEQUIN ® 🖤 *Silhouette*®

HARLEQUIN ®

Scandals

A passionate story of romance, where bold, daring characters set out to defy their world of propriety and strict social codes.

"Scandals—a story that will make your heart race and your pulse pound. Spectacular!"   —Suzanne Forster

"Devon is daring, dangerous and altogether delicious."
                                                    —Amanda Quick

Don't miss this wonderful full-length novel from Regency favorite Georgina Devon.

Available in December, wherever Harlequin books are sold.

SCAN